New York Times Bestselling Author

Vivian Arend

"If you've never read a Vivian Arend book you are missing out on one of the best contemporary authors writing today."
~ *Book Reading Gals*

"The bitter cold of Alberta, Canada, is made toasty warm by the super-sexy Coleman brothers of Six Pack Ranch."
~ *Publishers Weekly*

"Brilliant, raw, imaginative, irresistible!!"
~ Avon Romance

"This story will keep you reading from the first page to the last one. There is never a dull moment..."
~ *Landy Jimenez*

"I loved Mitch and Anna. Their chemistry was off the charts and it wasn't so much what they did that made it so hot (though it helped) it was the way they did it. If the Six Pack Ranch Series is as hot as this was, I'll definitely being going back to read it."
~ *Lost in a Book*

"This was my first Vivian Arend story, and I know I want more! "
~ *Red Hot Plus Blue Reads*

New York Times Bestselling Author

Vivian Arend

~*CONTEMPORARY TITLES*~
Six Pack Ranch
Rocky Mountain Heat
Rocky Mountain Haven
Rocky Mountain Desire
Rocky Mountain Angel
Rocky Mountain Rebel
Rocky Mountain Freedom
Rocky Mountain Romance
Rocky Retreat

Thompson & Sons
Rocky Ride
One Sexy Ride
Let It Ride
A Wild Ride

Adrenaline Search & Rescue
High Risk
High Passion
High Seduction

DreamMakers
All Fired Up
Love Is A Battlefield
Don't Walk Away

A full list of Vivian's paranormal print titles
is available on her website
www.vivianarend.com

Rocky Mountain Shelter

Vivian Arend

This is a work of fiction. Names, characters, places, and incidents either are the product of the author's imagination or are used fictitiously, and any resemblance to any persons, living or deal, business establishments, event, or locales is entirely coincidental.

Rocky Mountain Shelter
Copyright 2015 by Vivian Arend
ISBN: 978-1-516947-55-3
Edited by Anne Scott
Cover by Angela Waters
Proofed by Sharon Muha

Chapter One

May, Rocky Mountain House

A METALLIC shriek filled the air as Trevor Coleman stomped on the brakes, gravel flying as his oversized pickup skidded to a halt. On the ridgeline of the run-down rental house he'd been stalking for days, a dark silhouette teetered precariously, and he swore under his breath.

He shoved the truck back in gear and hurried onto the pothole-ridden private road. It took a minute to manoeuver the narrow driveway, his approach hidden behind a line of thick, overgrown pine trees. Barely into the main yard, he jolted to a halt, rushing out the door toward the house. He didn't want to scare whoever was on the roof into taking a fall, but no way could he turn a blind eye to what looked like a teenaged kid trespassing.

"Hey," he shouted. "What the hell do you think you're doing?"

His feet carried him forward as the youth spun to face him, arms flapping upward. The kid's feet slipped on the worn shingles, his body smacking down on the rooftop then sliding rapidly toward the edge. Trevor put on an extra burst of speed, aiming at where the kid would fall off the roof and plummet to the ground.

He was greeted by silence instead of a jet-propelled body.

Trevor stepped back a couple of paces to discover the kid sprawled belly down, arms spread wide as he clutched a hammer. The prongs had dug into the roof like an ice axe.

"Jeez, you've got horseshoes up your ass." Trevor whipped off his hat as he stared upward, trying to figure out the easiest way to get the kid down so he could kill him with his bare hands. "Stay put. I'll get the ladder."

"There isn't one."

Trevor jerked in surprise. That was no teenaged boy. That was a female voice.

He eased away another foot and examined her more carefully. "How'd you get up there?"

"I climbed. Do you mind? Go away."

Like hell he would. Trevor stayed alert as she got her feet under her, twisting to vertical to stare down like a disapproving angel.

Now that he was closer, it was very clear she was a woman—there was no disguising the way she filled out the flannel shirt and well-worn jeans. Dark brown curls stuck out from under the brim of her baseball cap, the rest of her hair tucked away, and he had the sudden hope the wind would gust and send the cap flying so he could see it all.

She was far enough away some details were lost. Like her eyes—definitely dark, but he wasn't sure if they were deep brown or dusted with lighter tones. Her lips were drawn tightly together into damn near a pout, which gave him all sorts of ideas about how to turn her frown into a smile, not the least of which would be planting a kiss on them.

Because the stubborn glare she was giving him was a challenge and a half, and Trevor liked challenges. Especially when they were delivered by mysterious, good-looking women, although he didn't know about the standing-on-the-neighbour's-roof part.

She wavered for a moment, arms shooting out again to catch her balance. She didn't make a sound, though, probably in an attempt to seem less frightened than she was.

If she wanted to pretend everything was cool, he could play that game as well. "You want a hand?" he drawled.

Her nose twitched. "Is this when you start clapping?"

"I wouldn't dream of it." He glanced along the roofline. The house had a higher section to the left of where she stood, the second-storey windows like wide eyes staring at him. "Seems a strange place to be taking a walk, that's all I'm saying."

"There's a leak," she offered finally as an explanation.

Now they were getting somewhere. Something to fix. He could deal with that. Not to mention, it would give him a chance to possibly pick up some information—details he'd been searching a long time to find. "Why don't I—"

Her feet slipped again, the sharp incline too much to control.

This time Trevor knew she couldn't recover, and he shot forward, keeping a wary eye out for the hammer. It flew off the edge barely a second before she rolled after it.

He expected to hear her shriek on the way down, but deep silence hung on the air in the seconds before he caught her against his body and momentum drove them both to the ground.

She was soft in all the right places, and warm—

—and gone. Vanished before he had a chance to truly appreciate a bit of bodily contact as a reward for his heroic rescue.

She'd scrambled to her feet, backing up until there was ample space between them. "Thank you."

Then damn if she didn't turn and walk away, snatching up her hammer as she passed it, headed straight for the front door.

"That's all you got to say? Thank you?" Trevor raced after her, incredulous. "Really?"

She laid a hand on the door, pausing to look him up and down. For a second he thought she was considering using the hammer on him. "What do you want?"

"I don't want anything. I mean, I want—" He fell silent, looking at her for inspiration.

What the hell *did* he want? She had him so muddled he sounded like an idiot. *Come on, brain in gear.*

He folded his arms over his chest and put on his most flirtatious smile. "Just wanted to say hello, and welcome to the neighbourhood. I heard you've got a leak in your roof. I've come to give you a hand."

There. That should get some kind of positive reaction from her. A smile, a nod, maybe a bit of flirting in return.

Nothing.

Instead, she tugged open the screen door and slipped through, offering one final comment over her shoulder before swinging the solid wood door shut. "Thanks, but I got it under control."

The door clicked. The sound of a deadbolt being turned followed.

Trevor stared in confusion.

The rental house was no longer empty, he'd just rescued a woman falling off the roof, and yet he was no further ahead than he'd been five minutes ago. This was all sorts of fucked up, and not very useful. He didn't know her name, didn't know how she'd gotten there...

A sharp *creak* sounded, and he jumped off the porch, glancing around cautiously. A second squeaking *bang* followed, and this time he looked upward in time to see one of the shutters on the second floor move, and a jean-clad leg extending over the sill.

Incredible. Damn woman was crawling out on the roof again.

He stepped back into her line of vision. "Are you trying to break your fool neck? You're going to fall."

"If you go away and stop distracting me, I won't."

Trevor couldn't believe it. "You've got some kind of a death wish, honey."

Silence in response.

And that was enough to push him over the edge. Trevor wasn't used to being ignored. Especially not by pretty girls.

He took a quick peek to make sure she was solid on her feet before he did anything. She seemed all right. She had an X-Acto blade out and was patiently trimming away the shingles from the lower section of roof.

Sending up a prayer she wouldn't lose her balance while she had the knife in hand, he hurried around the edge of the house to where a giant apple tree sat conveniently located. Convenient at least for his purposes. He shimmied up the trunk and into the first crook before he'd had time to consider what he was doing.

5

But even pausing to wipe his hands before tackling the more difficult part of the climb didn't change his mind.

No way was she leaving him on the ground without any information. He was just being neighbourly, he reasoned, as he stepped from branch to branch, going higher than the eaves trough.

His dad would give him hell if he didn't offer a lady a hand.

Trevor propelled himself from the tree to the roof, tipping forward to land on his hands and knees to catch his balance before scrambling upward, the old, worn tiles warm under his fingers. He moved in silence, not wanting to startle her again, especially when there was no one to catch her if she did fall.

He waited until her hands were empty, watching from barely over the ridge as she cleared away a section of what was clearly water-damaged roofing. She rose and moved cautiously back to the second storey windows, grabbing hold of the windowsill and leaning in for something.

Trevor took advantage of the moment and ran the lower ridgeline to her side. He caught hold of the window and her waist at the same moment he offered a warning.

"Don't panic."

She stiffened but otherwise didn't move. Didn't scream, didn't shout, didn't do anything except cautiously pivot her head toward him. His hopes he'd avoid getting reamed out faded when their gazes met, her eyes blazing.

Shit.

"I didn't want you to fall," he hurried to explain, withdrawing his hand from her waist reluctantly. She was a good-looking woman, and he had zero objections to having her in his arms.

6

But she wasn't only mad, she was white knuckling the windowsill. "How'd you get up here?" she demanded.

Trevor tilted his head toward the corner. "Apple tree. A lot of these old homes have big enough trees you can get upstairs pretty easily." The anger in her eyes flashed momentarily to an entirely different emotion. *Double shit.* "Don't worry, not many people around here have a habit of climbing onto roofs."

"I'm lucky you came over, is that what you're telling me?"

The snarky comment offered a tiny crack in the ice, and Trevor leapt on it with everything he had. He thrust his hand forward. "Can we try this again? I'm Trevor Coleman. You never did tell me your name."

She offered her hand slowly, her grip strong as her fingers wrapped briefly around his. "Becky Hall. I'd really prefer you not be on this roof with me."

"I'd really prefer you not be on the roof, period," Trevor confessed. "But you said you've got a leak. Maybe can we can work out a compromise."

She eyed him up and down, one hand still clutching the edge of the windowsill. It was obvious she was scared to death, but he wasn't sure if it was of him or their height above the ground.

Her pulse was visible at the base of her throat, and he watched it, fascinated, drawn to the soft texture of her skin. If they'd been at Traders Pub, or somewhere in town, he would have leaned in as he flirted, maybe even casually stroked a finger along her neck, just to see how she'd react.

Not the time. *Definitely* not the place. And something warned him to go a hell of a lot slower than

7

usual. Something more than the panic hovering in her eyes.

"How about we discuss a trade?" he offered.

"What kind of trade?"

"I'll fix your roof, and you help me get in touch with your landlord."

She stared at him long and hard, and then without a word, threw a leg over the windowsill and crawled inside.

He waited, hope rising. Maybe she was going to get some paper and give him the phone number.

Instead, she lowered the window between them with a snap and turned the old-fashioned latch firmly before meeting his gaze. "That's okay. I'll take care of the repairs myself." Her voice muffled behind the glass barrier. "I trust you can get down the way you came up."

She disappeared into the darkness as Trevor leaned his face against the window and peered in like some crazy peeping Tom.

Well, shit. That hadn't worked out at all the way he'd hoped.

———————

HE PULLED into the parking space outside the Coleman bachelor pad. Two of his cousins still lived there, and from the trucks parked in the yard, both were home. He hurried into the house to find the back screen door open and Raphael and Jesse sitting on the porch with long necks in their hands.

"Look what the cat drug in." Jesse held out a beer. "I thought you were going to be here half an hour ago. We started without you."

Trevor twisted the cap off his bottle as he dropped into one of the sturdy lawn chairs, taking a long drink of the cold liquid as he looked his cousins over.

In spite of their differences, he was pretty sure most strangers could tell at a glance the three of them were related. Rafe's hair was the blondest. Jesse's a touch darker and then his—a deep brown. His cousins had blue eyes; his were an unremarkable brown. They stood over six feet, solidly built from years of working the land. All of them got their share of female attention without much trouble.

They'd been teased before about their "cowboy uniforms"—jeans, boots and hats, and an unshaved jaw from nights spent tying one on a little too hard.

Trevor laughed. If he showed up looking worse for wear, it was far more likely he'd spent all night chasing down part of the herd or dealing with a ranching emergency. It wasn't easy trying to beat a living from land that seemed hell-bent against being tamed.

The three of them were the last of the Coleman men left unhitched, which was fine by Trevor. He liked playing the field, although he usually had far more luck with the ladies than he'd had that afternoon with Becky.

Rafe eased forward in his chair, curiosity in his eyes. "I met your brother on the road this afternoon. Lee said he was doing late chores, so you should've been done a while ago."

"I was. I headed into town to hit the library."

For some weird reason, Rafe stiffened before demanding, "What were you doing there?"

"Yeah," Jesse teased, "I didn't know you could read."

Trevor rolled his eyes. Jesse being an asshole outweighed poking at Rafe's strange behaviour. "Oh, a cutting blow. You're such a bastard, Jesse."

His cousin smirked harder.

"I can't go on. I'm going to curl up right here and cry in my beer."

"Asshole." Jesse laughed the word. "So... *what?* Why were you in town? Don't make us pull it out of you, because I'm sure it's not that interesting."

Trevor's amusement faded as frustration rushed in. He'd wanted to do this on his own, but after getting stuck without any forward progress, maybe it was time to call in reinforcements. "Trying to find out who owns the parcel of land that butts up to the west of the Moonshine property line. You'd think someone in town would know, especially if there's gossip involved, but everyone is surprisingly tight-lipped, and so far I haven't found anything on file in land records."

"You guys need extra pastureland?" Rafe asked.

"Maybe. Pasture some, hay the rest, but there's no use in making any plans until I know who to contact."

His lack of progress was more than annoying; it was becoming a personal taunt. Like a *fuck you* that he couldn't do as much for his family as the rest of his siblings. "My dad's still not feeling well, so we're all trying to take up the slack until he's back on his feet."

"And even short-handed, you want more land?" Rafe shook his head. "I wish we had your troubles."

"I thought the Angel clan was doing okay," Jesse said. "With going organic, and all that shit."

Rafe made a rude noise. "It's going better than it was, but we're still a long way off making it a complete success. I don't have to tell you why."

Trevor sympathized without saying anything.

10

They all knew that of the older generation of Coleman brothers to settle in the Rocky Mountain House area, Rafe's father Ben had proven to have the shittiest attitude and the least sense. Trevor would take his father—or Jesse's dad, Uncle Mike—any day of the week over Ben, but it wasn't the kind of sentiment you straight up said to another person. *Gee, yeah, it sucks that your dad is an asshole.*

Might be true, but it just wasn't said.

Rafe tipped his chair back on two legs, staring into space as he absently picked at the label on his bottle. "You know, I've never heard the story either. Seems like that land should belong to someone in the family, but I've only heard it called *the rental.*"

Which was what Trevor knew as well.

"We're the youngest, except for Lee, and nobody tells us shit," Jesse complained.

"There's never been a reason to tell us," Raphael pointed out. He finished his bottle and stood. "I'm starving. I'll get supper going."

Trevor lingered over his drink. He'd struck out for the past couple of months, but Becky moving in changed things. Maybe he'd be able to finally get ahead. "There's someone new renting it now," he said. "The house on the southwest quarter."

Jesse raised a brow. "What? The old-timers are gone?" He snapped his fingers. "Hey, you're right. I heard somebody say they decided it was too much work to take care of, so they moved into town. That was back a month or so ago."

"Well, someone else moved in already, so I might be able to find out who owns it from her."

Jesse's eyes widened. "Her? Tell me we've got new blood in the neighbourhood."

11

Something tightened in Trevor's gut. He had absolutely no reason to feel possessive, or protective, but damn if that wasn't what whipped through his veins the instant interest lit up Jesse's expression. "Yeah. Must be an old schoolteacher come to retire, or something," he lied.

Anticipation faded from Jesse's blue eyes. "Well, damn it all." He threw his beer bottle across the deck into the open garbage can, the glass ringing loudly off the metal frame. "I swear Rocky is where people come to die. Makes it difficult to find anybody to spend time with."

The utter dejection in his cousin's voice made Trevor laugh out loud. "What makes it difficult is the fact you've already dated all the women in the area and pissed off most of them, in this county and the next three over."

Jesse held his hands up in surrender, flashing a grin. "I can't help it if I'm too much for any one woman to handle."

Rafe made a gagging noise from the doorway. "If anyone has any appetite left after that load of crap got delivered, get your asses in here and help. Trevor, I take it you're staying for supper?"

Trevor had his own place down the road, but he liked company too much to spend his evenings alone. "I'll cook the vegetables and save your taste buds from Jesse's slam-bam-thank-you-ma'am cooking methods."

Jesse snorted as he rose to join them in the kitchen. "You two have no idea what culinary marvels I'm capable of. I keep my talent on the down-low, kind of like Superman in the kitchen."

"No argument here—you've got a stomach of steel. We're far too redneck for your class of cooking." Rafe shoved a dirty plate into Jesse's hands. "That's why you get to wash. And get a move on, 'cause there's nothing to eat off."

Trevor forgot his worries in the complaining and joking that followed. But one thing he didn't forget was the pair of light-brown eyes that had burned into him with all the fire he liked in a woman.

Intriguing. That's what she was. Not only did Becky Hall have the answers he needed, she was easy on the eyes, and he wanted to find out what made her tick. It was a good combination—one that made him eager to return to the old rental house.

Becky was going to find out just how determined he was to be neighbourly...

Chapter Two

BECKY GLANCED at her watch for the third time since leaving the house. Today it didn't matter how long the walk took, but if she was successful in finding work, she'd need to know for future trips.

Living in the country would have its drawbacks, especially come the winter, but she was too grateful for the roof over her head to complain.

A roof that needed work done before it rained again, but still...

Hard facts were easy to ignore on a day like this. It was a gorgeous morning, with the sun peeking through the morning clouds and a whole lot of birds going absolutely crazy in the bush beside the road. It was easy to have a light heart when everything was so beautiful, in spite of the impossible list of things she had to accomplish once she reached Rocky Mountain House. And the impossible things she had to accomplish at the homestead. And the—

She laughed. By this time she should be used to accomplishing impossible things before breakfast.

It'd barely been a week since she'd arrived, but it felt a lot longer in some ways. She'd explored the ranch house, and all the land within an hour walking radius.

She had a pretty good idea of what she could accomplish with a little hard labour, and that was the one thing she was more than willing to provide.

This was a new start. A new chance to make a better life not only for herself —

—but she couldn't get ahead and dream too quickly. She was still working one step at a time to keep her head above water. But having the opportunity sent a thrill through her every time she realized how much her life had changed.

Even this. Walking at the side of the road, quilt bag in hand and the urge to whistle breaking free as she strode along.

If she wanted to whistle, she could.

She pursed her lips and warbled back at the birds, the melody from her lips accompanied by their trills and chirps, and she didn't worry about how it *wasn't womanly* to be making such a loud racket.

In fact, she increased her volume and swung her arms harder, head lifted high as she marched toward town.

The honk of a vehicle horn directly behind her made her shoot nearly two feet in the air, heart pounding in panic.

Only when she turned, she made sure no sign of her fear showed, smoothing her expression, especially as she recognized the truck slowing to a snail's pace beside her.

Oh goody. Her meddlesome rescuer.

Becky kept walking, glancing into the cab as the truck pulled up beside her. The passenger window slid downward, the truck now rolling forward an inch at a time, keeping pace with her strides.

"Hop in, rodeo girl." Trevor adjusted the tan cowboy hat on his head as he flashed a smile.

"No, thank you."

Any normal person would have nodded then driven on, but considering the man had climbed a tree to get her attention the previous day, she should have known a simple *no* wouldn't be enough to get him to leave her alone.

"If you're going to town you may as well ride. I'm headed your way."

"It's a nice day," she said clearly, offering him a brief nod. "I'll enjoy my walk. Thanks. Maybe I'll see you around sometime."

She totally ignored him and went back to whistling.

Well, not *totally* ignored, because it was difficult to forget that a massive four-by-four traveled exactly ten feet behind her, and no matter how fast she walked, or how much she dawdled, he stayed put.

She covered another mile before turning to face him, arms folded across her chest as she glared at the truck and the stubborn man behind the wheel.

He eased all the way up until he was in line with her again. The smile in his brown eyes matched the one creasing his lips.

"Hop in, rodeo girl," he repeated. "I'm headed into town, how about a ride?"

"I don't want a ride," she insisted. "I really wish you'd leave me alone."

The sparkle of amusement faded from his eyes. "Oh, hey, if you're worried about getting a ride with a stranger, you can call anyone you'd like to let them know you're with me. But I promise I'm safe."

God. She *was* naïve—being worried about safety was the perfect excuse, although no way was she admitting she didn't have a phone. "I'm happy walking, but thanks for the offer. I appreciate it."

"How about I loan you my truck," he blurted out. "You can head into town on your own."

Shock made her feet come to a stop. "What is *wrong* with you?"

"What?"

She was tempted to take her bag off her shoulder and swing it at the truck. "You can't just give me your truck, or offer for me to leave you abandoned at the side of the road. That makes no sense."

He shrugged. "Makes no sense to me that you're walking when I'm driving the same direction you're headed." He tilted his head toward the seat. "Come on."

"I bet you were an annoying child," she snapped, resuming her march. But now she stared straight ahead to keep him from seeing the smile she was having difficulty hiding.

The truck was barely moving, inching its way down the highway. It was a good thing there was no other traffic, or they would've caused a traffic jam.

"Are you new to town, or visiting?" Trevor continued as if they were having a conversation somewhere normal and not at the side of the road with him driving in a one-car parade. "If you're sticking around, I can show you the sights. What're you interested in?"

"Being left alone?" she retorted. "But you don't seem to understand that concept."

"Just tagging along to keep you safe," he said, his deep voice tinged with amusement. "It can be tricky business, walking all the way into Rocky. I'd hate for you to get lost."

"The road doesn't turn once between here and town," Becky pointed out, glancing into the cab. She was losing her battle to keep a straight face.

Especially when he gasped in shock, his face twisting dramatically. "*No.* Jeez, you mean those four right turns I've been taking my entire life aren't necessary?" Becky snorted, and Trevor laughed, snapping up a hand to wiggle a finger at her. "I knew there was a sense of humour hiding in there."

She gave up. If he was going to be this persistent she might as well save her feet a bit of wear and tear. "Stop the truck. You win."

His grin grew wider as she hauled open the door and crawled inside. "Where to, rodeo girl?"

Suddenly she wasn't as certain. She had a whole bunch of places on her list, but she supposed the one that was the closest would be best.

"Anywhere on Main Street would be great. Thanks." She tightened the seatbelt over her chest and placed her bag in her lap.

"So, Becky Hall, what brings you to Rocky Mountain House?"

A perfectly civil question, and one she'd prepared for. "It was time to move out," she said with complete honesty.

Trevor nodded, his square jaw all the more noticeable in profile as he kept his gaze on the road, giving her plenty of time to study him. "There comes a time to do the next thing," he agreed.

She could agree with that. It was past time.

"You have a job in Rocky?" he asked.

"Nothing yet," she admitted. "That's what I need to do today. Drop off resumes, talk to people—get my bearings."

"I know a lot of folk in town," he said enticingly. "What are you looking for? Maybe I can put in a good word for you."

"Right. You don't even know me."

He laughed again, the sound echoing brightly in the cab, and somehow the sheer joy in it made little bubbles of happiness rise in her core as well, like the birdsong earlier in the day had lifted her spirits.

"Sure, I know you," he insisted. "You're my neighbour. Plus, you're determined enough to crawl on a second-storey roof even though you're afraid of heights. And you're stubborn enough to refuse to take the easy way out. I can honestly recommend you for a number of jobs based on those habits alone."

She leaned back in her seat and took a deep breath. "Okay, you can help me. You know anyone who's hiring?"

"Depends on your skills," he said. "You got any training or certificates?"

"No. Nothing official."

"What were the last three jobs you had?"

She had to give titles to what she'd done? She'd done everything, and nothing. Cook and nanny. Teacher and nurse.

Whore.

"I can cook, and clean, and sew," she replied firmly. She shouldn't try to work with children—she bet too many questions would be asked to get those types of jobs.

He nudged her arm lightly. "Did you sew that bag?"

19

She curled her arms around the sachet. She shouldn't have taken it, but leaving everything behind had been impossible. "Yes."

"That narrows it down then. You can quilt—which means first person you should talk to is Hope. Hope Coleman."

The familiar last name registered a second before panic set in. He'd been flirting with her, she was sure of it, and yet...

And yet it's not as if she hadn't had first-hand experience with worse.

"She your wife?"

He'd just lifted a Coke to his lips, but the instant she spoke he was choking, a thin trickle of liquid running down his shirt before he wiped at his mouth and coughed hard to clear his throat. "Jeez, Rodeo, you did that on purpose."

"Did what? And why are you calling me that?"

"Hope is my *cousin's* wife, and she owns the quilt shop in town. And I'm calling you Rodeo because of this." He ran a finger along the white fringe decorating the sleeve of her plaid shirt. "That's what barrel riders wear to rodeo."

The fancy shirts with the tassels were like nothing she'd ever worn before, but they'd come cheap from the thrift shop she'd visited. All she could stuff into a bag for two dollars.

"Sorry to disappoint you, but I don't rodeo. I just liked the shirts." Even as she spoke, a touch of anticipation was rising. She *could* quilt. "Do you think Hope needs help?"

"I happen to know she does," Trevor assured her, turning at the first set of lights and heading down Main

Street. "She's expecting, so she's looking for an assistant to ease the load."

He pulled to a stop at the side of the road, and she glanced over eagerly at a neat glass-fronted shop proudly declaring *The Stitching Post*.

"It looks nice." She turned to face him. "Thanks for the ride."

"No problem."

Only before she had both feet on the sidewalk, he had somehow gotten out and around the vehicle fast enough to offer her a helping hand.

Before she could complain, or stutter uncomfortably, Trevor pulled the wind from her sails. "Let me introduce you," he offered.

It was too strong of an incentive for her to turn down. Add in that he'd been nothing but charming for the last five minutes, Becky decided to stuff away her reservations for the moment.

"Thank you. Again."

"Just being neighbourly," he said with a wink as he pulled open the shop door and gestured her forward.

A small bell rang overhead as Becky eased past him, her body brushing his muscular frame in the tight doorway. She stepped quickly into the open to widen the gap between them, a riot of colour pulling her attention to the shop around her.

It was amazing. Sample quilts hung on the walls, while row after row of bright cotton fabrics were arranged by colour families on sturdy shelves. Tables and books and buttons and…if she'd ever dreamt of heaven it would have started with a room like this.

Becky pivoted in place and hoped with all her heart that Trevor's good word would be enough to get her the job.

Chapter Three

THE BELL on the door offered enough of a warning that Hope was already approaching, her pale-blue eyes taking in Trevor and the newcomer he'd brought along.

"You're not who I expected for the first customer of the day, Trevor. Does Aunt Kate need something?" Hope came to a stop directly in front of them, transferring her load of patterns to the opposite arm as she examined Becky more closely.

"Hope, I'd like you to meet Becky Hall. She's new to Rocky, living in the rental on the quarter west of Moonshine land."

"Nice to meet you, Becky." Hope glanced between them, probably trying to figure out how they knew each other. Being Hope, though, she tried to find a polite conversation topic. "Do you sew?"

Becky nodded, but her focus was elsewhere. She seemed distracted, her gaze darting around the room. "This is amazing. Did you make all the quilts?"

"Most of them. A few are local women who teach different techniques. If there's anything that catches your attention, we might have a class you could join."

"I think Becky knows how to do a lot of this stuff, already." Trevor slipped into the conversation since his mystery woman seemed more interested in scoping out the shop than selling her skills. "She's looking for work," he shared. "She's good—you should hire her."

Becky's head snapped toward him, a crease forming between her brows as if to warn him off.

Hope's demeanor changed slightly. A little less like she was talking to a potential customer, and more like dealing with a future employee.

"Trust Trevor to get straight to the point," she said with a laugh before waving him away. "Let us talk, then. We don't need your help."

Maybe not, but he was too curious to do more than drift away a few feet and pretend to be fascinated with one of the mechanic magazines Hope had stashed beside a comfortable chair. It was obviously a place set up for men to relax while their women shopped, but it was close enough to the front till he could overhear their conversation without *looking* like he was listening intently to every word.

"How about you tell me what you're looking for, and we'll take it from there," Hope suggested.

"Full-time work would be best, but part-time is fine." Becky twisted to face the counter, showing that intense concentration he'd seen while she was ignoring him. "I can work days or evenings—my schedule is wide open right now."

"Have you worked in a fabric store before?"

Becky hesitated before shaking her head. "No, but I know how to stock shelves and keep supplies in order. And I can help with questions when it comes to most quilt designs, as well as help gather the materials for people."

23

"What about the cash register, or ordering new supplies?" Hope leaned back, both hands pressed into her lower back. The move stretched the front of her jumper over the small round formed by her expanding belly, making it clear there was a baby on the way. "Sorry. I overdid it yesterday."

There was another pause while Becky looked over the machine, her nose wrinkling in the most adorable way. "I haven't used that kind of register, but I'm sure I could learn it. And ordering—it depends. What system do you use?"

Hope rattled off a list of numbers and letters that Trevor couldn't make heads or tails of.

Neither could Becky from the panic twisting her face.

Hope chuckled. "It's not much more than a basic Excel spreadsheet, if that helps."

Becky shook her head again. "Computers aren't my thing. This is." She pulled the bag off her shoulder and held it out.

Hope took the quilted fabric and nodded in admiration as she turned it over. "It's pretty. Hand pieced?"

"All my work is." Becky gestured to the bag. "There's a wall hanging inside, as well."

Hope's expression changed rapidly as she pulled fabric from the bag and laid it on the counter between them. "Holy *shit.*"

Trevor was still pretending to not be listening or he would've been on his feet in an instant. He tried to glance past the edge of the magazine, but he was too far away to see what had made Hope swear like a sailor. To him it looked as if she was staring wide-eyed at nothing more than a piece of painted fabric.

But he guessed not because his cousin-in-law seemed damned impressed.

"You've got some mad skills," Hope murmured. "I've never seen a watercolour design that detailed." She passed the quilt back with reluctance. "I don't know if it's enough, though. You being able to sew."

"What if I try for a week?" Becky offered. "No charge—I'll volunteer. See if it works for you, and if it does, then we can talk."

Hope glanced over and met Trevor's gaze.

He dipped his chin. Unless Becky was a far better actress than he'd guessed, it wasn't a risky move. He didn't think she'd take off with the cashbox or anything, and it would give Hope a chance to see if this was the help she needed. Seemed a win/win move to him.

"Okay, you can start tomorrow," Hope agreed. "Ten o'clock, and you can fill out the paperwork when you get here."

Behind them the bell rang as the door opened, and a group of a half dozen ladies slipped in, talking excitedly as they moved into the shop.

"I could start right now, if you want," Becky offered. She pointed to the half-empty box Hope must have been working on when they'd arrived. "I can stock that if you want to help your customers."

Hope seemed torn.

All of three seconds later, one of the women called her name and waved excitedly. "Oh, you got in that fabric I've been looking for. Hope, can you help me? I need to get started on this today."

"Of course, Mrs. Tate. I'll be right there." Hope hurried around the counter and pressed the box into Becky's open hands. "You're on, girl. Start today, and I'll buy you lunch. And I'll pay you for the week, no matter what. Deal?"

"Deal," Becky agreed quickly.

Hope went one way, and Becky the other, but she paused for a moment and her smile widened as she faced Trevor.

"Told you Hope was awesome," he offered.

She fidgeted then nodded sincerely. "Thank you."

"Hey, no prob. You're the one who has to do the work."

He tipped his hat and left the shop to get the things he needed from the hardware store. And after that he had a dozen urgent tasks all loudly calling his name.

But like the night before, he couldn't get the damn woman off his mind.

Hours passed as he worked with his older brother, checking and repairing the field equipment in preparation for the coming season. When he found himself drifting from his task yet again, Trevor gave up. He might as well call it quits and go see how her day had gone.

His tools were put away and he was stripping off the blue overalls he'd worn to keep the grease and oil from his clothes before Steve noticed.

His brother paused to wipe the sweat off his forehead with the back of his sleeve before frowning. "Where're you headed in such an all-fired hurry?"

For how much time Trevor had spent that day wondering how Becky was doing, he should've used at least thirty seconds to plan an excuse for cutting out early.

I need to go stalk our new neighbour probably wasn't good enough.

He opened his mouth and closed it a couple of times before giving up. "I'm meeting someone in town."

Steve sat in silence. Just sat there, drinking from his water bottle and waiting for Trevor to confess to... *something.*

It didn't take long for guilt to roll in like the bastard wanted. "I'll finish this later tonight, I promise. I want to be there on time."

"Well, that's fine. My time means shit, though, is that it?"

"No, of course not."

"Next time tell me you've got a date," Steve complained. "Finishing the swather is a two-person job. We would have worked on something else this afternoon if I'd known you were going to leave. And we can't finish it later because Melody and I are going riding tonight."

"I'm sorry." And now he felt like a shit for screwing up Steve's plans. "I can stay."

Steve waved a hand. "Forget it. Only don't make any plans for tomorrow morning because we're going to stick to this job until we're done, got it?"

He might've felt terrible, but he was also itching to leave. Trevor headed toward his truck as he called out a reply. "I promise. Tomorrow I'm all yours. For as long as it takes."

"You know I'm going to find out who's got you all rattled," Steve shouted after him as Trevor climbed into his truck and pulled the door shut. "And I will tease you unmercifully every chance I get."

Trevor stuck his hand out the window and gave his brother the finger as he drove away, hurrying home to grab the fastest shower ever.

Dressed in clean clothes, he tore down the back roads so he could make it to the door of the Stitching Post right at four thirty.

Only it was Hope's head that popped up when the bell announced his entrance.

"Hey."

She motioned him forward, waving her hand frantically. "What is going on?" she demanded.

"What?" He glanced around the shop, but no one else was there. No customers, no Becky. "Where is she?"

"The place emptied out about half an hour ago, so I sent her home. The shop is on short hours today."

Dammit. If he hadn't taken the shortcut, he might've spotted her on the road. Or maybe she'd gone to pick up some groceries...

Hope poked a finger into his chest. "Hey, stop your woolgathering and talk to me."

It finally registered. Hope's question when he walked into the place. "Is something wrong?"

She made a face. "I...I don't know."

He was still missing a bunch of details, but he hadn't meant to cause any trouble. "Hey, if Becky's not going to work out, don't feel obligated to keep her on because I brought her in. It's your shop."

"It's not that. She's great when it comes to the quilting stuff. She organized a whole bunch of projects I've been wanting to get to, cleaned up the storage room, *and* somehow convinced Mrs. Tyler to buy something instead of hanging out and talking my ear off for two hours."

Whoa. "She got Mrs. McScrooge to open her purse and spend some *money?*"

Hope nodded. "I'd call her a miracle worker, but it's the other stuff I don't understand. Hang on." She

28

marched to the door and peeked out for a moment before closing it firmly and turning the deadbolt. After flipping the *open* sign to *closed*, she rejoined him at the counter. "She has no ID, Trevor."

"She forgot it?" Damn. If he'd been there half an hour earlier he could have driven her home so she could get it.

"No, as in she outright told me she doesn't have a social insurance number. And that it'd be fine if I paid her under the table."

Not what he'd expected to hear. Not at all. "You can't do that. Can you?"

Hope hesitated. "I... And this is why I don't know what to think because I'd love to hire her, but I don't know if I want to risk getting in trouble. But we talked a bit while we worked, and I really like her, and it sounds as if she's got a lot to offer, but..."

"How could someone not have ID? That makes no sense."

"I don't know." Her face crinkled with concern. "There's an awful lot I don't know about her, yet."

"Do you trust her?" Trevor asked. "I mean, were you worried about being alone in the shop with her, or anything?"

"Of course not. It wasn't like that at all."

He tried to ease a few of her fears. "At least she was honest about not having the information you need."

"That made it better, and worse, at the same time," Hope complained. "If she'd lied I'd have no trouble kicking her to the curb, but the way she said it—as if she *expected* me to tell her to get out—damn near broke me."

He offered a consoling hug. Hope could be tenderhearted at the best of times, and pregnancy hormones were probably making this worse. He squeezed

29

her for a moment before a thought struck. "You know whoever she's renting from must have information, or they wouldn't have let her move in."

Hope backed away and nodded slowly. "You're right. I need to talk to Matt. See what he thinks."

"Is she going to finish out the week?"

"Yeah, and I feel okay about that. It'll give me time to make a decision how to deal with this."

And it would give Trevor time to dig up some more details as well. "Talk to Matt, but if either of you need anything, give me a shout. I'm going to go try and talk to her."

"I like her," Hope insisted again. "I want to help her, but not if it's going to get me in trouble. I can't risk it, Trev, I can't."

"No one expects you to, least of all Becky, from the sounds of it." He tweaked Hope's nose. "While I'm here, you need anything lifted or whatever?"

She shook her head. "Come on, I'll let you out the front door so you don't have to walk all the way around the block to your truck."

"Aww. I'm young and fit," Trevor taunted. "Unlike your husband who was sucking wind the last time we hauled bales. Looks like Matt's put on a few pounds."

"It's all muscle," Hope declared firmly. "And I bet he was tired that day because we'd stayed up all night playing grownup games."

Damn. "You play dirty, cousin," Trevor complained.

"Don't come to a battle of wits unarmed," she teased.

He was still chuckling when he hit the highway back to his place. Which, not so coincidentally, was also the highway to Becky's place.

Trevor caught up with her a mile from home, a plastic grocery bag in one hand as she marched double time along the side of the road. It only took a moment to do a reenactment of their morning's adventure, pulling beside her and lowering the window.

"Hey, Rodeo."

She stopped completely and gave him the most delicious dirty glare. Whatever else had happened that day, she still had enough *what the fuck* attitude in her to make him grin. "I don't rodeo."

"You also don't know you're supposed to walk on the highway facing the traffic," he pointed out. "Get in. I'll take you home."

Becky growled, but she jerked open the door and crawled in, resting her groceries on the seat between them. "You're stalking me."

"Maybe," he admitted. "Just a little," he hurriedly added when her eyes flashed wide with something that looked suspiciously like fear. "Not in that creepy *I'm going to bury you in a freezer in my backyard* kind of way. You intrigue me, Becky Hall. I want to know more about you."

She sat in silence for a moment. "Did Hope tell you?"

She'd been honest earlier. She'd probably appreciate the same now. "That she wants to hire you because you're really good, but that you don't have any identification she can use for taxes and all that stuff? Yeah, she told me."

Becky perked up. "She wants to hire me?"

"She does. So we need to figure out a solution to the other half of your problem."

"I sent in the requests for new papers, but it's going to take time for them to go through." She twisted

31

sideways in her seat so she could stare at him, her face far more expressive without the mask she seemed to drop into place at a moment's notice. Now she looked completely confounded. "Why're you being so nice?"

"Because I'm just a nice kinda guy," Trevor flashed back like he usually would before pausing. This wasn't the moment for trite humour. "Honestly? I don't know why. Other than you seem to need someone to give you a hand, and I feel like I should."

She didn't all of a sudden jump up and down and declare she trusted him, but some of the tension eased out of her shoulders.

Becky leaned back in the seat. "There've been so many good things happening lately I can't believe they're true. It's as if I'm waiting for a giant boot to drop out of the sky and crush me. That would be more like what I'm used to."

"And sometimes life changes," Trevor insisted. "Maybe there won't be a boot this time. Maybe whatever it is that's brought you to Rocky is because it's time for a change for the better. Everything bad in the past, and nothing but good ahead."

She sat quietly for a minute. "Part of me wants to say that that's impossible. Life doesn't change that fast, but the other part of me wants it to be true with every bit of my being."

He was approaching her driveway, which meant there was a deadline to deal with. If she didn't invite him in, he didn't know when they might get the chance to pick up this conversation again. "You have plans for tonight?" he asked.

"I'm going to work in the garden." Becky nudged the bag between them. "I bought some seeds, but the garden needs to be cleaned up before I can plant."

"Want to have supper with me first?" The invitation burst free without much forethought. "We could talk about your problem and figure out some solutions." Making it less of a date and more of a meeting, he supposed.

He didn't care what they called it as long as she didn't disappear again.

Trevor pulled to a stop on the road to wait for her answer, which let him look her square in the face as she considered his offer. Her nose twitched as she eyed him before slowly agreeing. "Okay."

He would've sworn somebody hit him with a cattle prod. A white-hot shot of excitement raced through him—he hadn't felt that kind of rush since the eighth grade when Tammy Janzten up and kissed him out of the blue.

He wasn't a teenager, and all Becky had done was agree to come over to his house for a meal. Still, reality didn't chase away the thrill running through his veins.

Trevor hoped like hell there was something in the cupboards at his place other than Kraft dinner.

Chapter Four

SHE WAS out of her mind.

In less than twenty-four hours, she'd gone from sticking to her plan of keeping to a solitary lifestyle to three times over accepting help from a virtual stranger.

Only...strangers were the ones who'd made the biggest difference in her life recently. The people she'd known for years had been the problem.

Still, there was enough anxiety hanging over her head to move cautiously.

The way Trevor rushed into the singlewide mobile home ahead of her was kind of endearing. She deliberately walked slower, figuring he needed a chance to clean up his bachelor pad, but the living room was surprisingly sparse except for the remote controls and car magazines on the coffee table.

"Give me a minute," he said, shifting his broad body through the small doorway into the kitchen to peer into the fridge. "I've got beer, juice and water."

"Juice is great."

Cupboards clattered and doors banged as she left him alone and instead took a closer look at her surroundings. The exterior screamed old, but inside everything was sparkling clean and bright.

On either side of the picture window, family portraits hung on the wall, a collection of smiling faces. She moved closer to examine them, picking out Hope in one group shot, her potential boss held tight against a good-looking man with a neat dark beard who had to be one of Trevor's cousins—the resemblance was uncanny.

"I see you've discovered the mug shots." Trevor marched back into the room and offered her a tall glass of cold orange juice. "Let me give you a tour."

"Hope told me there were a lot of family in town," Becky admitted, "but I thought she was exaggerating when she called you a horde." It wasn't an outrageous number of people by her standards, but she bet to most people in the area, they were an anomaly.

Trevor stepped beside her and tapped on pictures as he spoke. "Here's the whole lot of us. Four of the original Coleman brothers settled in Rocky. Mike, Ben, George, and that's my dad, Randy. This shot is our immediate family. Steve's the oldest, and Melody is his girlfriend. She's one of the local veterinarians. My younger brother Lee and his girlfriend, Rachel. My sister Anna—she's with the RCMP, and that's Mitch, her husband. Their family owns one of the local garages. Steve, Lee and I work with my parents." He pointed to another picture that showed his parents, the two of them standing under a flower-filled arbor. "They had a big anniversary party a few weeks ago."

She turned to the next set of pictures and was surprised when he didn't follow her. Instead, he stood back a few paces looking kind of sheepish.

"What's wrong?"

Trevor grimaced. "I didn't mean to talk your ear off. It's bad enough that there are million of us in the area. I don't want you to think you have to memorize names, or anything."

Becky laughed, snapping up a hand to cover her reaction. "I'm sorry, that was rude, but I honestly don't mind."

He still looked uncomfortable. "Just assume if you see someone who kinda looks like me, they're probably related. Heck, anyone you meet on the street, if you assume they're a Coleman, you'd be right fifty percent of the time."

"I'm sure it's not quite as bad as that," Becky assured him.

"I don't know. The locals gave up on calling us only Coleman a long time ago. My family are the Moonshine Colemans, then there are the Angel clan, Whiskey Creek and Six Pack to round out the mob."

She knew more about this kind of thing than he could imagine. "Only makes sense to use nicknames when there are a lot of you. From the sounds of it, though, there must be specific reasons *those* names came about."

Trevor gestured toward the kitchen. "Come on. Let me get something cooking, and then if you're still absolutely engrossed in this conversation, I'll tell you all kinds of stories."

She followed him into the small kitchen which was little more than a counter, a row of cabinets and sink, fridge and stove all tucked together as neat as could be into the small space.

Trevor opened the freezer and let out a happy hoot. "Hot dog. I mean, hamburgers." He offered a smile. "How many you want?"

Forget being polite, she was hungry. Lunch had been a long time ago. "Two, please. Can I get anything else together?"

He pointed at the fridge as he worked to unwrap the burgers and buns. "Grab all the fixings and the potato salad. It won't be fancy, but it'll fill the gaps."

He slipped out the front door with a plate in his hand, and she joined him a few minutes later, the scent of the burgers already making her mouth water. "Smells good."

"Food always smells good after you've put in a hard day's work."

Which reminded her all over of her problem. "Thank you for helping today with Hope. I'm sorry, though, to have gotten you tangled up in my troubles."

He eased a flipper under the edge of a burger to peek at the bottom before turning it over, the meat sizzling on the grill. "I told you I don't mind helping however I can."

She rested her elbows on the railing behind her as she looked him over and debated how much to say. "It's a long story, but like I told you, I'm working on getting new ID. Until it arrives, I don't know what to do. I mean, I don't want to get Hope in trouble, but I really need a job."

"Makes sense to me," Trevor said. "You know how long it might take for things to come through?"

"No idea."

He closed the lid on the grill and matched position opposite her, leaning against the wall of the trailer. He folded his arms, his long legs stretching in front of him. He'd taken off his light jacket when they'd gotten to the house, and he wore a simple T-shirt, his biceps fighting with the fabric. He was long and lean and a whole lot more muscular than—

37

"Let's figure out how you can work and make some money without government approval, for the moment."

His words distracted her away from dangerous territory. No—that wasn't right. His words were edging *into* dangerous territory. "I don't want to get you into trouble, either," she insisted.

"Of course, you don't, but we can find a solution without anybody getting into trouble." He tilted his head slightly as he examined her more closely. "Two questions before we go any further." His tone suddenly serious.

"If I can, I'll answer them."

"Are you on the run from the police? Like, my sister's not going to take one look at you and announce you're on an armed-and-dangerous poster somewhere in the RCMP office?"

She raised a hand in the air like she was swearing an oath. "I'm not in trouble with the police."

"Good. Although I was hoping you were some kind of mafia overlord moving to Rocky to set up an underground trade in quilts. That would've offered a little excitement for the summer."

"Quilts?" He was deliberately being silly, and a smile escaped. "If I get to choose, I'd like a nice *quiet* summer. What's your second question?"

If anything his expression grew more serious. "Are you in danger?" He hurried on before she could take a breath to deny it. "And I'm not asking you to tell me secrets that will make things worse, and don't tell me if I'm guessing right, but if you're on the run from an abusive ex, or something, I hope you'd let me know. Or let Hope know. That way we can keep you safe. Safer."

The longer Trevor spoke, the tighter her throat grew, and she was once again floored by exactly how miraculously good her luck had been right when she needed it most. "I'm okay. I'm pretty sure, but thank you for the offer. You have no idea what it means..."

And that was it. Her voice was choked off by the tears she refused to let fall. She would *not* weep—not when what she was being offered was good and kind, and everything she'd never dreamed possible.

Trevor's eyes widened and he put down the flipper. "Oh, hey. I didn't mean to go and make you cry."

He looked absolutely horrified. Becky swallowed hard and forced a smile back to her lips. "Trust me, these are happy tears."

"If you say so."

And then he changed the topic, thank God, until the burgers were done and they were sitting in lawn chairs with plates balanced on their knees. He told her all about the family nicknames and the land around them, using his hands excitedly as he pointed in different directions toward landmarks.

The food went down well. Went down like she'd barely eaten anything in the past week, which was not too far from the truth. And Trevor seemed content to ramble without her contributing much. Everything he shared was interesting, but even more, his going on and on was a chance for her to get her bearings and not have to be careful about every word she said.

Mentally picturing the two of them gave her another moment of sheer, overwhelming wonderment. She and this handsome man sat together, sharing a meal without any obligation on either part other than to be a good neighbour.

She was suddenly very glad she'd taken a chance and accepted the help of strangers.

TREVOR LOGAN Coleman was utterly smitten. His mystery woman turned out to have the appetite of a linebacker and more secrets than a crazy whodunit novel.

She'd eaten both the burgers he'd grilled for her, plus a huge serving of potato salad, *and* a bowl of ice cream served up Jesse Coleman style—three giant scoops.

Even as he enjoyed her company, he was very aware whatever was haunting her had its teeth in tight. She tensed at every loud noise in the background. Something as innocuous as the rumble of a truck rolling down the secondary highway nearby his trailer set her on high alert. But just like she'd been stubborn enough to get up on the roof in spite of her fears, after a second's pause, she'd pull herself together and ask him the next question.

He'd felt uncomfortable talking about his family earlier, but it seemed getting to know everything about them made her relax. When she relaxed, this little smile would sneak out and send a thrill up his spine.

The more she smiled, the more he worked to make her do it again.

Yep. Absolutely and *completely* smitten.

Which was why once they had consumed an extraordinary amount of calories, Trevor was still not ready to call it a night. "Do you know if you've got any tools over at the rental? A shovel, or a hoe?"

"One of each," she said, adjusting her jacket over her shoulders as she prepared to leave. "Why?"

"Wanted to know what to bring along to help with the garden."

And...they were back to her staring evilly at him.

"You don't need to help me."

"Of course I do," he insisted. "It's in the *Just Being Neighbourly* manual."

A small noise escaped her, as if she was growling at him in annoyance. Sick bastard that he was, he liked that as much as one of her smiles.

She stood on the path leading to his truck and the road past her house. "If I refuse to let you help me, am I gonna wake up and find you've done it anyway?"

"Hell, no."

"Really." Totally deadpan voice. Amusing as all get out.

Trevor shook his head and drew an X over his heart. "Wouldn't be me. It would be those pesky garden gnomes we've got in the area. Had a real infestation a few years back, and we've never been able to figure out how to get rid of them."

Jackpot. Becky smiled, admittedly a kind of a twisted thing because her lips were pursed together as if she was trying not to laugh.

"If I let you help me get everything ready, you have to promise that once I have a garden growing, you'll take some produce. Or baking, or something like that."

"Saskatoon muffins. I'd sell my soul for a batch."

Becky shot out a hand, and he took it, her firm grip the first thing he noticed followed rapidly by vivid images of her using that grip on him.

Damn, he had it bad.

He pointed past her to the shed at the back of his property. "I've got a small tractor in there. How about I put some tools in the truck, and you drive it home? I'll

41

bring over the tractor, and we'll see what kind of damage we can do to your weed patch."

"What is it with you trying to give away your truck all the time?" she asked.

Trevor laughed. "You can drive the tractor if you'd like." She held out her hand palm up. He shrugged before dropping the keys into her hand. "Talented woman."

"Anything I need to know?"

"It's a John Deere. Is there anything else to know?"

She adjusted her bag over her shoulder and marched away from him, completely focused on her destination. Trevor was focused on the swing of her hips.

Damn, again.

Smitten *and* very keen on getting to know the mysterious Becky Hall better in more ways than one.

He beat her to the rental by a few minutes. He'd waited in his yard until the tractor engine kicked over in case she had trouble with the old beast, but from the way she backed it out of the shed and through the narrow gate into the back forty, this wasn't her first time behind the wheel.

"Nice job, Rodeo," he said, joining her beside the tractor she'd left idling. He eyed the garden space before hiding a wince. Unfortunately, weed patch had been an optimistic term for the mess they faced. "I don't think anyone's tackled that for a long time."

"That's why the renters before me left. Once they couldn't take care of the garden anymore, they figured it was time."

The momentary drop of information threatened to distract him, but Trevor pushed it away for now. "How big do you like it?"

Shit, that came out dirtier than he'd intended. Thankfully, she was already stepping away to mark the perimeter without giving him grief.

"You want to drive, or you want me to?" he shouted after her.

"You go ahead. I'll grab everything else I need from the shed and follow behind with a shovel."

Which meant she'd be the one doing the hard physical labour, but it was too late now to go back without making it sound like he was trying to protect her.

Over an hour later he turned off the engine, climbing down to be greeted by the scent of fresh-turned spring dirt, an instant *put him in a good mood* scent. He grabbed a set of gloves from the tractor box and moved toward where Becky was working, a clean line of pristine topsoil behind her. A massive pile of weeds lay stacked along the edge of the garden.

He grabbed a second shovel and went to work beside her.

Becky startled, her eyes going wide before she took a deep breath and let it out slowly. "Wow. I didn't even notice the tractor stopped."

"It's my catlike ways. Silent and mysterious."

Her lips twitched as she stood, stretching her back before leaning her rake against a fence post. "You want a bowl of milk?"

It took him a second to get it. "Cold water?"

She tilted her head toward the house. "Come on. That's enough for today. I really appreciate all your help, but the sun's about to go behind the mountains. I think you've put in a long enough day."

So had she. If it took him stopping to get her to stop, that was fine.

He joined her in the tiny back area where paving stones created a small patio, albeit frost heaved and uneven. There was barely enough space for the two ancient straight-backed chairs he pulled from under the eaves.

He didn't ask to go into the house. That look in her eyes from earlier in the day when he'd asked if someone was stalking her—she hadn't said yes, but she hadn't said straight-out no, either. Trevor figured she probably wasn't ready to let anyone into her safe zones.

So he sat in the rock-hard chair and gazed toward the west where the sun was shooting streaks of gold and red skyward as the fiery ball dipped below the ridgeline. They sat in silence and drank the glasses of ice-cold water she'd brought out.

It was peaceful and perfect, and it was crazy how happy he was to be sitting there with a virtual stranger.

He heard the horses before he saw them. Steve, his brother, and his fiancée turned off the road into Becky's yard, dismounting and leading their rides closer.

Trevor offered a warning to Becky. "Remember that ugly guy in the pictures I pointed out? My oldest brother, Steve? That's him now."

She didn't bolt, but he could tell she wanted to. "Did you miss curfew, or something?"

"Probably want to say hello." Although how Steve had tracked him down, Trevor had no idea. He hadn't said a word about where he was going. He rose to his feet and moved forward.

Becky still looked worried, and Trevor hurried to reassure her, motioning her to join him.

"Come on, he's pretty safe. And Melody is cool enough to more than make up for any stupidity on my brother's part."

44

"I heard that," Steve said, leaning his elbows on the other side of the wooden railing separating the garden space from the front yard, his horse's reins dangling from his hands.

"I heard it too," Melody smirked, bumping Steve with her hip. "I've always liked your brother. He's got a good head on his shoulders."

Trevor gestured toward his family. "The Moonshine Colemans, or at least another small part. Guys, this is Becky."

Becky stepped forward and offered a hand. "Nice to meet you." She glanced around them to the horses. "Good-looking animals."

Way to make a hit with Melody. His sister-in-law-to-be smiled harder. "They're sound and even-tempered. I'm training them to drive, but it's still nice to take them out solo every now and then."

The woman at his side nodded. "Wagon, cart or carriage?" she asked.

Melody lit up. She waved a hand at Trevor and Steve. "You boys go play. I'm dying for a conversation about driving with somebody who doesn't nod politely while their eyes glaze over."

"I don't know that much," Becky insisted. She glanced at Trevor, concern in her eyes again.

"Remember, I told you Melody's a vet. If you run out of carriage things to talk about, ask her what she's been working on. If you don't mind all the gory details."

It was strangely difficult to step away to where Steve stood just out of earshot. There was no reason on earth why he had to worry about leaving Becky with Melody.

There was no reason on earth he should worry about her in the first place, but that ship had sailed.

Steve glanced between him and Becky. "Made a new friend?"

"Seems that way. What's up?"

"Matt phoned. Sounds as if your new friend has had a difficult time of it."

Not that he could fill in many details, the few he had might ease the tension that had rolled in faster than a Chinook wind. "I asked her if she's in trouble and she insists she's not. At least not with the police."

Steve gave him a look. "Right, because every person who's in trouble is going to up and tell you in the first thirty seconds of meeting you."

Trevor thought about it for moment. "Actually, if a criminal was going to up and confess to anyone, it would be me. People like to tell me shit."

His brother laughed softly. "You're probably right. Bastard."

He shared his biggest concern. "I do think she's in some kind of mess, though. She didn't tell me anybody's coming after her, but there's got to be a reason why she has no ID."

Steve patted him on the shoulder. "It's not as big of a concern as you think. Matt and I have a bit more background, so we're going to let her know what she can do to ease things along."

What did they know that he didn't? Trevor wanted to ask, no, *demand* his brother spill the beans right that instant, but with the girls standing nearby, and Becky still glancing over every few seconds, this wasn't the time.

"If you've got something to tell her, do it," Trevor suggested.

Steve held him back and lowered his voice. "I don't know what you're thinking regarding the girl, but I

46

need to tell you something, and I need you to not question me about it, okay?"

"Right." Like that was ever going to happen.

"It's great that you're helping her out, but don't— don't get too close until we hear back from the landlord. There are reasons, good reasons, but we'll leave it at that for now."

For fuck's sake. "Well, that was clear as mud."

"I swear I'll explain as soon as I can."

"Fine, whatever."

Steve sighed like only a long-suffering older brother could. "I'm serious. Don't be an ass about this, and trust me."

Trevor glared at him. "Don't push me around."

He wasn't going to drag details out of Steve right now, because it was more important to let Becky know whatever news there was to share. But he would be having a conversation with his older brother soon, and if that meant that he had to beat the information out of him, so be it.

It wouldn't be the first time.

Trevor resisted the urge to shove Steve between the shoulder blades en route to rejoin Melody and Becky.

"Sorry to interrupt," Steve said, sliding back beside Melody, "but I have a message to pass on."

Becky's body went rigid and she swallowed nervously. "Yes?"

Steve looked pointedly at Melody and Trevor.

Instead of backing down, Becky folded her arms, the expression on her face hardening to the stubborn one Trevor had already grown familiar with. "If it can't be said in front of your fiancée, then I don't want to hear it."

Steve shrugged. "Your choice. It's nothing bad, just wanted to let you know that Hope's husband and I talked about your situation tonight, and he's good with her hiring you at the shop."

She swayed hard enough Trevor reached out a hand instinctively to be sure she didn't fall off her feet. "Really? Even before my ID arrives?"

"One condition. Do you know your landlord?"

Trevor didn't think it was a trick question, but by how long Becky paused, it had to be. "A little."

Steve smiled, the expression lighting his face and eyes. "Get him to send a letter vouching for you. Hope will work it out so you get paid in trade until the paperwork comes through. It's a little underhanded, but it's not outright illegal if things get squared away before the end of the year."

She didn't seem one hundred percent happy with that demand. "It'll take me a few days to set something like that in motion."

"We figured. No rush. In the meantime." Steve reached into his back pocket and pulled out his wallet, handing over a thin pile of twenties. "Here's an advance on your wages. You and Hope track your hours, and when it comes time, she'll make sure it all gets squared away."

Becky took the money, slipping it into her pocket carefully. "I'm not sure what to say. Thank you."

Melody caught hold of Steve's arm. "It's time we headed home. It's been good to meet you, Becky. I look forward to seeing you around. If you want to stop by the house, give me a call to make sure I'm home."

Steve held the reins as Melody mounted up, swinging a leg over his own ride a moment later. The two of them waved farewell as the horses left the yard at a slow walk.

The sky was all sunset yellow and springtime reds, reflecting off the pale siding of the house and setting a warm glow to Becky's skin as she shuffled back slightly.

"I should head home too," Trevor admitted, reluctant to make the move, but hanging around any longer would be pushing his luck. "I'll leave the tractor here, if you don't mind. If we need it tomorrow, I'll grab it. If not, you may as well keep it until you're done."

"That's very generous." Becky caught her arms around herself, face lifted to the mountains for a moment before tossing him another one of those addictive smiles. "Thanks for all your help. I really appreciate it."

"No prob."

He wanted to say more. Wanted to *offer* more, but that was stupid. He'd already made a fool of himself by the way he'd stalked her.

Trevor pulled himself together—tomorrow was another day, and he knew where to find her.

He tipped his hat and offered a wink before strolling to the front and crawling into his truck. She stood beside the rail fence as he left, still there when he glanced back as he hit the road.

The fading light shone around her as Becky changed position. She disappeared for a moment before her head popped up above the solid wood slats—she'd crawled on top of the fence and was staring into the distance, a feminine silhouette against a glowing sky.

So many mysteries—so many things he had yet to discover about Becky Hall.

Trevor could hardly wait.

Chapter Five

Two months earlier, Paradise, Saskatchewan

SHE LAY in the dark, body aching, until he fell sleep, his breathing thickening to a loud, steady snore. The old worn mattress dipped toward his body, and Rebekah held herself rigid to keep from rolling into the hollow formed by the weight of his body. There was a stickiness between her thighs, and a knot of disgust in her throat, and for one horrid second she wondered how difficult it would be to kill herself.

The thought was fleeting, disappearing immediately. The urge to survive was far stronger—*she* was far stronger—she had to be.

There had to be more to life than what she'd been handed. She *knew* there was more than this, and she was determined to find it, no matter what the short-term cost. She already knew staying was equal to accepting hell. If she left, there was a glimmer of hope for her future.

So she waited until there was no doubt the heavy body beside her was sound asleep, his snore building to a solid, unmistakable rumble.

Rebekah slid from the bed, feet hitting the icy-cold hardwood boards. She landed like a cat, silent and cautious as she made her way out of the bedroom toward the narrow flight of stairs. A light shone from under the door to her sister's room, but she ignored it, sliding silently past even as she longed to say goodbye. She pulled on a pair of runners from the back door—not her own—crossing the yard wearing nothing but her thin nightshirt, the threadbare fabric offering little protection against the cold March night.

She hurried without looking as if she was rushing, moving down the packed snow trail to the nearest barn. Only once she was safely out of sight did she kick into high gear, sprinting across the open space to the wooden slats that formed a ladder up the side of the barn wall.

If she were caught now, it would mean the end of more than her dream of a new life.

Up in the hayloft, she hurriedly moved aside the bales until she found the old backpack where she'd hidden her supplies. Rebekah jerked on the clothes, a massive shiver rocking her as she layered up with an assortment of things taken from various members of the community. All of it stolen in dribs and drabs so that no one was aware of the thefts.

She grabbed the backpack and slipped from the warmth of the barn back into the cold night, running past the men's house down the trail in the snow she knew they had packed all the way to the highway. If she was lucky, everyone would be asleep. If she was lucky, someone would be passing by on the highway who'd pick her up.

If she was lucky she would make it...

...but up till then she hadn't had much luck.

She didn't have any reason to expect that to change.

Chapter Six

Rocky Mountain House, present day

BECKY STARED at the envelope in her hands. The pale pink material had been left behind by the previous tenants, part of the mess of abandoned boxes and possessions scattered around the rental house. The faded paper inside held her request for more help as her future hung in the balance.

None of it belonged to her. Not the paper, not the house—even the stamp she was about to buy would be purchased with borrowed money.

"You ready to mail that?"

She snapped to attention as the woman behind the post office counter thrust forward a hand, already glancing past her to assess the next customer.

Becky handed over her future. "Yes."

"Express or regular?"

She supposed the message was urgent, but...what if the answer was no? It made no sense to rush to get her feet kicked out from under her. "How much?"

The difference wasn't outrageous, so Becky handed over the cash, carefully putting away her change. Then she walked out into the morning sunshine and took a deep breath. One more obstacle passed—now she had nothing more to do but wait.

And…possibly make herself so indispensable to Hope that even if her other benefactor didn't come through again, maybe she wouldn't be thrown into the street.

The door to the quilt shop was still locked when she got there, which made sense because she'd left extra time to hit the post office before the shop opened. But even after stopping to grab a few needed groceries, she was there ahead of Hope.

So she sat on the bench outside the shop, took a deep breath, and people-watched.

Traffic at nine thirty in the morning on a weekday was slow. Maybe Main Street Rocky Mountain House never got much busier than this, but it was fascinating all the same. The coffee shop across the way had a steady stream of customers passing through their door, most of them older men in worn coveralls and baseball caps. The retired or semi-retired, who'd finished their "chores" and now had time to shoot the breeze with their friends while their kids and grandkids did the real work.

She'd seen it before in the small town near the Paradise Settlement the few times she'd been part of the family who'd gone to town. Rocky didn't seem that much different at first glance, but it was. Hugely.

Because she was sitting on that bench all by herself, waiting for her *boss* to open the door. Waiting to put in a day of labour that was for *her* benefit, and no one else's. Maybe she didn't own anything now, but she could, possibly, in the future.

The thought made her giddy. The idea of that much freedom forced her to take deep breaths until her trembling hands calmed. The vivid dreams she'd had of the night she'd left Paradise behind had shaken her, waking her with a pounding heart and aching head, but now the truth sank in.

She'd made it this far.

The door swung open, and Hope's cheerful voice carried on the air. "You're early. Come on, and we'll figure out what the plan is for the day."

Becky tucked her shopping onto the shelf Hope had cleared for her in the back, then joined the other woman in the cozy fabric-filled store. "Stocking shelves?"

"That, and we need to make up some kits for the summer—things for people to do with grandkids who are off school, stuff like that. If you have any ideas."

Hope pulled out a notepad and together they made a list. Brainstorming for ideas was enjoyable because finding ways to keep young girls busy was something Becky knew how to do.

They moved from that to gathering supplies and laying out fabrics with an ease she hadn't expected for her second day on the job, except it made sense. She knew what she was doing, at least right now. She might be fumbling and faking it for a whole lot of other things, but this? She knew.

Hope caught it too, laughing as Becky authoritatively pulled one bolt of fabric away from the stash and replaced it with a slightly different one. "I'm not going to argue with you. You've got a great eye for colour."

"Lots of experience," Becky admitted. "And you have the most amazing stock on hand. It's easy to make good choices when there's tons of options."

The shop opened, and customers came in, and they were busy and the day moved on wonderfully, up until Hope got caught in the middle of organizing a big order and asked Becky to deal with ringing in another customer's sale.

"No problem."

Except, there was. The old register wasn't a register. The metal contraption she'd spotted that was familiar to what she'd seen in the old mercantile near Paradise Settlement was for display only. Tricked out with small sewing notions and a little quilted sign that read *My stash is totally legal.*

She didn't get the saying, nor did she see anything that would allow her to tap in prices or numbers on a keyboard. "Umm, Hope?"

Her boss glanced over her shoulder before continuing to measure off fabric. "Oh, right. The iPad is under the counter, and the scanner is next to it."

Gibberish. Hope was speaking total gibberish.

Still, with a customer waiting on the other side of the counter, there was no use in wishing they'd gone over this before someone got to witness her complete cluelessness.

Becky bent over and spotted books, papers and a lot of things she could identify. And two things she had no idea about—those had to be her targets.

She lifted them onto the counter, the one a rectangular object like a picture frame connected to a power cord, the other, a small plastic gun. She took her time laying them on the counter carefully in the hopes that they'd magically transform into something recognizable.

Nope. No such luck.

Mrs. Jordon cleared her throat softly. "You need a hand?"

Becky made a face. The grandma in front of her probably knew more about this than she did. "Please."

The older woman nodded before spinning the

rectangle halfway around so it faced both of them. "I had to show my husband too—he hates Macs. Always insisted PCs were the way to go, so when my daughter gave him an iPad, I thought he was going to have a bird. Power button is here."

She slipped her fingers over the top and the thing turned on, a picture of a pretty quilt filling the frame. Then Mrs. Jordon said something about "swiping" and "passwords", and Becky shook her hands and backed up.

"I'm sorry, I'll get Hope to help you."

"I'm here. What's up?"

She resisted the urge to flee. "I can't work this."

Hope rested a hand on Becky's shoulder. "I should have shown you before—sorry, Mrs. Jordon. Rookie boss on the floor. I didn't teach Becky how to use our register yet."

"We all need to learn sometime," she assured them. "I'm in no rush."

Hope stepped beside Becky. "Here. Watch me, then you can ring in the next couple things."

The scanner was the gun, the iPad instantly recording and totaling the information off the price tags. That part was interesting, but when Mrs. Jordon used her finger to sign her name on the screen and sent the receipt to her email—Becky knew this wasn't something she could fake her way through.

She copied Hope's moves, and managed to ring in the next order without too much difficulty, but once the customers left and they were alone, she bolted from behind the counter, running for the safety of the fabric stacks. "That was awkward."

Hope snickered, immediately looking contrite. "Sorry, that wasn't nice. You tried your best, and I'm sorry I didn't run you through the system right off the bat."

"Not your fault I didn't understand." So many things that were obviously part of a typical twenty-one-year-old's vocabulary and life skills, but hadn't been used much in Paradise. "I'll do better next time."

"You will," Hope encouraged her, and that was that.

The taunting voice inside that sneered at Becky that she had so much to learn was quickly silenced by the truth her ignorance wasn't her fault. She *would* learn.

If she had a few fumbles along the way, it would be worth it.

TREVOR SLOWED the tractor, staring at the nearby gravel road until he was certain the RCMP cruiser that had been tracking him was his sister behind the wheel, and not one of the other officers doing a routine check.

Anna pulled over to the side of the road and offered a wave, strolling to the front of her cruiser and leaning against the grill as she waited, tilting her head to let the sun shine on her face.

He left the tractor and hopped the nearby fence, offering her a happy greeting in spite of the strange meeting spot. "You don't know how good it is seeing you abandon your vehicle and sunglasses. Once that happens I figure I *might* have a chance of getting out of whatever it is you pulled me over for."

"Handing out tickets to the Coleman family is the most fun I get," she teased. "How're you doing?"

"Working hard," he said earnestly, "Or at least

that's what I want you to report to Steve if you see him later today."

She straightened, resting her hands on her hips as she looked him up and down. "So. I have something I have to tell you."

"You're pregnant."

"Oh my God, *no*. Don't do that to me."

"You got a transfer?"

She rolled her eyes. "You're determined to come up with the worst possible scenarios. Shut up and let me tell you before you give me a heart attack."

"Sorry."

She wrinkled her nose. "You're such a brat. You out of all of us Moonshine kids—you've always been the biggest pain in my butt."

"I'm just so talented and creative. Means you had to work harder to stay ahead of me. You should be thankful. I'm the reason you're such a success."

Anna made a hacking sound. "And on that note, I hear you've taken a fancy to the new renter on the western quarter."

For fuck's sake. "What is this? It's freaky even for Rocky how much everybody's up in my business about that. Yes, she's a pretty girl, and I like her. Or I like what I've got to see of her so far."

"I want to let you know..." Anna wrinkled her nose again. "Jeez, I thought this would be easy, but it's worse than I imagined."

"Spit it out," Trevor demanded. "Before I tell Steve it's your fault I'm not finished on time."

"First, I heard you've been trying to find out who owns that section of land, and I want to suggest you lay off."

Shit. "Don't tell me you *know things* too?" He

58

made air quotes around the words.

Anna shrugged. "It's not up to me who people tell secrets, but once I joined the RCMP, yes, Dad told me some things."

"But he didn't tell me or Lee?"

"Or Steve. Not everything."

This got crazier by the minute. First Steve going all cryptic, and now Anna? Trevor was more annoyed than he'd expected. "I've been trying to find out if we could rent that land. You mean you know how to contact whoever owns it? That's all I need."

"It's not my secret to tell," Anna snapped. "Bottom line, you want more information, you've got to convince Dad to let you know. The second thing is if you like Becky, go for it. There's nothing stopping you, as far as I know."

Which seemed the exact opposite of what Steve had implied.

What the fuck was going on?

Trevor didn't bring up Becky's lack of identification, because he didn't know for sure Anna knew, and if his sister wanted to get shitty about him later for withholding information, Trevor was fine tossing *it's not my secret to tell* back in her face anytime she wanted.

"You're not making a hell of a lot of sense," he muttered in frustration.

"I know, but in case you hear...*something*, and then get to thinking...*things*, I know enough to be able to say that if you want to date her, it won't be weird."

"But this conversation—*this* is weird," Trevor drawled.

"Even for us," Anna admitted.

He shook his head. "Anna—"

"Go talk to Dad," she insisted. "Other than that, I can't suggest anything."

She marched back to the cruiser. Trevor waited until she pulled away before stomping back to the tractor. Maybe he wasn't the smartest one in the family, but this all seemed more convoluted than it needed to be.

He guessed he couldn't blame Anna for not giving him contact details on who owned the land before this point. He'd been keeping it pretty secret that he wanted to do something.

But now? To know he wanted the information and still shut him down?

Fine. Maybe he wouldn't be able to step forward like a conquering hero and have the "I tracked down more land for us to use, look at me, aren't I wonderful for helping the family" moment he'd envisioned. But the damn secrets were getting out of hand, and he only had time and energy for so much. Tomorrow he was going to sit down with his father and find out what the heck was going on.

Tonight?

Tonight he was going to follow his sister's encouragement and track down a certain young woman who was also full of secrets, because *those* were the ones he wanted to spend his time and energy unraveling.

The tractor wheels clicked in time with the pulse in his veins as he drove the beast over the field at a faster-than-normal speed. He was going to see Becky again. He was going to convince her that the *Good Neighbour manual* included a section on getting to know each other better outside of chores.

But even with plans that made him move eagerly through the final tasks of his day, the thought of all sorts of secrets remained tangled together.

Family wasn't supposed to be this complicated. Frustrating? Annoying? Always.

Complicated?

Maybe he'd been too busy before to notice, or too stupid, but now that he'd gotten a peek into Pandora's box, he wasn't going to simply slide back into ignorance and silence.

Trevor Coleman was ready to figure shit out. But first things first— He had a neighbour to check in on.

Chapter Seven

SHE'D NEARLY made it home before Trevor caught up with her, rolling down the driver-side window to lean on his elbow and greet her with a laugh. "Looking good, Rodeo."

"What do you want, Trevor?" Becky continued to step briskly though her feet were sore from being on them all day in the shop, and the long walk to and from town.

She didn't want to admit to the bubble of happiness inside that had risen unasked at the sight of his truck.

"You're walking on the right side of the road. I mean, the wrong side of the road, which is the right side," Trevor joked. "Good for you."

"I knew the rule before you told me. I didn't think there was enough traffic to worry about it."

"No, I guess not. Good point."

And with that, the damn man crossed the centerline. He ended up right beside her, driving on the wrong side of the road, grinning through the open window from only a couple feet away.

"Are you crazy? Get back where you belong," she snapped. "If someone comes along and you crash, you'll kill me at the same time, and I don't need that today, thanks."

"The only people on this stretch of the road will be my cousins or my family, and the road is dead straight forever, so I'll see them coming. You're safe."

Good grief. "You're amazing."

"I'm glad you think so. I also have this lovely air-conditioned truck, if you'd like a ride."

"I'm nearly home, thanks."

"Becky." The cheesy joking and laughter vanished, his voice dipping deeper, and his new serious tone sent a shiver up her spine. "Let me give you a ride the rest of the way. Please?"

If he'd ordered her, she would've ignored him, but it was the *please* that made her pause. She glanced up, catching his gaze, and it was there too. That bit of something in his eyes beyond goofing around. "I really am too close to home to make it worth your while," she pointed out. "If I cross the field here, I can be in the back door quicker than it takes for you to drive."

He shrugged his acceptance. "Fine. Then can I come over later? I can help you clean up the garden patch some more."

She was torn. After her full day she'd had a date with the bathtub in mind. But he looked so enticing, with those puppy dog eyes, and whatever strange magic he'd cast over her to make her agree to nearly every one of his suggestions so far. "I will put you to work again," she warned.

"I don't mind."

Of course he minded. He'd put in a full day's labour by now, too, and the last thing he needed was to do her chores as well as his own.

Stubborn man.

63

"Pull over," she ordered. She crossed in front of the massive truck to reach the other side before climbing into the passenger seat. "You win this time, but you're staying for supper," she warned. "If I'm going to make you work, the least I can do is feed you."

"Ha, is that supposed to be a threat? Because, sweetheart, you don't scare off a guy by offering him food. We're pretty much empty stomachs, all the time."

"You don't know if I can cook," she teased back, shocked at her daring as she drew a chuckle from him. "I have a liver and lima bean recipe I've been dying to try."

"As long as you've got ketchup, I can eat anything."

She pressed her lips together to stop from laughing out loud, glancing out the window at the line of trees forming the windbreak in front of the house. The light spring breeze made the pine branches sway, shadows flickering on the dry grass at the base of the tall sentinels.

The row ended and the house came into view, and this time she checked it over with a more critical eye. The weathered home was the answer to so many of her problems, but it was looking a little disreputable. "Do you think it's worthwhile painting the place?"

Trevor pulled to a stop beside the front steps. "While you're renting? Doubt it. You could give the boards a good power wash if you wanted to spruce it up a little, but it needs more than a coat of paint to make it look new."

Becky joined him on the steps, staring up and assessing. "You're right, it would be a little like putting lipstick on a pig."

He chuckled softly, leaning back on the porch railing as she unlocked the door. "By the way, did you figure out how to fix your leak?"

"Yes," Becky answered quickly, not mentioning her fix was an oversized bucket she'd found in one of the sheds. It would have to do until she had the time and money to do the repairs up right.

She ducked down the hallway ahead of him, feeling a touch uncomfortable as she glanced around. The week she'd had in the house hadn't been nearly long enough to make any big improvements. "I know it's a mess," she called over her shoulder. "The kitchen is clean, and the bathroom—I've gotten those under control. Follow me."

Trevor obediently followed in her wake as she dodged boxes and led him to the back of the house. "What can I do to help with dinner?"

"Nothing—it'll only take me a minute to get things started."

He sat in the chair she pointed him at, but his face spoke volumes. "Interesting decorating scheme in the living room, hallway and dining room. Bet the place is warm in the winter."

The piles of paper and other "treasures" stacked nearly to the ceiling were hard to miss.

This was one tidbit she felt comfortable sharing. "You know the couple who lived here before me? They weren't doing that well, I guess. Things got out of control, and they couldn't handle getting rid of the stuff they'd accumulated."

"They'd been here for a long time," Trevor noted.

Becky nodded as she put on a pot of water. "Over ten years, I think. I don't know all the details, but I said I'd go through and clean it up."

"No wonder I didn't notice them moving out. They just up and left." He made a noise. "I hope you're getting paid."

"Lower rent, and the stuff that stayed with the house is basically mine to use. I don't need to find furniture or kitchen supplies, that kind of thing," she offered. "It was worth it."

Trevor eyed the kitchen. "You cleaned this room up nice."

"Thanks. It took a bit of elbow grease, and there're a couple piles of things I'm not sure what to do with that I've got under tarps."

"Not in one of the sheds?" He figured it out before she said anything. "Oh, for fuck's sake—I bet the sheds are full to the brim as well, aren't they?"

Becky couldn't stop her amusement from showing. "You sound scandalized. Don't you know any packrats?"

"I know enough to feel sorry for you having to clean up after them." He reached a hand her direction, and she offered up the jar of pasta sauce she'd been failing to open. "But, hey, if it got you a good deal with your landlord, good for you."

She put the pasta on to cook, eyeing the amount and adding extra to make up for the fact she didn't have much else to go with the plain meal.

It was still worth it, a hundred, million times over to be able to be in her own kitchen, cooking a meal for herself and a...neighbour. Someone she wanted there, if she was honest.

Twisting her body to one side let her stir the pots and watch Trevor out of the corner of her eye at the same time. He couldn't have come straight from the ranch. Not with the clean jeans and the crisp cut of his flannel shirt. His dark hair was cut short and neat, and his hands were well scrubbed as he turned the pages of a gardening magazine she'd saved during her cleanup of the mess in the kitchen.

He glanced up, catching her eye. "What?"

"You're..."

Oh, *great*. Way to back herself into a corner and all but have to admit that she'd been admiring him. Or at least looking close enough to notice that the colours he wore complemented the layer of scruff darkening his jaw. No way was she going to blurt out that his muscular body intrigued her more than she cared to think about, or that the scent of him, clean and fresh, was doing something to her insides.

Trevor's smile widened as if he'd overheard her racing thoughts. "Tongue-tied?"

"...sitting in a bad spot to read. The lighting is terrible. Why don't you move to the right?"

"Because the lighting might be bad, but the view is great." Trevor deliberately let his gaze drift up her body, from her ankles all the way past her flaming hot cheeks until their eyes met again.

She wasn't ready for this. Not to have those kinds of feelings for someone. A tremor of fear started inside, and Becky turned to the stove, deliberately putting her back between them as she stirred their supper.

Having a good neighbour was another thing to be grateful for—a blessing she'd never expected, and she wanted to hold on to that good thing with both hands.

More than that?

She stared into the pot of boiling water and stirred extra hard to avoid having to answer her mental question.

"DO YOU have an extra burning barrel?" she asked.

The obvious change of topic away from his light flirting was abrupt. He wasn't sure what had happened, but Trevor could go with the flow. "I know where one is. Anything else?"

"Right now? A wheelbarrow. There's probably one in the shed, but..."

Jeez. "You'll never find it. Sure—there's got to be an extra one or two of those around somewhere in the Coleman clan. That'll make it easier to wheel the stuff to the burn pile."

She nodded, putting two sparkling clean but chipped plates on the table, and for the second time in two days they shared a meal.

This time Trevor focused on finding out more about Becky, but she was good at evading his questions without seeming to evade them. Sticking to talking about house improvements seemed safer.

And vehicles—

"Do you need help finding wheels for you?" He swore as soon as he said the words. "Shit—you're waiting for your ID. That's why you don't have a car."

Becky twirled her fork in the bit of pasta remaining on her plate. "I'm in limbo for a bit, yes. It's okay. Walking to town isn't bad in the summer. And I hope to get things straightened out over the next while."

Curiosity demanded he ask what the hell had happened. Why she had no ID. Self-control forced him to hold his tongue and wait for her to offer up details when she was ready. It wasn't any of his business, not yet.

Didn't mean he couldn't help in other ways. "I can drive—" Trevor began before being offered the evil eye once again. "Wow, you're good with that Icy Stare of

68

Death. You whipped it out in under three seconds flat."

Her lips twitched. "Icy Stare of Death?"

"Kind of like you're daring me to do something stupid. Hate to tell you, this is another warning that doesn't work with guys. Just like food, we're always willing to be stupid."

Becky shook her head. "Don't offer me your truck, since I can't drive it. And I like walking, so don't *accidentally* show up every morning 'going my direction' or I'll be pissed."

He didn't like her ultimatum. "What if it's raining? Or I'm going on a coffee run? Or I need something from town? Can I pick you up then?"

"You can be really annoying," she muttered as she pulled their empty plates from the table and stacked them in the sink. "You get on a topic and keep going at it and going at it."

He laughed as he followed her to the back door and opened it for her. "My mom's nickname for me when I was little was Tigger. She said I'd get wound up tight like a spring, and then bounce and bounce until I'd crash."

Absolute confusion flooded her face as she walked past him.

"Oh, come on. Winnie the Pooh? Hundred Acre Woods? Tigger with the spring in his tail...?"

Nope, she clearly had no idea.

Well, then. "You've never read *Winnie the Pooh*?"

She pulled the basket of seeds from a shelf beside the door and they walked together to the garden. "Never."

"Want to go to the library to grab a copy tomorrow? You can use my library card, since you don't have one yet."

Her eyes widened, and her mouth opened excitedly before she made a face. "I'm working tomorrow night. And Hope asked if I'd make a list of some designs I might want to teach, so I'll be doing that as well."

"No rush," he said, casually taking the rake and getting ready to be her flunky. "What section do you want to do first?"

They worked for an hour, getting areas prepped for Becky to drop in the first of the seeds. His muscles ached from the long day, and his stomach was growling because as good as the food had been, he hadn't had enough to eat, not that he'd ever tell Becky.

He didn't care one bit about those faint annoyances—he was having a blast. His mysterious woman was becoming more intriguing by the minute, and he couldn't wait to start untangling the little bits and pieces that made up the whole.

Trevor lasted until they'd plotted out where the beans were going to go, a thin cotton string drawn between two stakes setting a straight guide to plant the seeds. Becky had been so insistent how she wanted to organize things, and he'd carefully followed her orders, wondering if she realized she was bossing him around like they'd been friends for years.

It burst out of him.

"You want to go out sometime?" Trevor asked in a rush.

Becky stared as if he'd spoken in some foreign language. "What do you mean? Like a date?"

Her shock amused him all over again. "Yes. A date. Exactly like a date. How about we go out for dinner. Or to the movies, or—"

"I don't think so." Becky avoided his gaze, absolutely fixated on the line she'd drawn in the soil.

Bean seeds fell from her fingers one after the other exactly the same distance apart, and she moved away at a steady pace.

"Oh, come on," Trevor teased. "I'm even more entertaining on a date. You've only seen me at moderately charming while I've been hanging around here."

"Well, then, it's a definite no. I can barely handle you at *moderately charming*."

That was part of the trouble. She wasn't handling him, and he wanted her to be. Those hands of hers that were meticulously planting the garden—he'd prefer to have them all over his body, shaping and touching *him*, driving him wild.

"No, I think it's a *really* good idea," he insisted.

She finally looked up. "Which? For you to be charming, or for us to go on a date?"

"How about both the same time? I multitask really well."

Becky sat back on her heels and stared at him for a good long time. Long enough he felt uncomfortable looming over her, so he got down in the dirt too, reaching for her hand and taking it in his.

"What are you doing?" She wiggled uncomfortably. "I'm dirty, my fingers are a mess, and you're wearing clean jeans."

"Who cares? Becky, I like you, and I think you like me, so why don't we go out. Just say yes."

Her hand was warm and strong in his, and yet femininely soft. But she was trembling, so he stroked her fingers, trying to figure out what was making her gun shy so he could talk his way through it and get her to accept.

For one moment her fingers closed over his in a

71

gentle caress, and he was sure she would say yes—and then she was gone.

Not only gone, but standing a good two feet away, looking down at him with an expression verging on terror. "Thanks for your help today. I'm really tired. I'll see you around."

And she fled, leaving her basket abandoned behind as she escaped through the back door. It closed with solid *snick* behind her, the door lock twisting into place.

Something twisted inside Trevor as well. He'd never had a woman look at him like that. Like he was someone to be afraid of. Like he was the enemy at the gates. He'd thought his banter and teasing had been lighthearted, yet he'd clearly crossed a line.

What had he done?

Trevor took a deep breath and sat there on his heels to figure out his next move. It had to be something that wouldn't involve crawling on her roof, or knocking on her door, or anything else that might frighten her even more.

He didn't know her phone number—hell, did she have a phone?

It suddenly sank in exactly how strange this whole situation was. How far from the norm her life must feel, how out of control, being in complete limbo. He'd pushed her too fast. That much was sure.

Time. He had to give her time.

Trevor gathered the beans that had fallen to the ground when she'd bolted and slowly finished the row she'd begun. He mounded the soil over the line, patting it down firmly before taking three trips to and from the rain barrel to water them.

Then he tucked the rest of the seeds away into the

72

basket, returning it to where she'd stored it by the door.

Inspiration struck, and he jogged to his truck, digging into the storage box behind the cab and coming up with a giant hand bell they used when moving cattle. They'd trained the herd so that like Pavlovian dogs, the cows knew when that sucker rang there was fresh feed being dropped nearby.

It was loud enough to be heard clear across the distance between their homes.

He left it on the back stairs where she'd be sure to see it, along with a note. He made sure to make no mention of her running away. He didn't think apologizing was the thing to do right now, even though he felt like a shit.

Putting control back in her court was the only thing he could think to do.

Hey, Rodeo

Didn't realize until now that you probably have no phone. Stupid brain didn't register how isolated you might feel. If you have an emergency, give this a shake. It's loud enough I'll hear it at my place, or Steve and Melody will. Heck, you could probably wake people in Drayton Valley if you're at an upstairs window and really give it a go.

And if you ever need it, go ahead and take my truck—yeah, I do like to offer to give that baby away. I know, I'm bad, but I mean well.

My door is always open.

Trevor

Chapter Eight

IT WAS too early to go home, and too late for him to spend more time working, so Trevor turned the truck around and headed into town. He had some thought of hitting Traders Pub and finding a game of darts along with a beer, but a block before Main Street he spotted Rafe's truck outside the library.

His cousin had acted suspicious over nothing a few days ago, and it looked as if Trevor might be able to find out why.

He parked in the space next to Rafe, edging up tight to block the driver door just to be an ass, because that's what cousins did—they went out of their way to annoy the hell out of each other.

Inside the library doors the scent of books hit him hard, and he paused near the checkout desk to look around and let the wave of memories subside.

The Moonshine clan got teased about being bookworms. His mom had hauled them down once a week from the time they were babies until they hit high school to take part in whatever program was being offered that month. Lee and Anna had eaten it up like candy. His dad had shuffled along, heading straight for the magazines, while Kate would vanish into a quiet reading area, and woe to anyone who disturbed her when she had a book in her hands.

Steve admitted once that he didn't mind going because it meant they weren't out doing chores, and Trevor mostly agreed with him.

He and books had a love/hate relationship. He loved stories and storytelling, but had hated language in school. Hated being called up and pointed out as the slowest one in the class when it came to getting words down on the page.

Or reading out loud—*God*, the thought made his skin crawl.

But the library was magic. It had high-speed Internet and graphic novels, and the best part? During high school he discovered some of his female classmates went there after school to spend time and do their homework before their parents got home from work.

Trevor might be slow, but he wasn't stupid. Pretty girls he could walk home? He got more kisses and action in high school because of the library than any other dating venture since.

Now with the thought of Becky fresh on his mind he wasn't looking for a pickup, but maybe...a pick-me-up for her.

"Can I help you?"

He twisted to discover a vaguely familiar face peering expectantly from behind the counter. The pretty blonde had her hair braided back neatly, collar fastened demurely high and the faintest wash of pale pink colour on her lips.

He glanced at her nametag. One of the Baptist pastor's kids—that's why she seemed familiar. "Laurel Sitko. You're not old enough to be working here."

She flashed a smile. "Finished my two years of Librarian Technician training, and I'm home to do my practicum."

"Cool. Technician, huh? Sounds fancy," he teased. "Does that mean you can find me a copy of *Winnie the Pooh*?"

"Going for the classics, are you?" She lifted the center of the wooden counter and slipped out. "Disney version or the originals?"

"Like you said, go for the classics."

She nodded. "Follow me to Christopher Robin's."

He let her lead the way, peeking down the side paths for a glimpse of Rafe. Nothing, not before they reached the kids section.

Laurel happily passed over a set of books with black and white illustrations. "Is this what you were looking for?"

He flipped a few pages, nostalgia striking again. "Perfect."

She grabbed a few out-of-place books from the top of the nearest bookcase and waved goodbye before wandering away, slipping the books back onto their shelves. Trevor tucked the box set under his arm and decided he might as well copy his father's example and hit the magazines. It was cheaper than buying a bunch of them every month.

Rafe sat in one of the easy chairs grouped together in a quiet corner section of the library. He seemed so intent on his magazine he didn't notice as Trevor paced up silently, grabbed a random mag off the shelf then dropped into the chair behind him.

Trevor lifted his own reading material so he could peek from behind it to spot whatever had Rafe so mesmerized.

There was a story time for tots going on in the opposite corner, little bodies in pyjamas squirming like worms while the senior librarian attempted to keep their attention.

A shudder shook him. Rugrats. Nope, he could tolerate them when they were family, but random, underaged vermin were definitely not his thing.

He checked out the young moms in the group, though, wondering if Rafe was sweet on one of them. That notion was blown away in less than a minute as Laurel strolled into view, drifting toward the playgroup, and Rafe did that thing where he stiffened up like he was a pointer on guard, his nose tracking the pretty, young librarian perfectly.

Trevor was proud he held back his amusement and avoided laughing out loud like a ninny. Instead, he rose and stepped over to Rafe's chair, plucked the magazine from his cousin's hands and plopped himself down on the armrest like he'd just arrived.

"Yo, cuz," he muttered softly. "Happening night at the library. You're going to get a rep for being a badass if you keep this up."

"Shut up," Rafe snapped a little too loud.

"*Shhhhhhh.*" A field of faces turned toward them. Frowny faces with pointer fingers pressed in warning to their lips.

Trevor was going to die, he really was. "See. Shit disturber," he whispered.

"Go away," Rafe forced out through clenched teeth.

Trevor leaned over. "Do that again. How did you get words out while making that face?"

His cousin jabbed his thumb toward Trevor's thigh hard enough to leave a bruise, but he'd seen it coming and leapt to his feet in time to get only a passing hit.

"Actually, there're some new interesting items I'd like to *check out* more closely," Trevor taunted.

Rafe had stood as well, following Trevor's deliberate gaze before snapping his head back and all but growling out a response. "She's too young for you."

He was mean to tease, but he did it anyway. "You're not seriously considering trying to get a date with sweet Laurel, are you?"

"Shut. Up," Rafe snapped. "Not here."

"Shhhhhhhhh." The warning sounded again.

Trevor bit the inside of his cheek to control himself.

Rafe offered a final tormented glance toward Laurel who was moving rapidly in their direction. "Don't you dare say a word," his cousin all but begged.

"Me? Never."

Rafe tossed him a dirtier glance than the last one. "I swear I will take you apart and put you back together inside out."

A soft cough sounded beside them.

Laurel stood a few feet away, hands held together in front of her primly as she made deliberate eye contact with them in turn, her cheeks flushing noticeably before she jerked her gaze away from Rafe. "Would you guys take your conversation outside, please?"

Trevor turned on her with a wide smile, sweeping his books forward. "No problem. Can you help me check these out, first?"

She took them and his card and all but ran back to the counter ahead of them.

Rafe leaned in as they walked. "You're a bastard."

"Yup." He slapped a hand on his cousin's shoulder. "Don't worry, I'll be good."

He was. He didn't say a word to Laurel about Rafe

even through he was tempted. "What does somebody new to town need to get a library card? I can't remember what I used."

Laurel seemed relieved he'd asked a question she knew how to answer. "If they have a utility bill to show they're local, they can get a card for no charge."

"That's it?"

She nodded. "For now. It might change in the future, but that's all."

"Great. And thanks for the books." He gave her a wink and stepped outside with a happier heart than when he'd arrived.

He burst out laughing as he discovered Rafe leaning on his tailgate with a pissed-off expression.

"Forgot about that," he said when he could speak.

"You're such a bastard." But Rafe was grinning too. "And before you say anything else, yes, I was there to check out Laurel, but don't bother teasing. Me and her is an impossible idea. Doesn't make her any less sweet to look at knowing she's forbidden fruit."

Oh, well, that changed things. It was one thing to torment Rafe, and another totally to have anyone *outside* the family give him grief. "Who says she's forbidden fruit? If you like her, ask her out."

Rafe made a rude noise. "Right. You're not thinking very hard, Trevor. We don't travel in the same circles."

Fuck this. He straightened up and gave Rafe a focused stare, pointing a finger in his face. "We live in Rocky, cuz. There is no Royal Palace or shit, not in this neck of the woods. There're people who are good, and a few who are assholes, and you're kind of in the middle of those two rankings, so if you're interested, don't let anyone tell you you're not good enough to ask her out,

79

especially not yourself."

Rafe gave in, or at least gave up for the moment. "Thanks."

"Anytime."

"Now can you get your fat-ass truck out of my way?"

Trevor shrugged. "Keys were in the ignition. I figured you'd move it to the back lot and hide it or something to get even with me."

"Dickwad," Rafe shouted in farewell as Trevor crawled into the cab and started it up.

He drove toward home feeling a lot more lighthearted than earlier. He was still worried about Becky, but when he stopped in her yard, library books in hand, there was a hint of the pep talk he'd given Rafe still ringing in his veins.

Becky and him—it could work. He'd have to go slow and not be scary.

Books weren't scary.

He checked around the back of the house and found the bell and his note where gone, which made him happy. And it made him even happier when he went to knock on the door and found it opening before him.

Her whiskey brown eyes were wide, but her back was straight and she seemed determined to face him. Like he was a too-tall ladder or something else she was strong enough to tackle.

"Hey, Rodeo. You got a minute? I brought you a present."

———◦⟲◦———

SHE FIGURED he'd show up. Knowing what she

did of the man, it made total sense for her to open her door and find him standing on the doorstep.

Slightly embarrassed by her rapid disappearing trick, she shuffled from side to side. "Sorry about earlier."

He waved it away. "You did nothing to apologize for. I was the one being a jackass, and I'm sorry. You've got an awful lot on your plate right now, and it's not my place to make your life more difficult."

They stared at each other for a moment, and it wasn't nearly as awkward as it should have been. "You want some ice tea?"

He hesitated. "Only if I'm not in your way. I mean it, I need a minute then I can get out of your hair."

"I'd like you to stay," she admitted.

Trevor tilted his head toward the patio area. "Wait for you there."

Becky hurried inside to get them two glasses of ice-cold tea. She returned, setting the drinks on the small table she'd found while burning off steam after he left.

"That's new."

She nodded. "I may as well use the things I find."

"I found something else for you tonight. It's only a loaner, but I hope you enjoy it."

He handed over some hard-covered children's books, and another bit of tension escaped. "*Winnie the Pooh*. That's how they spell it."

"Right? Instant way to make a roomful of kids giggle."

"These are from the library? Thank you."

"You're welcome." He took a long sip of his drink, sighing contentedly as he put the glass back on the table. "It sounded like you hadn't read them, and I'll admit it's been years since I did. I thought you might like to check them out."

There was a whole lot she hadn't read. A whole lot she didn't know. That's what she'd been obsessing over after making a fool of herself and running away earlier in the evening.

Her attraction to Trevor shouldn't even be on her mind yet. All the other things were what she needed to focus on. "I have a favour to ask."

The words burst out, kind of like his invitation earlier in the evening.

Trevor looked suitably serious. "Go on."

She wasn't sure where to begin. "I had to use a computer today at work, and I've never used one before. I'm worried that there's going to be things that I don't know that will make me lose my job, and I know—"

"Hope would never fire you for not knowing how to do something before she's trained you." He looked at her intently. "Back up. You've never used a computer before? How is that possible?"

"Trust me, it's possible." She took a deep breath. "I can't tell you everything, but I need help. I need to learn some of the things that you probably learned when you were a kid."

He was nodding slowly. "I'm not that good on computers, but I know a little. Just the basic stuff that most people know, if that's enough."

"It's not only computers," she explained. "It's things like the library, and what books you read in school, and how to drive a car."

"A car—wait, you knew how to drive the tractor."

"A tractor and a car are not the same thing, Trevor."

He was nodding in agreement before she'd finished speaking. "You're right. I was surprised, that's all."

"And I get it. My life hasn't been very typical, and I have a lot of things I need to work on. I'm waiting to hear back from my landlord, and that's why it threw me a little when you asked me out." She wasn't nervous anymore. Either he was going to understand, or it was better that she knew differently right now. "Trevor, what I need right now is a friend. Someone I can ask questions without it getting all tangled up in other complications."

Trevor offered her touch of a smile. "Yeah, I am a complicated fellow."

He was one of the most accepting and caring guys she'd ever met. "It's been fun getting to know you these last couple of days. Can we go back to that?" she asked. "Nothing too fast—there's no rush."

"Sure." He finished his drink then rose to his feet. "I should be going. But how about I make a list of some of the things I think you need to learn, and we can get together sometime and start working on it."

He didn't sound annoyed or upset, and the final bit of tension in her stomach eased.

"That sounds really good." She walked after him toward the gate. "Trevor?"

He paused with a hand on the door to his truck. "Yeah, Rodeo?"

"I promise not to take your truck until I know how to drive it."

She got the smile out of him she was hoping for. "Good night."

"Thanks. For everything."

She waited until he'd driven away, and then she took the books with her and retreated to her room so she could curl up and disappear into a different world.

Although...this world had taken a decidedly good turn for the better.

Chapter Nine

THE NEXT days passed in a blur. She saw Trevor twice, for exactly ten minutes at a time.

"Don't think this is me copping out on you, or anything." He stood on her front porch, covered from head to foot in a fine layer of dust. "The family decided this was a good week to seed, so we've been going sunrise to sunset most days."

"I understand." She rushed off and returned with a glass of water before he could refuse. "Planting happens when it's time for it to happen."

"Did you want me to—?"

"Nothing. Go home, have a shower and put your feet up. I'm keeping myself busy cleaning up around here."

"But I promised to help you learn some stuff," he complained.

Becky laughed. "Trust me, I'll still have things to learn next week."

"If I survive this week, I will be very happy to sit behind a computer with you."

On that issue she was happy to have good news to report. "I made Hope show me one step at a time, at least for the thingy we use at work. I can do it now if I concentrate."

He chuckled. "The *thingy* is an iPad."

She shook her head. "I suppose if you think about it, that makes sense, but not really."

"It's a computer. It's not supposed to make sense, it just follows rules."

Becky shooed him away, smiling after he'd left.

Between the walk to and from work, because there were no rides this week, and full days helping Hope, and hours going though stuff at the house, Becky fell into bed every night exhausted, but happy.

Friday morning at the store turned out to be insanely busy. The small warning bell rang again and again until both Becky and Hope were turning toward the door with a laugh each time it happened.

"I've never seen such a rush," Becky said when they finally had a moment to breathe. A calm in the middle of the storm.

"I hope we don't see the end of it," Hope joked. "Days like this help the store survive the winter snowstorms when everyone curls up and stays home. I swear, last year I got to hate the weather forecast—"

The bell sang out, interrupting her story. Hope's face lit up with delight even though it wasn't more customers slipping through the stacks of fabric. It was her husband who hurried forward to meet her before she could take more than a couple of steps.

"Hey, beautiful." Matt tucked his fingers under Hope's chin and tilted her head back so he could press a kiss to her lips.

It was a proper enough public greeting, but at the same time Becky's toes were ready to curl just watching them. He finished with a caress of his hand over Hope's cheek as if he hadn't had enough of her, and the way he gently slid a hand around her waist to keep her by his side spoke of an intimacy that ran deep.

Hope let out a happy sigh. "Well, I was going to say it's nice to see you in the middle of the day, but that was far better than nice."

"I was about to grab the fire extinguisher," Becky teased, fanning a hand in front of her face.

Matt offered a smile to both of them before tilting his head toward the cash desk where he'd left a paper bag. "I picked up lunch for you girls, since I was in town. For when you have a moment to eat."

"Are you joining us?" Hope asked.

He shook his head regretfully. "I promised Blake I'd be back as soon as I could. I had to drop off blades to be sharpened. And..." He turned to Becky, his smile brightening further as he reached under his jacket and pulled out a slim envelope. "I checked the post office. Your landlord got in touch with me."

His expression meant everything was fine, but she still needed it said out loud. "And I can keep working here?"

Matt nodded. "We'll still need your identification once that comes through, but in the meantime, we've got your back."

Becky fought for control, but sheer relief hit harder than expected. She buried her face in her hands to hide the tears that rushed to escape.

"Hey, this is supposed to be *good* news," Hope said, dropping an arm around Becky's shoulders and hugging her.

"I'm happy, really I am," Becky insisted, the words a little tangled and tight.

"Don't worry," Matt teased. "Hope is pretty much a watering can these days with pregnancy hormones. I know crying women are happy."

"Hey," Hope warned. "Watch it, bucko."

Their loving banter was as wonderful to witness as their earlier passion.

"You don't know how much this means to me." She wiped tears from her eyes and offered Matt another smile. "I know I haven't shared everything that's going on, but the fact you were willing to take a chance on me—it really is changing my life."

Matt pressed a kiss to Hope's temple where she'd slipped back into his arms for a brief moment, the two of them looking at her with kindness in their eyes.

"Oh, by the way, I have a feeling you're going to see a lot more of a certain someone in the coming days. If he's too big of a pain in the ass, tell him to go fly a kite, okay? Just because he's your neighbour doesn't mean he's got any rights to you." Matt shook a finger at her. "You decide who you hang out with, even if that means telling my overeager cousin he's not welcome."

Matt left. More customers came in. She and Hope ended up trading off to sneak bites of their lunch between working.

The whole time Becky pondered how her life could have changed so much in such a short time. She certainly hadn't done anything to deserve all the good things coming her way.

Didn't mean she wanted any of it to stop. Not the job, or the house. Maybe not even having someone dance attention on her. Although he'd been so good about her request to slow it down.

Trevor made her feel...

Well, that was the point. He made her *feel*. She'd never had a relationship with a man that hadn't involved a lot of ice-cold sensation in her gut, or worse.

87

She was daydreaming about him, in fact, as they got ready to close the shop at the end of the day.

"I'd tease you about your dreamy expression, but I don't want you to take it the wrong way and stop." Hope nudged her with a shoulder as she hurried past. "I'd like to keep that smile on your face. You look good happy."

"So do you," Becky teased. "You should have seen your face when Matt showed up here at lunch."

Hope clutched the fabric she was tidying to her chest as if she'd forgotten it was there, her eyes going hazy with pleasure. "That man is a wonderful, terrific husband, and I'm very lucky to have someone who gets me as hard as he does."

A shot of something raced through Becky, and she fought to identify the emotion. It wasn't covetousness. She was honestly glad that Hope had Matt.

She didn't *think* it was jealousy, wanting what the other woman had. Right now freedom and a future were pretty potent highs to wallow in. Having someone to share the joys with—she could handle that.

It was the wide, gaping chasm between Hope's life and her own that made her hesitate. Hope had Matt, and the Coleman family, *and* her own family on the way. Becky had...

Herself.

At least for now, that was it.

She wanted more, but without the demands *more* would put on her, and that wasn't fair to anyone.

Sadness crept in. She liked Trevor, but it wouldn't be fair for him to get involved with her as more than a friend. Knowing that changed things.

She was still delighted with the good news the day had brought, and she wouldn't hurry to change their relationship, but at some point she would have to make the situation clear. She had a future, but it was one where she'd be alone, and that was fine.

Or at least, she spent the walk home trying to convince herself of that.

THE EVENING they finished seeding the fields, as many of the Moonshine clan as possible gathered together around the family table to raise a glass to another successful start to the season. Now they had to wait until the fall to see how things would turn out.

Typical rancher's life—work like crazy to find out if their dreams would be met, or dashed to pieces by bad weather or a million other disasters. Maybe it was a smart thing to celebrate every single success along the way, because there were no guarantees.

His mom was a firm believer in the *celebrate life* philosophy, which is why everyone, except for Melody who'd been called out on a veterinarian emergency, was in the room. Food vanished, plates wiped clean by the hungry crowd as they visited and laughed.

His dad was the quietest of the lot, his food picked over like it had been for the last year. Indigestion had been the first complaint, and now Randy was having troubles with his joints. He absently rubbed his hand and wrist with his other hand as he listened to the family squabble, complain and brag about what they'd accomplished.

The volume in the house was enough for a dozen people, but when any group included his brother-in-law Mitch and his younger brother's partner, Rachel, gatherings tended to get a little loud. The two of them were like oil and water, in a good way. They didn't fight, but they never let the other get in the last word.

Trevor found the changing family dynamics fascinating.

He sat beside Lee at the table in their old spots, the ones their mom had put them in so she could keep an eye on them, as if they weren't well behaved all the time growing up, or something.

Trevor gestured across the table to where Rachel was poking Mitch in the arm as he pretended to not hear her, his smile twisted into a smirk. "You want to lay odds on them breaking into a fistfight?"

Lee chuckled. "Rachel won't punch him again like she did last time, she promised. I bet you a case of beer, though, that in the next five minutes, someone proposes they arm wrestle."

"You're on." Trevor snatched the peaches from under his mom's hand before she could take them away. He poured the last few into his bowl then handed her the empty jar. "I don't want them to go to waste. I'm surprised you have canning left on the shelf."

Kate lifted a brow as if he'd insulted her. "What kind of comment is that? Of course I still have stuff left in the pantry. It's only June."

"Except you're all out of bacon," Trevor's oldest brother muttered under his breath.

His dad gave his Steve the evil eye, but it was too late.

Kate turned on her husband. "I thought we talked about you raiding the freezer. Hands off the back bacon."

"I haven't touched it in months," Randy insisted. "Honest."

"That's because he finished it months ago," Lee said quietly to Trevor.

90

Chaos. It was all chaos, and it was perfect...except for the way his thoughts kept drifting back to wondering what Becky was doing for supper tonight on her own. He'd missed her the past week, which was crazy to admit, but the truth.

"Thank you, Kate. That was delicious, as usual." His dad blew a kiss at his wife as he rose slowly out of his chair. "You all deserve a cheer for getting the job done, especially since I slacked my ass off most of the time. So—" He raised both arms in the air and gave a shout, shaking his hands as if he were waving pompoms.

Steve snickered and ducked his head.

Dad laughed. "There we go. I'm not doing my job if I haven't embarrassed one of you every family dinner."

"Never embarrassed, Dad, just making sure you don't signal for us all to join in."

Randy patted Steve on the shoulder. "I'm going to watch a little television. Don't break the house, kids."

He moved gingerly toward the La-Z-Boy recliner he'd spent a lot more time in lately than years before. Whatever was wrong was turning him old ahead of his time.

On the other side of the table Mitch and Rachel were pushing their chairs aside, a burst of laughter going up from Anna.

"What's going on?" Kate demanded. "Don't you dare start a food fight, or break any of my dishes this time."

"It's not my fault," Anna exclaimed as the two in front of her squared off like Lee had predicted, lifting their hands into position for an arm wrestle. "Blame Rachel for this one. Mitch was being good."

"That's open for debate. We're using left hands," Rachel insisted, wiggling her way forward to place her

91

elbow on the table as she made a face at Mitch. "And Anna holds your elbow in place."

Mitch offered her a silent mocking grin, flexing his flame-covered biceps a few times as he eyed her less-than-pumped upper arms.

How the heck had Lee known?

"You cheated. Somehow, you cheated." Trevor jabbed his brother as Anna stepped behind Mitch, curling her arms around his body and pressing her lips to his neck in what had to be a very distracting manner.

"Don't think that's gonna help Rachel win," Mitch grumbled, amusement in his voice. He loosened his grip on Rachel's fingers, adjusting to allow her into a better position with her shorter forearms. "You have no chance of taking me down. Glutton for punishment."

Rachel and the rest of them laughed, while Kate kept gathering plates, headed for the kitchen. "I swear none of you are grown up yet. I still have a parcel of kids to wrangle every time you get around my table."

Steve moved into position to referee the match. "Ready? Three, two one—"

Anna set her teeth into Mitch's earlobe right when Steve said *go*, and Mitch sucked in a breath of air.

Rachel nearly got the back of his fist to the table before he recovered, steadily powering their hands back to vertical. "Anna Thompson, I'm going to smack your ass if you don't stop."

Trevor couldn't see what else was going on, and he didn't want to because it had to be something dirty—his brother-in-law's face was turning red, and it wasn't from exertion. The muscles in his tattooed arm barely popped as he carefully controlled his strength and took Rachel to the table to win.

Anna relented, leaning over his shoulder to plant

a final kiss to his cheek. "Sorry, Rach, I tried to help."

"I'm still right, even though you won," Rachel said as she made her way over to the opposite side of the table and bumped Lee's chair until there was enough room she could crawl into his lap.

Steve took off to join their father, and Trevor decided he'd clear the table instead of sitting around chatting with the two couples like a fifth wheel.

The kitchen smelt glorious, even with his stomach more than comfortably full.

"Did you want take some leftovers home?" Kate asked.

"I'll never say no to that." Trevor snuck over and offered his mom a hug because she seemed to need one. "How're you doing?"

She glanced over her shoulder to make sure they were alone. "I'm doing good, but your dad's having a tough week," she confessed.

"I saw that. When's the next set of tests?"

"Never."

Shit. "What do you mean?

Kate shrugged. "Your dad said he'd had enough of being poked and prodded. Said trying to find a cure was worse than suffering through whatever's wrong. He's being stubborn, and I don't agree, but it's like arguing with a brick wall. I don't have the energy to do it anymore."

Trevor stood there feeling hopeless and helpless. His mom never spoke like that, her tone one of despair. "Is there something else they can try?"

"There's always something more they can try, but it means going to Calgary or Edmonton for testing, and you know your father."

Trevor nodded. "And you know me. Mom, why

93

didn't you say something earlier?"

"Because it's his decision," she said softly. "It's the *wrong* decision, but I'm not going to bully him into doing something he doesn't want."

"Then I will," Trevor declared. "Don't worry, I'll go to work on him, and see if we can find out once and for all something that's gonna help. In the meantime, let me know if you need anything."

She nodded, a big sigh escaping her. "You are helping a lot, you know. You boys, and Mitch, and the girls—it's been good to have you all around more often, pitching in on more than the chores."

It's what family did. They took care of each other.

And looking out for each other was something you did for a friend, as well. "Do you have any extra canning, or things in the freezer you might not get through before this coming harvest?"

Kate looked thoughtful. "Probably. I'd have to look. Do you want anything specific?"

"It's for my neighbour. In the rental, on the west quarter."

His mom's eyes widened.

"She'd really appreciate it," he said. "Anything you've got."

"I'll look." Her tone of voice and expression changed to curiosity. "So, getting to know someone new?"

"Don't start, Mom," he warned with a laugh, moving to the sink as Steve stepped into the room behind them.

"Dad informed me I needed to get my butt in here and send you out—there's some documentary starting up he said you wanted to see."

Their mom dried her hands as she gave Trevor a meaningful stare. "I will be asking more questions later," she warned him. "Don't forget to wash the pot on the stove."

Trevor and Steve looked at each other. "Heads or tails?" Steve asked, hauling a coin out his pocket.

"Heads."

Trevor got stuck washing—his least favourite task. But with a little conversation, time moved along quick enough.

And Steve took the opportunity to share the good news. "Matt said everything's okay. Got a letter from Becky's landlord, and that thing that I warned you about, you can forget it. It's nothing."

He still didn't have a clue what Steve had been implying in the first place. He was more interested in the other bits of information. "So her job is okay?"

"Hope said she's doing really well, and in the end, that's the part that's most important." Steve dried another pot and placed it on the table behind him. "I guess the landlord asked for a list of things that need to be done around the place to fix it up. We thought maybe you'd like to give her a hand putting that together."

Interesting. "So you've gone from warning me off to trying to matchmake?"

Steve gave him a startled look. "Of course not. Only she seems to trust you, and we don't want to make a big deal out of this and involve a lot of people. She didn't seem your type, actually."

"What's that supposed to mean?"

His brother shrugged. "She's young, that's all."

"Hey, I'm not the one on the wrong side of thirty," Trevor said.

"Wait until your next birthday—you hit the big three-oh this year, don't you?"

"That's just a number. I'm much more mature

95

than you, yet young inside, old man."

Steve snapped the drying cloth, the sharp sting on his thigh drawing a shout from Trevor's lips.

Which brought in the rest of the clan, which turned into a water fight that only stopped when Kate kicked them all out after they'd mopped up the mess.

Trevor stopped to offer his dad a goodbye handshake. "Want to ride the fence line with me tomorrow before we bring in the herd from the east fields?" he asked. "If you're feeling up to it?"

His dad's eyes lit up. "Want to ride horses or quads?

"Horses." They couldn't talk as easily on the quads, and there was a whole lot he wanted to bend his father's ear about. Luckily, horseback was the method he knew his dad would prefer.

Randy hesitated. "If we take the horses, we'll be gone all day. You sure you don't mind?"

His dad looked too excited to disappoint. "It's a been a while since we've had a full day together. We can pack a lunch."

"I'll pack for us both," Randy promised. "Five a.m.?"

God. The sun got up too early in June. "I'm surprised you didn't suggest four thirty."

"You need your beauty sleep," his dad teased.

Trevor headed home with a whole lot of plans rumbling through his brain. He didn't have time to stop in at Becky's, not if he had to be saddled up and ready by five.

He slowed as he drove past her house, a faint light shining in one of the upper rooms, the rest of the house dark.

Like a single star shining in a dark sky.

Chapter Ten

Two months earlier, Paradise, Saskatchewan

SHE'D HIT the asphalt and kept running, not toward town like people might've expected, but away from it.

The edge of the road was slick with ice where the plows had scraped away the recent snowfall and left behind a thin layer. The clothes she'd stolen weren't warm enough to fight off the weather, but she kept moving fast enough it didn't matter. Her exertions sent her heart pumping, her breath escaping rapidly.

Whenever a set of lights appeared in front of her, she'd duck into the ditch and hide. The fewer people who saw her on the road, the better. The way she wanted to go was west, and every time a set of high beams showed in the distance at her back, she'd glanced behind to see if it was a possible ride.

She'd taught herself what big-rig lights looked like, and that was the only thing she'd dare to flag down. Anyone else might be related to the family, or think she was being delusional.

Or worse, they might insist on taking her to the police, and that wouldn't end well either.

It was probably four in the morning before she

finally heard the rumble of a diesel. Her fingers were numb, and her toes icy cold, and she'd settled into a shuffling trot because she had no energy left to run anymore. She turned and raised a hand, waving at the fast-approaching truck.

His brakes engaging was the most terrifying and wonderful sound she'd ever heard in her life.

The truck came to a stop on the edge of the highway far enough ahead that she had to hurry forward. The high door swung open, and she glanced up as warmth poured out of the cab, and she shivered involuntarily.

Blue eyes in a weathered face looked down at her. An older man, with a baseball cap on his head and serious expression on his face. "What the *hell* are you doing out here at this time of night, girl?"

"I need a ride."

He looked her up and down, and she was dreading further questions. Thankfully, he nodded briskly and motioned for her to join him.

Becky scrambled into the cab as quickly as possible, closing the door behind her and pulling the seatbelt across her body without thinking too hard that she might've stepped out of the frying pan and into the fire.

"Where are you headed?"

She couldn't read his emotions, one way or another, in the gruff tone of his voice. She'd planned this part out. "Calgary. But if you're not going that far, you can drop me wherever." Her fingers tightened on the backpack clutched in her lap. "I can give you gas money. I appreciate the ride."

He nodded, slipping back onto the highway, then they sat in silence for a bit while the road stretched in front of them in a razor-straight line. She stared out the window at the mile markers, and the snow fences, and tried to will her heart rate back to normal.

"Are you hungry?"

She snapped her head to the side as something jabbed her arm. Her ride held a granola bar. It was obviously what he'd used to get her attention.

He nodded toward it. "Go on. We won't be stopping to eat breakfast for over an hour, so you may as well have this now."

She promised herself to get through this she'd do *anything* to make it somewhere safe. And if that meant taking a bit of charity along the way, her ego would have to get over it.

She pulled the snack from his fingers gratefully. "Thank you."

The heat inside the cab, the exhaustion from her escape, plus a little food in her stomach meant her eyes were rocking closed before too much longer.

It wasn't until the noises changed that she woke from her hazy sleep. The wheels were slowing, and the turn indicator clicked in a steady rhythm. She looked out the window, horrified to discover they weren't outside the gas station. He was pulling off in a way station in the middle of nowhere, with no signs of another vehicle.

Becky dropped her fingers to the seatbelt release, ready to make an escape if needed, as he brought the massive vehicle to a complete stop.

He glanced her way and swore softly.

"Damn, you should see your face. I'm not going to hurt you." He shook his head. "I wish to hell I could go back and give whoever put that look in your eyes a taste of his own medicine."

She let out the breath she'd been holding. "Why'd

we stop?"

He stared at her with those blue-edged knives. "Because I want to know what the hell I'm doing before I pull into a truck stop and get arrested for kidnapping some teenager. It doesn't matter that you were hitchhiking, no one will believe me if you decide to start screaming for help."

"I won't. I mean, I'm not." This wasn't something she had considered in her plan. "I'm not a teenage runaway. I'm twenty-one, and I—"

He choked. "Twenty-one? Shit. Okay, that helps. But why were you on the road at four a.m. willing to get a ride to Calgary or *wherever?*"

She forced herself to look him in the eyes. "I don't want to tell you."

He grunted, his lips twisting into a wry smile. "At least you didn't give me some bullshit story about going to see family."

Rebekah shivered. "I don't want to tell you anything. I'm not trying to make trouble, but I think it's best I do this on my own, except for the ride. I need a ride."

"As far away from here, as fast as possible?"
She nodded.

He stared back, his expression sad and yet kind. He didn't say anything for the longest time, and she fidgeted on the spot, seconds away from bolting before he finally nodded. "Girl, you need more than a ride, you need a friend. Let's see what we can do to get you straightened up."

Chapter Eleven

Rocky Mountain House, present day

INSTEAD OF his father, Trevor's mom met him at the barns at the bleary-eyed hour just shy of five a.m. Her expression said it all.

"He's sick, isn't he?" Trevor asked, looping Tigger's reins around the post while he talked.

Kate nodded. "He was looking forward to going, but he can't. Something threw him off last night, whether it was the food, or the excitement."

"Family dinners aren't *that* thrilling, Mom." Trevor was disappointed. Not only that he'd miss the chance to talk to his dad about a few pointed items, but he'd been looking forward to a day with just the two of them a surprising amount. "Tell him we can wait. We don't have to move the cattle to new fields for a couple weeks, so if he's feeling better in a few days, we'll go then."

His mom offered him a beaming smile. "He'll be happy to hear that. Now, can I entice you into taking some fresh-baked muffins with you before you go?"

"Twist my arm."

His mom forced a half dozen on him. Once they were out of the yard, he let Tigger take her head, peeling back the paper wrappers and enjoying the warm buttery muffins as the sun inched its way skyward to paint the fields with a gentle light.

Too many jobs called his name to laze about all morning and simply ride, but he enjoyed the interlude, putting Tigger back in her stall in the barn behind Rafe and Jesse's place, a final pat to her rump before focusing on work.

He and his brothers met a dozen times over the day as they worked. At one point he passed his dad going the opposite direction, albeit in the tractor. Randy waved but didn't stop.

His dad looked green around the gills. Stubborn man. Couldn't even let himself be sick for a full twenty-four hours.

Trevor packed it in early since he'd started before five. By the time he grabbed a shower and headed into town in the hopes of catching Becky before she started walking, it was still early afternoon.

He pulled to a stop outside the rental shocked to see she'd beat him home.

Damn stubborn *woman*.

Once again Becky was in a high place, although clearly not happy about it. She stood on a tall ladder, her jawline tight as she focused intently on the window in front of her. She had a scraper in one hand, and a spray bottle of something hanging off the top of the ladder as she worked on the exterior seals.

He approached as cautiously as possible, driving into the yard and getting out of the truck quietly, but once again he was stuck in the position of saying nothing until she noticed him because he didn't want her to fall. They'd been lucky that first time when he'd spooked her off the roof. He wasn't willing to risk it happening again and have her hurt.

Instead he waited, ready to move in an instant, but in the meantime, he enjoyed the show. The late-spring day had warmed up enough that with the heat reflecting off the white-board siding, she'd stripped to nothing but a T-shirt and shorts. Her arms were smooth and muscular. Strong enough for the task she was doing without losing her feminine curves.

And those *legs*. She was shorter than him, but she was all legs. Yeah, he wasn't sad to have to watch for a minute or two.

He breathed a sigh of relief nearly as loud as hers when she finally climbed down and her feet hit the ground.

"Head's up. I'm here," he warned.

"Of course, you're there," Becky replied without missing a beat. "That's what stalkers do. They lurk in the shadows, watching." She tilted her head to the side and examined him more closely. "Dare I ask what you're doing?"

"I came to give you a hand."

"That much I figured. The *Good Neighbour* manual again."

"It's amazing how often it has relevant information for us."

She went to get the ladder but he anticipated her, grabbing hold and taking it down.

"Face it, Trevor, you're not being neighbourly, you're nosy."

He couldn't even pretend to be shocked. "Well, that too."

Becky shook her head. "I meant, what are you doing here at this time of day?"

"I was going to ask you the same thing. I started

103

early."

"The shop closed at two. Hope says nobody comes shopping the afternoon the schools have early dismissal, and she keeps consistent hours all through the summer because it's easier."

A coincidence he was happy to use to their benefit. "Perfect timing, then."

She followed him to the shed where he hung the ladder along the sidewall. "You're sticking around?"

"Steve suggested I could help you with that list your landlord wanted." He pointed above their heads. "Like checking the caulking around the windows."

"Which I've got nicely in hand, thank you."

"Never said you didn't, but some jobs go faster with two people."

She rolled her eyes. "Don't you dare get in trouble with your family, hanging out helping me while you're supposed to be doing stuff for them."

That was the last thing he was worried about. "It's my time. I can spend it how I choose."

She shrugged. "It's okay with me, I guess."

She rambled off a list of things she planned on checking, and Trevor listened, but he also thoroughly enjoyed a chance to keep looking her over.

She'd pulled her hair into a ponytail, and the dark length poured down behind her like a soft waterfall his fingers itched to dip into. Her lips were a deep red, soft and plump, and he bet if he bit softly on the plump lower one, he could make her moan.

Trevor snapped his gaze back up to meet hers, forcing aside his distracting but very entertaining ideas for a moment.

He could tell what projects she was more enthusiastic about, and which ones she was dreading by

104

her face. Although not really her face, but her eyes.

When she spoke, her eyes dipping toward the ground, he knew she was either worried or as excited as he was about dishwashing. At other moments, her face would light up and glow.

It was like watching a wild spring storm through a window, with all the changing moods that entailed.

"What's the main goal for tonight?" he asked.

Becky paused. "I have to find what needs fixing, and we should talk about what you think I need to learn, but I *really* want to empty the living room so I have somewhere other than the kitchen to sit."

"Makes sense to me. Let's clean it out. Garbage first?"

She nodded. "I've got a couple boxes I can tuck aside for the stuff that should be saved or given away, but most of it can be burned. Part of the packrat collection."

They went to work, the first loads filling up fast as Becky tipped a towering stack of newspapers and magazines into her box, and he did the same. She was efficient and direct in all her motions. No wasted time, no wasted energy, but always mesmerizing.

Until she zigged and he zagged when they met in the middle of the hallway, her box piled too high.

He caught the top item before it could topple to the ground, reaching underneath to catch the load. His knuckles brushed the sides of her body as she pulled away, and she took a little breath, seemingly as aware of him as he was of her.

"How about I'll wait at the door, and you bring the boxes there," he suggested. "We'll be able to move a lot faster."

"Good idea."

They moved faster, but it still gave him plenty of time to enjoy watching her both coming and going, her trips taking slightly longer to gather the bits and pieces into the boxes than for him to march to the burn pile and dump the contents.

He leaned against the doorframe and waited for her to come around the corner, hips swaying as she stepped. The frayed edges at the bottom of her shorts caressed her thighs. Trevor's gaze dropped happily along smooth limbs all the way to her bare feet as she padded down the hall. Bare toes he wanted to nibble on.

He took the box she passed him then paused long enough for her to turn away. This time he got to enjoy watching her sweet heart-shaped ass waving at him like a flag. With her T-shirt tucked in neatly at the waist, the curve of her breast would appear for a second before she'd turn the corner and disappear from sight.

He had his short journey to and from the burn pit to wait in anticipation for the next enticing visual tease.

Trevor strode through the door to find Becky standing on a small stool with old paint cans in her hands, lifting them toward a shelf in the hall. Only they must have been heavy, and with her hands full, it was impossible for her to keep her balance.

He rushed forward, matching his hands over hers and steadying the buckets, suddenly aware of their proximity. Of the way her ass rested back against his groin, and how the heat of her body pressed his through her thin T-shirt. The silky-smooth touch of her skin under his hands as his fingers grasped hers over the thin metal handles of the buckets.

"Are you steady?" he asked, but it came out half a breath above a growl, lust riding him hard as his cock reacted and the urge to drop the pails and kiss her senseless shot skyward.

The next second a subtle change in her body position screamed a warning. She was breathing hard, but not in a good way. Not as if she were feeling the lust that had fired his blood to maximum.

It was fear. Fear made her fingers tremble where he held her trapped—

Shit, he was such a fool.

"I'm sorry, baby, I didn't mean to scare you. Slip your hands out from under mine, I've got the pails."

There was none of the false *oh, I'm okay* some other woman might have said. He loosened his grasp, and she stole away, disappearing like a ghostly wind. The final caress of her torso against his enough to remind him what he couldn't have.

But only a bastard took what he wanted when a woman wasn't ready. He moved quickly, placing the pails on the floor and turning to face her. "You okay?"

Becky had retreated to the other end of the hallway, arms wrapped around her, fingers clutching her upper arms tightly. She made a face. "You didn't do anything wrong."

"Doesn't matter, I still scared you."

She nodded. Slowly she twisted to look at him, forcing a reluctant smile to her lips. "You're a good man, Trevor Coleman. I mean that, and I sure like doing things with you. And you've been a big help already, in more ways than you know, but I don't know if I'm someone you should be hanging around with."

Now she was talking bullshit. Trevor brushed his hands on his jeans as he marched forward, moving slow enough she could escape if she needed, but she didn't seem afraid anymore. Him grabbing her had done that. "Sounds like you're getting ready for a goodbye, or to shove me out the door, or something."

Becky shrugged. "Honestly? You said you liked me. I assume that means all the ways a man can like a woman, and..." Her chin trembled for a moment before she fixed him with steely gaze. "I'm an awful lot broken inside. Even though you make me feel things I never expected to feel, I won't be a good girlfriend. You deserve somebody else."

Trevor reached a hand up slowly, gentling his movement to keep from spooking her. "Now, maybe you need to let me decide what type of girlfriend I need."

"I can't give you the things a girlfriend usually gives," Becky insisted.

"You're right," Trevor agreed.

Her eyes widened.

He brushed the tips of his fingers over her cheek, sliding back until he was able to stroke his thumb over the curve of her blushing skin. Moving carefully, watching for any cues to back off. Grateful when none came.

"But considering everything I've been taught by my brothers and cousins, it's not about what a woman can give me that's the bit that counts. It's a hell of a lot more about what I can give *you* that matters."

She was about to protest, those beautiful lips opening so she could explain probably in more detail why she was the worst thing ever for him, but Trevor didn't give a damn what the details were, or what demons she was fighting—

Wait. No. He cared a hell of a lot about what was wrong, but it didn't matter right this instant.

"I like you, Becky. You make me smile, and you make me think." He reached out and slid his hand down her arm until his fingers linked with hers. He squeezed lightly then brought her hand toward him to rest on his chest. "You make me feel things in here that turn my brain to mush, and if that goes along with the laughter we've already proved we know how to do? Let's get to know each other, and we can focus on things we *can* do instead of the things we can't."

Her eyes were sparkling, not with delight this time, but with a dash of emotion and moisture he was pretty sure she didn't want him to mention.

"As long as you don't feel obligated," she began.

"Ha, it doesn't say anything in the *Good Neighbour* manual about doing things out of obligation. It says you do them because you want to, and that's pretty much where I'm at."

He slipped his hand lower to curl his fingers under her chin and rub his thumb lightly over those lips that he'd been craving ever since the first day. A craving he had every intention of finally satisfying, if he could convince her to say he could.

"I'm not trying to push you too hard, but I sure would like to kiss you. While we're being honest, and all that."

She swallowed hard, her tongue slipping out for an instant as she moistened her lips. Her tongue darted against his thumb, and another shock rolled through him, making him hard. Making him ache.

"Just a kiss," he teased softly. "If you'd like."

Instead of answering with words, Becky's fingers moved. From where they rested against his chest she slid them upward slowly, oh so slowly, until her hand rested at the back of his neck. Her fingers gently curled around him then tentatively tugged him forward.

Trevor's heart pounded like he'd been going full speed all day, but he waited, watching closely. Moving the instant she applied the barest pressure to his neck, bringing him toward her lips.

She tilted her head slightly, and he copied her, and a moment later they made contact, the sweet warm air of her breath striking first, sending the taste of her into his mouth as he inhaled the split second before their lips met.

He was a kid again, when every touch from the girl he was sweet on was enough to send his system whirling.

Oh, he'd kissed a few girls over the years, and had always enjoyed it, and it had always given him a rush, but this? Like taking a hard shot of proof whiskey.

Trevor was reeling, drunk on one taste. She tasted like innocence and sin. Becky might think she wasn't the right woman to be his girlfriend, but she was wrong. This was what he'd been craving without knowing it.

He deepened the kiss, pleasure rattling through his system like a runaway train.

Oh, hell *yeah.*

Chapter Twelve

SHE WASN'T sure how she'd ended up in this situation. Not after being so convinced the only choice was to tell Trevor they needed to remain strictly friends. That there could never be anything more between them...

Becky was *very* glad things hadn't gone the way she'd planned.

A swirling sensation tickled her stomach as adrenaline raced through her body, but it wasn't a flight-or-fight response. It wasn't like any sexual experience she'd had before.

Trevor touched her as if she were precious. As if she were breakable, and maybe she was, but she also wanted this much. This much at *least.*

A kiss, willingly given and willingly accepted. He pressed closer, his lips warm on hers, and his simple closeness triggered a riot of emotions. Becky savoured it all.

His touch. His nearness, the scent of him around her. Strong and masculine and fresh, in spite of the work they'd been doing. It was honest labour on top of a clean body, with strong hands that touched her with infinite care, and as his tongue teased briefly against her lips,

111

she opened willingly, a soft moan escaping at the pleasure turning her limbs soft and trembling.

All too soon he pulled back, a low groan escaping him as well as he pressed their foreheads together and looked deep into her eyes. "Becky Hall, you taste damn good."

She laughed, the sound bubbling up from deep inside her. Not boisterous or loud, but it rang in her ears as if she'd shouted. An expression of joy at experiencing something she'd never had before.

Suddenly it was important she tell him that, although the news was probably going to freak him out.

"That was my first."

He frowned, and she saw the gears turning as he tried to figure out what she meant.

She took pity on him. "My first kiss. Or at least the first one that counts."

He turned his shock pretty smoothly into a smile. "Well, for a beginner, you're pretty damn good. I'll have to do it again to be certain, if that's okay with you."

"I guess we could," she teased, breathless to repeat the experience. "Just to be sure."

He rested his hands on her hips and kissed her. This time less an outpouring of passion and more kiss of a friend. Not a fire that turned her limbs molten, but a sweet, tender caress that had her leaning in, eager for more.

When he pulled away this time he stayed close. The firm grasp where he held her reassuring instead of frightening. His fingers rested on the top of her butt, his thumbs sliding back and forth slowly along the edge of her shorts. He wasn't touching skin, but it felt as if he were lighting a fire. It had to be the friction causing flames to burst out all over her skin.

Her fingers were still around his neck, and she boldly stroked him as well, their body positions the closest thing to a hug she'd had in ages.

She'd daydreamed about moments like this, but it was different than what she'd imagined. How simply touching lips could cause her heart rate to increase and small tingles to dance all over her skin—it was pretty amazing.

Trevor slid his hands lower, easing off on the pressure, but he was definitely cupping her butt as he leaned in for another go-around. It was addictive—touching him, and being touched—and the longer they went on, the more aware she became of the changes in his body. His muscular hips pressed forward, and he held her snugly against him, and if kissing made her feel tingly inside, it had made him hard, the solid length of his arousal pressing through his jeans against her belly.

He pulled back not even a second later, voice full of concern. "Becky? You okay?"

She nodded. "I wasn't scared."

He tapped his fingers under her chin and tilted her head back. "You gasped. Like something frightened you."

Whoops. She hesitated, not quite ready to admit that maybe she should be scared, but she was more curious than anything. "We should talk."

Trevor held out a hand. "Then let's go talk," he said.

She threaded her fingers through his and followed along. "The cleaning..."

"Really?" He gave her a look. "I'll interrupt kissing to talk, but not to clean."

A small laugh escaped. "Good to know you have your priorities. I do need to finish cleaning, though."

113

He tugged her after him, back into the kitchen. "I'll call in the clan to help. There's too much for us to do. With their help, we could have the garbage out of the entire house in a few hours."

"We can't do that," she protested. "I think it's supposed to be kept secret—the bit about how the Rylers weren't taking care of the place. I don't want everyone in town to know and have them embarrassed."

"Fine, we'll deal with it together with just a little help. Lee and Rachel know how to keep their mouths shut. We'll double date.

"And clean my house? Sounds like so much fun," she deadpanned.

"It will be," Trevor assured her.

Then instead of pulling out a chair for her to sit in, he picked her up and plopped her on top of the sturdy kitchen table.

"*Trevor.*" Her hands flew instinctively to his shoulders to catch her balance.

He gave her a wink before his expression edged toward serious. "The talking we need to do— Should I break out a bottle of something strong?"

She wasn't sure exactly how much she was going to tell him. If she told him the whole thing, he'd probably appreciate having had a few shots first.

But then again, *she'd* probably have to drink most of the bottle to be able to get it all out in the first place.

Nope. Start small.

"We don't need to get drunk."

He nodded sharply. "You've got secrets, and I don't want you to feel like you have to spill them all right now, but is there anything you *want* me to know?"

"I'd like a hug," she confessed. That much was easy to admit.

114

Trevor laughed. He stepped between her legs and enveloped her in his strong arms. Becky closed her eyes as she slipped her arms around his body and squeezed tight.

They stayed like that for what felt like a long time, and yet not nearly long enough, his muscular body a rock-solid wall to cling to. The scent of him another layer of what made it perfect.

"How come you don't know things? How come that was your first official kiss?" Trevor asked softly. "Are those safe things to ask?"

She dipped her head, her cheek rubbing his shirt. It was kind of nice not looking him in the eye while they had this conversation. "I grew up with very strict rules. We weren't allowed televisions or computers, and we only got approved books and magazines. I didn't go to the local school or the library. Lots of stuff like that."

He held her protectively, one hand rubbing small circles between her shoulder blades, and it felt nice. "Were your parents really strict, or is this something else?"

Oh boy. Already she was going to have to throw herself onto his mercy and hope what she said went no further.

She clung to his shirt tightly so she could stare at the wall instead of his face. "We lived in a small community in rural Manitoba. My parents were with a group of families that all belonged to the same church. They set the rules, and they were...not typical, I guess."

Call a spade a spade, Mark had said—her rescuer on the road, and the first person outside the family she could honestly call a friend.

But it felt too soon. She trusted Trevor, but some stories weren't ready to be shared. So she kept it simple

115

and skipped about a dozen intermediate steps.

"I ran away. I didn't agree with the things they thought were important, and I didn't like how I was being treated, and I didn't see any other way to make things change other than to get out."

"Gutsy move."

She hadn't been gutsy; she'd been desperate.

Becky broke their embrace so she could push him back, needing to see his expression. She still had to look up to meet his eyes, even with her sitting on the table.

"I've got an awful lot to learn, so if you want to go back to just being friends, I'm okay with that."

Trevor tilted his head to the side. "Now why would I want to go back to being *just friends* after I've gotten to kiss you?"

"Because I have a lot of what they call *baggage*."

Trevor took a deep breath and let it out slowly, his gaze examining her face, his expression thoughtful. "You don't understand why I kissed you if you think I'm going to tuck tail and run because you admit you've had a shitty time of it."

Becky tilted her chin up. "Maybe I don't know why you kissed me, but I'm saying if you want easy and uncomplicated, I'm not it."

"Then we're a matched pair. I'm complicated too, remember?"

The sensation in her gut was confusing. *Sheer utter relief.* She caught hold of his shirt and tugged him toward her to steal another hug.

A protective cage of warmth wrapped around her. His hugs were even better than kissing.

—or maybe not.

She might have to do a lot of both before making a decision on that.

HIS MIND raced, and the list of questions he wanted answers to grew by the second. But the way she'd looked at him, with such sadness and desperation in her eyes—the need he'd seen was enough to keep him where he was. Silence fell as he held her. Giving as much support as he could, although a simple hug couldn't be enough.

He totally lacked the smarts to know what to say next that would be brilliant or soothing or...whatever Becky needed.

Lee would know what to ask. Or Anna. Even Steve was better at figuring things out than Trevor was, and at that moment as he held Becky in his arms, he wished for a cheat sheet like he'd made to study for his ninth-grade departmental exams.

She'd run away from a bad situation, getting out with no ID, no *nothing* except herself from the sound of it. Thankfulness for his own solid upbringing turned bitter an instant later because it wasn't fair—neither of them had done a thing to deserve the hand they'd been dealt.

Thinking of family caused a question to escape. "Is there anyone you want to talk to?"

So much for being brilliant. Becky stiffened up like he'd dropped her into a snow bank in mid-January. "You can't tell anyone where I am. Oh, God, please don't—"

"No, that's not what I meant." *Shit.* He'd known he would screw this up. Trevor cupped her chin so she'd look him in the eye again. "You ran away, and you had

117

your reasons, and I sure the hell am not going to say you were wrong. But if there's anyone you need to get a message to. To let them know you're okay...?"

Becky took a deep breath, her body shaking as she clutched his arms. "I've thought about that, and there are some, but until I get my new ID, and everything is straightened out, I don't think it's a good idea."

"Okay." Which said not everyone where she'd been was horrid—that was good to know. He looked her over carefully. Stupid question number two, coming right up, but he figured it needed to be asked, if she grew up religious. "Did you want to talk to a pastor, or some church people? Like, normal ones?"

Her lips twitched. "You're trying really hard not to freak out, aren't you?"

"I'm trying to think of things that will help," he admitted. "The Coleman clan's not much for church-going, although my mom and Aunt Marion do a bit. And my mom is like the least scary person on the face of the earth, except when I was fourteen and talked back to her. Then she was damn scary."

Her amusement lit her face with another of those addictive smiles. "I don't think I'm going to hell, or something, for running away, but if I feel the urge to discuss God, I'll remember that."

"You can talk to me too," Trevor offered. "I mean, I don't go to church, but I got taught the golden rule and the rest."

Becky's hands rested on his waist, the heat of her palms a small connection between them. "I will, but really, I'm good."

Trevor found himself nodding, worry rising again. While he didn't want to discount how bothersome dealing with religious fallout could be, he was more concerned about real physical threats. "I asked you once if you were in danger, and you said no. Anything you want to add to that? Like, I'm not sure why you had to run away. Why couldn't you simply leave? You're old enough."

She hesitated for long enough he figured he'd pushed it too far.

Shit. Trevor hugged her again, trying to ease the tension as he stroked her back. He spoke softly, but he meant every word. "If it's too soon, forget I asked."

Her voice was muffled against him. "No one will come after me. I'm being cautious."

"Makes sense." He ignored the other unanswered part of his question—why she'd had to run away. It *was* too soon. He could wait. "I'll always listen if you need to talk about stuff, but if you want to focus on the future more than the past, I'm good with that too. I kissed the Becky I've gotten to know—the one who crawls out on the roof and goes up ladders even when she's scared, and the one who wears fancy-ass shirts to work in the garden."

A gentle laugh escaped her. "They're from the thrift shop, you know. It's not like I'm trying to make a fashion statement."

"Doesn't matter," he insisted. "Anybody smart in these parts shops at the thrift shop for clothes to wear, especially for doing dirty chores, but you picked out something fun and happy, and it feels like you. You're passionate about things. I like that."

She let out a deep breath. "I want to be passionate about things. I feel like I'm coming out of a fog, and just starting to learn how."

She'd never had a kiss before—

Trevor's mind was filled to overload, but he was smart enough not to push it extra far and ask if she was a virgin. Chances were, strict religious parents and all?

119

The answer would be yes.

But then again, she'd said she was broken...

Oh, boy. All his protective instincts shot to the highest level. He'd do his damnedest to keep her from being hurt, even if that meant reining in himself and his overeager libido. Slowing down, here and now. He'd have to let her set the pace—

"Enjoying life is a good thing. And the rest of it..." He shrugged. "We'll see what happens. I've got no agenda other than I like you and want to spend time with you."

She'd begun to move her fingers again, and the fleeting touch on his torso was driving him crazy. "I like spending time with you, Trevor. I appreciate your help, and if you want to keep doing that, I'd really like to as well."

"And dating. And doing the things you need to learn. Remember those bits. It's not just about chores."

"You might find some of it boring," she warned.

"And I might find some of it interesting. More interesting than you think. Let's give it a shot."

"Does it involve more kissing?" Becky teased, seeming to find her balance.

"Hell, yeah," Trevor acknowledged. "And I think we could fool around a little bit, but only as much you want. No agenda," he promised again.

Becky curled her fingers into the front of his shirt. "What if I have an agenda?" she warned a split second before tugging hard and bringing him close enough for another kiss.

He was gone. His body was back on full alert in seconds, his heart racing, and his cock rock solid. But he planted his feet on the floor and refused to rock against her, savouring instead the sweet touch of her lips over his. Enjoying the way she spread her palms against his chest and stroked in circles before becoming fascinated with his abdomen muscles.

Every muscle in his body was clenched tight as he fought for control, the little noises she made as he kissed her back enthusiastically revving his engine higher and higher.

Slow. *Slow*, his brain shouted.

He caught hold of her hips and lifted her off the table, ignoring his brain as he slipped his tongue past her lips and took the kiss deeper. Becky wrapped her legs around his hips and clung to him, fingernails biting into his shoulders. Adrenaline and lust fought for dominance as he blindly backed into a chair, settling with her in his lap.

Then he grabbed hold of the wooden base of the seat and held on for dear life to stop from touching her. To stop from ripping up her shirt and stripping away her bra and *taking*.

Kisses only—deep, drugging-to-the-senses kisses that made him shake. They went on and on, both of them moaning and panting and making far too much noise, but it was right and it was fucking hot, and he was about to fucking die from pleasure.

Becky finally pulled back, sucking for air hard. She stared at him, the golden flecks in her eyes sparkling, lips trembling slightly.

"Holy, moly, that's—" She let out a shaky breath, her face lit up with sheer delight. "I like kissing. I like kissing *you*," she admitted.

Jeez, understatement of the year. "I like kissing you too."

They sat there grinning at each other like fools. It was perfect, and it was right, and even if his cock was trying to escape his jeans and he was going to have to jerk off later tonight to deal with himself, there was nowhere he'd rather be, and no one he'd rather be with.

It appeared he had a girlfriend.

Chapter Thirteen

GOOD TO his word, Trevor asked his brother Lee for a hand on the down-low to make a dent in the mess filling her house. The next time slot that worked for them all was Becky's half day, and she slipped out the shop door the instant Hope gave her the nod.

A tall brunette was waiting for her street side, leaning on a familiar truck. "Becky?"

She nodded. "Don't tell me. Trevor is hiding around the corner, right?"

The other woman laughed, hauling open the door and gesturing her in. "Nope. I'm Rachel, Lee's girlfriend, and I got orders to pick you up when I was done work. Hop in."

Becky obeyed, laughing softly as Rachel crawled behind the wheel. "Trevor constantly offers to give away his truck, but I didn't realize until now he'd actually do it."

Rachel shoulder-checked the traffic before pulling onto Main Street. "No kidding. That guy is missing the macho 'this is my baby, no little women behind the wheel' gene. I don't even get to drive when I go places with Lee. But Trevor came into the café this morning and tossed me his keys without offering a single warning to make sure I drove carefully."

With the doors closed, an amazing aroma filled the cab as Rachel took them down the side streets, looping around to the road home.

"Is there fried chicken in here?" Becky asked, her mouth watering involuntarily.

Rachel patted the bag on the seat between them. "Yup. Hope you're hungry. I made us lunch before my shift ended, and my boss sent along one of the day-old pies."

Well, that was embarrassing. "I didn't expect you to feed me as well as come and work," Becky complained.

"Of course you didn't, but you can consider this your welcome-to-the-neighbourhood dinner." Rachel offered her a quick glance before focusing back on the road. "Sorry I didn't stop by sooner."

"Don't apologize. It's been a bit crazy since I got here." Silence fell for a while as Becky glanced out the window, staring at the sky where big grey clouds were rolling like someone was mashing potatoes vigorously. "I hope the weather holds off for a while. It'll make cleanup easier."

"We'll get it done, no matter what." Rachel tapped her fingers on the steering wheel. "And in case *you* feel the need to apologize for the mess we're going to deal with, let me tell you a story first. You know the Rylers?"

"That's the people who lived in my house before."

Rachel nodded. "They've been coming in for breakfast two or three times a week since they moved into town. They sit in the same spot every time, and just this past week my boss and I finally realized they take absolutely everything home with them at the end of the meal, except for the plates and utensils."

Becky wasn't sure she understood. "They're

stealing stuff?"

"Oh, no. Not really. We put things on the table for the customers' convenience, but they don't stop at using what they need. It's like they take the extra stuff *just in case.*" Rachel slowed as she approached Becky's driveway. "The packages of sugar, all the jams, the napkins—my boss said it's not the first time she's seen it. A bit of fallout still from the war generation. They don't know when they might get another opportunity, so they stash away everything they can."

It made sense, Becky supposed. To squirrel away things. "That would explain some of what I found when I cleaned the kitchen."

Rachel parked next to a dark-blue truck, waving out the window at a muscular young man standing on Becky's front porch as he dumped a load of garbage into the bucket of the tractor. "Looks like the boys got a head start on us. That's my Lee."

Trevor marched out the door right behind his brother, emptying his armload before hurrying to Becky's side. "Right on time," he said, curling an arm around her and tugging her to the side. "Hey, Rodeo."

Becky glanced at the other couple, but they weren't looking at anything except each other. Lee held Rachel with one hand and the lunch in his other as he welcomed her with a vigorous kiss.

Trevor cleared his throat. "Where's *my* kiss?"

Her cheeks heated up like she'd been in the sun all day long. "Really? Right now?"

"Right now," he agreed, although he moved slowly enough she could have evaded him.

She wasn't stupid. She'd been looking forward to their next kiss since the instant they'd stopped the other night.

He kept it short, but definitely not sweet, and she imagined her cheeks were flaming red to go with the tingling he'd triggered in her entire body. Then he took her by the hand and led her onto the porch to where a table and four chairs had appeared.

Rachel put the lunch bag in the middle as Lee stood waiting for them. He offered her a crisp handshake. "I'm Trevor's younger and much handsomer brother."

His girlfriend smacked him across the shoulders lightly as she laughed. "Stop flirting, or you don't get any dessert."

Lee tossed a wink at Becky before hurrying to soothe Rachel, but the teasing was obviously good-natured and all meant in fun as Trevor pulled out her chair and sat her at the table, and they filled plates with food from the café.

Trevor dropped a third drumstick on his plate. "Lee had the idea of using the tractor bucket to help with cleanup. We can get an awful lot in there before driving it to the burn pile."

"That's smart. I wish you could open up the walls and use the tractor inside the house," Becky grumbled. "I did another walk-through the other day, and so much of it is trash."

"If that's the case..." Rachel looked thoughtful for a moment. "Why don't you and I go through and grab anything that needs saving? The rest can be shoved toward the door for the boys to deal with."

Lee nodded. "Even the furniture—I took a quick peek, and whatever you do want to keep is going to need a thorough cleaning. Trevor and I can haul it onto the porch, then after the floors are done, anything you need can be brought back inside. The rest of it will be easier to haul away if it's out here."

Becky felt a little overwhelmed by the amount of work they were offering to help her with. "I don't know how to thank you."

"It's what neighbours do," Trevor reminded her.

"Heck to being neighbourly." Lee broke out into an enormous grin. "I'm doing it because I get to watch Trevor be all goo-goo eyed over a girl. That's payment enough for me."

"Lee," Rachel whispered as if she were scandalized. "What if Becky doesn't know?"

Her cheeks were heating up again. "What if Becky doesn't know, *what?*"

Trevor caught her fingers in his under the table and squeezed lightly. "That I'm goo-goo eyed. It's a terribly distracting condition caused by being in the presence of a woman you're very attracted to."

An imp of mischief jumped on her shoulder. "You mean like the way Lee can't keep from staring at Rachel every chance he gets?"

Trevor hooted, and Rachel laughed. Lee shook his finger at her before draping his arm along the back of Rachel's chair and nuzzling the side of her neck. "Guilty. It seems Becky is a secret physician."

"She certainly diagnosed you on the first try." Trevor let go of her fingers, but only to rest his hand on her thigh, stroking softly as they finished the meal.

Every time he touched her, he set off a chain reaction, and by the time they put away the remains of the lunch and got to work, she was glad for the break. Her skin felt sensitive, as if she was headed toward overload, but she wouldn't trade away a single touch.

They worked for three solid hours, and by that time the main floor was stripped bare, and the upstairs rooms reduced to nothing but furniture.

127

And Becky was in love.

Rachel was funny, energetic, and instantly made decisions Becky hesitated over. The older woman hadn't once judged or said a thing to make her feel anything but happy to spend time together.

Becky had shared bits and pieces of her situation, a little worried about it, but willing to take a chance and open up more. Rachel needed to know why it was important to keep some things that otherwise would've been sent to the dump.

Starting with nothing meant it was easy to find value in someone else's trash.

But Rachel shook her head as Becky debated keeping the boxes of books they'd found tucked into the back of a closet. "We could put them in the pile for giving away, but they smell. Even if there were a valuable book in there, which I doubt since I see a bunch of encyclopedias, the pages are mildewed and moldy." Rachel wrinkled her nose. "Let them go, hon."

"But...they're *books*," Becky protested.

Rachel hesitated then came over and caught Becky by the hands. "Oh, sweetie, I know. But I *promise* I'll make sure you get all the books you can handle, and more."

The words were matter-of-fact, but the touch was caring and real, and for a moment, a wave of homesickness for her sister struck hard enough Becky felt it in her heart. "Thank you."

"And not only kid's books, like *Winnie the Pooh*." Her fingers got another squeeze before Rachel set her free.

Becky took a quick glance toward the door, but they were still alone. "By the way, I was looking for a mention of Tigger, but I didn't find it yet."

Rachel's lips hitched up into a smile. "Does Tigger have some deep significance I don't know about?"

"It's supposed to be Trevor's nickname," she shared.

This time Rachel's amusement escaped in a loud laugh. "Okay, I can totally see that. I'll see what I can find out. We'll deal with that the next time we get together, which will be soon. If you're okay with spending more time with me," she teased.

It was hard to not be overeager and suggest they get together the next day. "I'm not busy, except for work and cleaning up around here."

"And spending time with me," a deep voice interrupted as Trevor stuck his head into the room. He gave Becky this look that made her knees shake in a good way. "Dammit, woman. Don't you go getting yourself booked solid with dates with other people."

Rachel planted her hands on her hips and gave him a cocky grin. "You snooze, you lose, sucker. She's my girlfriend now, too."

"Nope. I don't share. Besides, your boyfriend is downstairs waiting for you. He said something about taking you to a movie."

Becky followed them as they continued to banter, but she'd lost track of the conversation the instant Trevor had said *I don't share.*

Memory slammed into her, as if all the garbage they'd hauled out of the house had been picked up and dumped on her. It was hard to breathe, and she had to concentrate on every step down the stairs to stay vertical.

I don't share.

It was like the load lifted, vanishing between one second and the next. Becky took a deep breath and firmly

129

put a smile back into place.

These were good people, *good friends*, and her thanks to Lee and Rachel were sincere as she offered them.

Rachel climbed onto the bench seat and sat in the middle as Lee settled behind the wheel, lifting his arm over her shoulders to nestle her closer. "Glad we could help. If you need another hand, give us a shout."

Rachel leaned around him toward the open window. "And I'll stop by at work to chat. We'll figure out when our next date is," she teased.

"A book date?" Becky asked.

"Sure. And sometime we'll have a girls' night out, but we'll work up to that," Rachel said with a laugh.

Lee rolled his eyes. "That's like telling the newbie runner to look forward to her first marathon. You're mean."

"But you like me this way." Rachel snuggled against him.

"I *love* you this way," he corrected her, offering Trevor and Becky a wink as he put the truck into gear. "See you tomorrow, bro. Becky, it was great to meet you."

The air got quiet as the truck left the yard, and suddenly Becky felt a little shy. So she stuck to what she knew. "That was amazing."

"My family? Yeah. They kind of rock," Trevor admitted. "Except for Lee. He sucks at times, but I like Rachel, so I won't toss him out on his ass anytime soon."

Shyness vanished. "Rachel said you helped set them up."

"Let's talk while we drive," Trevor suggested, guiding her toward his truck and opening the door for her.

She paused. "Are we going somewhere?"

130

"We've worked for hours. We're taking a break before supper. If you're good with that."

Becky crawled in without another complaint. "Breaks are good. And you guys saved me a couple weeks' worth of work."

"Glad you're happy."

He turned left instead of right out of her driveway.

"I thought the only thing this way was Coleman land."

"Yup," Trevor agreed. "And some of the prettiest countryside in the Foothills. Wait. I think you'll like this surprise."

He took her to the river.

The instant he led her down the narrow path to the water's side, she abandoned her shoes and socks, then stepped into the mud, the deep brown mess squishing up between her toes. She didn't care if she was getting filthy—the place called to her. It was glorious.

And when Trevor sat without a word and pulled off his boots as well, something warm lit inside.

The river was wide, the slow-moving surface drifting past them like a speckled board, the sun filtering through the leaves. "I always loved walking by the river. Of course, our river was more like a creek, and it's not there all year long."

Trevor didn't squeeze her fingers, or show any outward sign that he was aware she'd shared something new. But he'd noticed. She was sure of it.

Then he turned it around and shared as well.

"The water meanders through all the Coleman land, except ours. We call it Whiskey Creek, but it's got a strong source, and most of the year it keeps chugging along nicely until the late fall. Over the years we've found different places along the creek to get into all sorts of mischief. The section close by the original homesteads is deep enough to go swimming, and there're a couple of really good spots for rope swings." He glanced over. "God, I love that. That's one of my favourite things on a hot summer day."

She could picture him, all wild and excited. "You'll have to take me sometime."

He curled a hand around hers, guiding her slowly as they left a set of barefoot prints behind them in the mud. "What about you? Did you ever go swimming at this creek you grew up by, or was it too small?"

"Where I grew up, yes, there was water all the time. But swimming wasn't approved of, so on hot days I'd hurry through my chores to find a moment to be down by the water. And I'd take off my shoes and socks, stick my feet in, and it was like I was in my own special world. Nobody was going to find me."

He brushed his thumb over the back of her neck. "You said that's where you were little...?"

Secrets were bundled up so tight inside of her she didn't know which string to pull to begin the unraveling.

"I moved to Saskatchewan when I was about sixteen..."

There was no *about* regarding the date. She'd been sixteen the day she'd arrived at Paradise Settlement to be scrubbed and dressed and made ready.

The sacrificial lamb prepared for slaughter.

It was too much—she wasn't ready for those memories. She twisted toward him, trying to revive the happy glow from moments earlier.

"I don't want to talk about that here." She waved a hand at the water. "This is a special place, and I don't want to mix up these new memories with those old ones."

132

Trevor stepped closer, slipping his arms around her and resting her protectively against him. "Then we'll have to do something other than talk."

He offered an exaggerated wink that set her off laughing.

She slid her hands up until she could link her fingers behind his neck, close and safe at the same time. "You know for us not doing anything other than kissing, we sure do find ourselves in this position a lot," she teased.

Guilt drifted over his face. "I'm not rushing you, really I'm not," he said, rubbing her lower back gently. "But I figured if you got comfy being close, it wasn't a bad thing. I like having you in my arms."

"I like being here. I like getting hugs." She turned her head and rested her cheek against his broad chest, and another wave of affection for him surged. She was safe, she was protected—things that a man who was important to her should provide.

They got quiet, until there was nothing but the sound of the birds and the river moving lazily past. He swayed them from side to side a little, his hands drifting lower as he rubbed her back. That hot, heavy sensation was back in her gut, but she didn't feel rushed or pushed, just a steadily increasing desire for more.

"Can I ask you something?" The words escaped her like they were propelled from a shotgun.

"Anything," Trevor promised.

It was easier when she wasn't looking into his eyes. "Can I see you naked?"

133

Chapter Fourteen

A SOFT curse escaped before he regained control of his brain.

The entire afternoon he'd watched Becky with something near obsession. Making sure she was okay with his family. Making sure she was comfortable with all of them being in her space. When he'd heard her laugh out loud from somewhere upstairs, working with Rachel, his gut had done backflips from relief.

That reaction had nothing on what was churning inside him at her out-of-the-blue request.

Slow. Remember? She probably didn't mean what he thought she meant.

He went for casual. "Well, that's an interesting proposition. Do you mean right here? Because there're no guarantees we won't have company at any moment, and while I don't care who I flash, this is a small town. We'll be teased for a long time. It could make for some awkward family-dinner discussions."

Becky adjusted position so she could stare up at him with those big brown eyes. "I was thinking maybe at your place."

He nodded slowly. "And does this *me getting naked* business involve you getting naked as well?"

She hesitated, chewing for a second on her lower lip. "Not yet."

That's what he figured. "Sweetheart, I don't know what you're looking so all-fired worried about. You want me to strip, I'm there. Don't expect me to do any dance moves, but if you're looking to do a little exploring, I'm more than willing to let you research."

"You want to know why?"

"Well, it's obviously because you're totally enamored with me, and want to admire me in all my most glorious bare-assedness."

"I know you're joking, but that's not far off," Becky offered in return. "And I didn't mean this minute." She flushed adorably and changed the subject. "What's the most fun you've ever had down by the river?"

Right now was the first answer that popped to mind.

Trevor took her by the hand and started walking again, following her lead and ignoring the *oh, my fucking God* request she'd made moments before. "Let's see. There've been float parties that were a lot of fun. Giant inner tubes and blowup rubber boats from the hardware store loaded with beer and munchies. We drive upstream till we're on the outskirts of Coleman property and then drift all the way to the other end. Those times hold a lot of good memories."

"You took beer in the rafts with you?"

"Sure. Coolers fit in the boats just fine. The best was the year that Travis set up a barbecue on a plank of wood over an inner tube, lashed it behind his rubber dingy, and roasted dogs and hamburgers while we floated. That was a hell of a lot of fun."

Her eyes had gone wide. "Now I know you're pulling my leg."

135

"Seriously, he actually floated a barbecue down the river, no problems at all. Joel was the one who tipped one year and lost the picnic cooler."

"It sounds incredible."

"Then we'll do it," Trevor promised. "Not until late July, or August, because the water is still cold as hell until then."

They reached the section of the river where they either had to turn around or cross over to the other side. Trevor eyed the rustic bridge he and the cousins had made years ago. It was looking a little worse for wear, winter debris tucked up against the slowly decaying logs. "I think we need to head back."

Becky nodded, slipping from his side to walk in the water. Every step she kicked up splashes that grew bigger and bigger as she swung her legs more vigorously. Trevor didn't bother to fight his grin as she played on the trip back, sheer delight in all her motions.

Until she turned toward him too rapidly and lost her footing, falling into the shallow river with a massive splash. The shock on her face and the loud shout of dismay from her lips had him rushing forward, barely keeping his balance as he hit the slick surface made worse by its recent dousing of water.

Only she wasn't hurt. Becky was laughing so hard she couldn't stand up. Every time she tried, her feet slipped out from under her again and she landed with another squawk in the icy water.

By the time Trevor closed the distance between them she was soaked and muddy from head to toe.

"You're going to get yourself all dirty," she scolded between laughs as he scooped her out of the water and marched back toward their shoes, carrying her in his arms.

Trevor ignored her halfhearted fist banging into his biceps, because she was still laughing. "Rodeo, I *told* you that water was cold. Could have saved yourself the experiment if you'd just listen to me."

"You didn't tell me that the mud was muddy," she said with a giggle that escalated to a shriek as he hoisted her in the air, draping her over his shoulder. "*Trevor*. Put me down."

"Nope."

"I can walk," she insisted.

"I noticed you walking. It seemed to involve a lot of arm waving and splashing."

Becky snorted in a most unladylike way, the sound making him chuckle as he snatched up their shoes and made his way cautiously back to the truck. Her laughing complaints continued to ring in his ears, his heart light at her good-natured response to her mishap.

He tossed their shoes into the truck bed then went to open the driver's door.

"No, please." Becky's amusement faded, and she sounded seriously concerned. "I'll sit in the back. I don't want to get mud all over your truck."

"You won't," he promised, keeping hold of her as he adjusted the seat and wheel to the maximum distance.

Then he twisted her in his arms until he had her back against his chest, one arm tucked under her legs to support her until he had sat himself down with her in his lap. It took a little work, but they ended up with her behind the driver's seat facing forward, just like him.

Again her sense of humour snuck out. "I don't know that it's the best time for a driver's lesson."

"We'll kill two birds with one stone." The river water was wicked cold at this time of year, and he was worried she'd feel it soon enough. "I'll get you home to a hot bath, but in the meantime, yeah, this is how you drive a truck."

He started a running monologue describing his actions to distract her from her wet and chilled situation.

It was a good thing he could drive while barely paying attention. Having her in his lap was making him crazy. The trip was so short he was tempted to drive around the section a few more times to enjoy the weight of her resting against him.

She reached up to the steering wheel, resting her hands on top of his, and moving with him. Trevor had a sudden vision of her naked, back in this position, riding his cock, and he stifled a groan as they hit her yard.

Then he ignored her protests again and carried her from the truck to the upstairs bathroom. "No use in getting two sets of muddy footprints on the floor," he pointed out.

"Oh, right."

He lowered her carefully into the old-fashioned claw-foot tub. "Got your balance?"

Her hand rested on his shoulder for a moment. "My feet are slippery."

"Sit down," he ordered, tossing a towel on the floor to stand on so he wouldn't make more of a mess with his muddy feet. Then he turned on the water taps and adjusted the temperature as she sat, jeans and all, in the tub.

A shiver rocked her hard. Damn, he should have known better. "Slip off your pants."

She hesitated.

"Look, you're cold and wet, and I promise I won't do anything but get you warmed up. Take them off."

He twisted away so he wasn't watching, but the sounds of her struggling were clear. A bar of soap rattled off the tub edge, rolling past his feet.

When a borderline bad word escaped her, he couldn't help himself. "You need a hand, Rodeo?"

"Maybe?"

So softly said.

Trevor made sure he kept his eyes on her legs as he checked to see what the trouble was.

She'd gotten the fabric only halfway pulled off, shoved together into a knot by her knees. "Relax. I'll untangle you."

Easier said than done at this point. He had to turn the fabric inside out, holding her by the knee as he jerked at the wet fabric that was stuck like glue to her smooth shins.

The water splashing into the tub was sending up billows of steam, while bits of mud knocked from her toes clung to the white porcelain like illegible hieroglyphics. Trevor tossed the wet mess of her jeans into the sink and returned an instant later to catch hold of her foot and dunk it under the running water.

Becky giggled. Full-out giggled as her foot jerked in his hand. "That tickles."

"Good to know." Trevor offered a smile as he kept a firm grasp on her, slipping his fingers between her toes to get out the stubborn mud. "Why did we think getting a mud pack was a good idea, again?"

"It's supposed to be go-*o-o-o-od* for the—*stop* it, you're killing me," she begged, wiggling harder.

"Nearly done," he promised. "At least this foot."

"I can reach my toes to wash them," she said, another giggle accompanying the words.

"I can reach them even better," he smirked, glancing at her with a mouth that had suddenly gone dry.

She'd wiggled out of her flannel shirt revealing the thin wife-beater underneath. The fabric was white, so it would have been a pretty meager cover to start with, but with the water wicking up the material from the tub, and the moisture from her earlier dousing, her torso was as close to naked as possible while still being covered.

Trevor might have swallowed his tongue while fighting the urge to whisper *Sweet Lord Almighty.*

Becky wasn't wearing a bra.

That bit took a moment more to register. Not because it wasn't plain as plain could be, but because, *holy fucking shit,* she wasn't wearing a bra, only a see-through white shirt, and he was supposed to go slow...

Fuck his life.

ANOTHER SHIVER took her, but this time she swore it wasn't the cold.

It was the look in Trevor's eyes.

He'd frozen in place, eyes locked on her torso, and the instant flush of heat that struck was most definitely centered deep in her core.

He swallowed hard, then dragged his gaze higher, meeting her eyes briefly with such a heated desire she broke into a sweat.

"Other foot," he ordered, breaking the spell between them, but leaving her fighting for air, as if the steam in the room was wall-to-wall and thick as cotton.

She lifted her left foot into his hand then leaned back, resting her arms along the top of the tub. Tilting her head back until it rested on the ledge behind her as she watched him with fascination.

Trevor had turned on the water, but left the drain open, probably to let the mud escape. It meant there were only a couple inches of water collecting in the bottom of the massive tub. Her panties were soaking, and her undershirt, but the fact she was nearly naked in front of him wasn't the bit making her heart pound like crazy.

He was *touching* her. Over and over, like an artist working with delicate materials, Trevor stroked her skin in small motions, wiping away the mud, flushing any remaining smears clean with fresh water.

It was the most innocent of acts, and she was more turned on than she'd ever been in her life.

She wiggled slightly, trying to do something about the ache between her legs without making it clear how much she was enjoying this unexpected situation.

Silence fell between them. Silence, but for the laughing trickle of the water, and the sound of their beating hearts. God, she swore hers was pounding loud enough Trevor should be staring at her in concern.

"Stand up."

His voice, tight and deep. A command, but one he was as forced to make as she was to obey. Her limbs moved without hesitation.

Trevor waited, kneeling by the tub as she rested a hand on his shoulder. A shiver rippled over her skin, although that should have been impossible since she was on fire. He grabbed the cup from beside the sink and methodically washed all traces of mud from the tub.

His dark head bent forward as he focused on his task, the muscles in his biceps flexing as he moved— power and passion bundled together in one appetizing package.

She was nearly drooling, breathing hard as she watched him care for her.

There were so many things she wasn't ready for, but this? She was ready for this. Sexual tension stretched taut between them, and while she didn't know what she wanted, she knew she *wanted*.

He put the plug in the drain before standing. Her hand slid down his arm, over firm muscles and barely leashed passion.

Trevor stared into her eyes, wicked heat held in control with an iron-firm grip. "You need to take off your things so you can soak and get warmed up. I'll step outside and go see—"

"What if I slip?" she interrupted, gratified to see his eyes widen with shock.

If she was going to hell, she was going to go on her own terms.

"Hold me," Becky ordered, not sure where she found the boldness.

But then he moved to obey, and she didn't care how it had happened. She reached under the edge of the shirt and caught hold of her panties, dragging them down her legs until they fell to her feet. She stepped out of them, stooping to snatch them up and toss them past Trevor into the bathroom sink.

She made the mistake of looking at him. If his eyes had been full of fire before, they were now twin infernos, scalding hot as he gripped her elbow, supposedly to support her.

"Rodeo. I don't think you're ready for what you're asking for." He licked his lips, as if desperate for moisture. "You said earlier you weren't ready to be naked in front of me. There's no need to rush. I'm not going anywhere, I promise, so whatever wild thing's got hold of you, you tell it to ease off for a little while."

He was probably right, but it was hard to resist temptation with fire flowing through her veins. "I want something more," she confessed. "I don't know what, but I don't want to let go of this feeling. Not yet."

Trevor nodded, a glimmer of mischief returning to break the tension. "You find any bubble bath when you cleaned the house?"

Curiosity struck as Becky motioned toward the drawers under the sink. "Second one down."

He placed her hands carefully on the edge of the tub as she dropped to her knees, her private parts still covered, as much as a soaking-wet shirt could stop her pebbled nipples from being visible.

Then he grabbed one of the small travel bottles of bubble bath and upended it into the tub, tossing the empty container in the garbage before fixing her with another one of those heart-palpitating looks. "Take off your shirt when I leave, and get comfy."

He must've sensed her disappointment because a wicked chuckle escaped.

"Don't worry, Rodeo. I promise to come back in about twenty minutes. We'll see what we can do about that *something more* you want."

He left before she could ask any questions, the bathroom door closing with solid *click.*

Becky stripped away her final layer, balling it up and tossing it in the sink with the rest of her clothes before she settled back and luxuriated in the hot water.

Only it wasn't like taking a bath any other day. Small bubbles escaping from the bottom of the tub caressed her skin as they made their way to the water surface. Every brush a tease, her anticipation growing stronger.

Without a watch, twenty minutes was impossible to gauge, but by the time the door opened she was a bundle of tightly wound cravings. She'd turned off the taps a while ago, but not before the falling water had produced a mass of bubbles covering the entire water surface up to her neck.

Trevor walked in, bold as could be, to settle on the lowered toilet seat as he checked her out with a self-satisfied grin. A moment's glance was enough to see he'd washed his feet elsewhere in the house, his bare feet tanned and strong like the rest of him.

"You're looking mighty comfy," he teased.

"I'm not cold anymore." Becky lifted her arms out of the water and laid them on the tub edge again. The position made the bubbles sway, the top curves of her breasts lifting the floating layer slightly and turning it into a rolling landscape.

"You okay with me being in here?" She must've made an annoyed face because he lifted a brow. "Hey, I need to check. You were awfully full of vim and vigor a while ago, and I don't mind one bit. But if you *ever* change your mind when we're fooling around, all you ever have to say is *no*, got it?"

She nodded even as she had to ask. "Are we going to fool around?"

He dropped to his knees beside the tub, his gaze drifting over the bubbles as his smile took on a decidedly dirty cast. "I think we might be able to do something."

The steam had mostly vanished, so she couldn't blame it for her instant difficulty in breathing.

Trevor placed a hand on either side of her shoulders and leaned in over her. His lips took hers with

144

a kiss that kick-started all of the earlier sensations back to high gear.

He kept kissing her, one hand rising to cup the side of her cheek as he turned up the heat. Owning her mouth, his tongue and teeth surprising her at every turn. He gentled the kiss to let her breathe, then went and stole her breath away the next second by sliding his hand down her neck and under the surface of the water.

He couldn't see under the layers of bubbles, but he didn't seem to need visuals to get where he wanted to go.

A gentle touch. A ghostly caress, barely using his fingertips over her skin, but every second the connection grew more intense. He scooped his hand to one side, brushing over her nipple, and a low moan escaped her, captured by his continuing kiss.

She had no idea what he would do next, but she had no complaints so far. His kisses continued to tease and entice as his fingers lay briefly over her ribs. His wide grip briefly circled her waist before dropping lower to tease her hip.

His thumb rested on the fold between her thigh and torso, the narrow crease that led down between her legs. She gasped for air as he broke away, staring into her eyes as he slowly followed the line. A gentle touch, but unwavering. Becky did everything she could to keep her face and body language showing him she was completely on board with what he was doing.

And what he was doing was cupping her, his big hand settling intimately over her sex.

"You okay, Rodeo?"

"Don't stop," she begged, not sure what she was begging for. All she knew was this was right. So right, and so long in coming.

It was as if she'd never been cold in her life. Never hurt or been afraid. Not with the lava bubbling inside her, burning away all sorts of bad memories and any ice that had lingered in her soul.

And then he moved his fingers higher, slipping between her folds to brush against the sweetest spot.

"You should see your face," he whispered. "So much pleasure. Relax, and let me make you see stars."

She was already halfway to the heavens, a delicious tension growing in her core as he caressed, slowly increasing the pressure. Becky let one hand fall into the water, brushing along his arm and the moving tendons of his forearm until her hand settled over his as he stroked her. It was magical, and perfect, and exactly the *something more* she never would've imagined to ask for.

"Relax," he ordered again.

"How do I relax when I'm about to explode?" she asked on an exhale, because there was no way she could take a breath to speak normally.

Trevor *growled*. Seriously, growled. This deep, rumbling noise escaped him that touched her inside in a caress as potent as his fingers on her sex.

Pleasure swamped her rapidly, like the cold water had surrounded her when she'd slipped, only now heat and intense arousal took her under as she climaxed. Core tightening under his touch as his strokes grew softer, slower.

The wide, dark centers of his eyes were the first things she saw as she opened her eyes, shocked to discover sometime in the last few seconds she'd clutched his wrist, holding him tightly to her. As if she was scared he'd run away.

As if she was scared this wasn't really happening...only it was. The languid satisfaction in her limbs made that clear.

So did the satisfaction on his face.

Becky found her voice. "You look like you were the one who just got *something more* in the tub."

"I did." His gaze drifted over her, lips curling upward, his breathing as unsteady as hers. "I got to put that expression on your face, and trust me, Rodeo, it might be our first, but no fucking way will it be the last. I had just as much fun as you."

He rocked forward on his heels and kissed her again, and it was like dessert, and a bow on top of a present, and the most beautiful sunset sky. All the things that made a day end perfectly.

Right before he stood and pretended to tip his hat at her. "I'll see you tomorrow. Sweet dreams."

The water was still hot, and the scent of ginger-and-peach bubble bath lingered in the air, but the most vivid detail filling her mind was the image of a sweet, incredible, *sexy* man who'd rocked her world and never asked for a single thing in return.

He'd said he'd make her see stars. Holy moly.

Trevor Coleman delivered on his promises.

Chapter Fifteen

BY NOW the low rumble of Trevor's truck had grown familiar enough she could recognize it without turning. Becky kept walking, but it was difficult to consider refusing the man anything after the magic he'd performed a few days ago.

Life being what it was, she hadn't seen him since her day off, although she'd spotted him in the fields at a distance. And that was fine. She didn't expect him to be around all the time.

If he were around more often, she'd never get anything done.

As the truck closed in, she turned to greet him, confusion rushing in. That wasn't his familiar face smiling at her through the driver's window. Instead an older woman rolled down the window and offered a greeting.

"Hi, Becky. I'm Kate Coleman—Trevor's mom. Can I give you a ride? I'm headed into town to the quilt shop."

"Thanks." She wasn't about to argue with Trevor's mom about how she was just fine walking. Still, she wished she knew how much he'd shared with his family. "We're going be there before it opens," she warned as she crawled into the passenger seat. "I was giving myself enough time to make it on foot."

Mrs. Coleman waved off her concern. "We'll grab a coffee first." She glanced quickly at Becky before fixing her eyes on the road ahead of them. "Are you enjoying working in Rocky?"

"It's been wonderful," Becky said honestly. "Hope has an amazing shop, and everyone has been so nice."

"All the quilts I made when I was growing up were from scrap fabric and old clothes. Sometimes I feel scandalized buying a piece of material and chopping it up."

That was exactly how Becky felt. "Almost all my previous projects have been the same. You use what you can get, I suppose."

"Speaking of which, Trevor mentioned you might be interested in some extra canning. I didn't want to stop by with anything before I checked to see what you needed."

She might be a little embarrassed at the offer, but Becky wasn't going to turn it down. Everything would be a huge help at this point. "I would appreciate anything you have extra of, but can I offer a trade? If there's anything you need help with, let me know."

"I'll take you up on that," Kate said. "We try to get the whole Coleman family together a couple times a year, and we alternate where we meet. Dana—that's the Angel Coleman family—asked if I'd mind hosting the family Canada Day picnic again this year."

"And you need help?"

Kate nodded. "I wasn't expecting it, and there's a lot to get ready before next weekend. It's too short notice for my daughter Anna to take time off, and the other girls will help when they can, but even with Melody and

Rachel coming over, I could use another set of hands."

That Rachel would be there was the icing on the cake. "I'll help. Just let me know when you need me."

"I'll talk to them, and if it works out, why don't you come over tomorrow night for dinner? We can work for a couple hours, and when we're done, you can raid the pantry for some canning and one of the girls can drive you home." She was turning into the drive-through of Tim Hortons. "What do you want?"

"A coffee would be great. Thank you."

"Cream? Sugar? Or are you one of those tough types who takes it black?"

She was the type who rarely got coffee from a coffee shop. Coffee was a treat in the first place, these days. "A little cream and sugar, please."

Kate put in an order for two *single-singles*, and a dozen donuts, smiling as she passed over Becky's drink. "I know you didn't ask for any, but help yourself to the donuts. I'll take the rest home, and the boys will devour them like a hoard of locusts, so we may as well enjoy our favourites while we have a chance."

It was still too early to suggest Kate drop her off, especially since the woman had bought her a treat. So Becky sat firm and struggled to think of something to add to the conversation.

The only thing that leapt to mind was to rave about Trevor, and she didn't know if either he or his mom would appreciate that.

Except Kate was the one to bring him up. She'd pulled off to the side of the road beside a park area, taking a long drink of her steaming-hot coffee before selecting a chocolate-covered doughnut out of the box. "I heard Trevor and Lee were out a few days ago giving you a hand."

"Rachel, as well," Becky said. "You raised some very hard workers, Mrs. Coleman. And very giving sons."

"That they are, although I don't know that I should take credit for them. After kids reach a certain age, it's a lot less about how you raised them, and more about the choices they make all on their own. And what their nature is like, I suppose." She gave Becky a quick glance before focusing out the front window. "Lee has always been the one to think things through before he started a task. He'd figure out the best and easiest solution to any problem. Anna would dig in her heels and fight until she got the job done."

This had to be leading to some kind of warning. Bells were going off in her head as Becky nibbled on her doughnut and waited for the other shoe to fall.

"Steve and Trevor—they were my easygoing kids. Steve's grown up a lot over the past year, but Trevor?" Mrs. Coleman shook her head, an indulgent smile on her lips. "That boy has always been willing to give the shirt off his back to anyone, at any time."

Becky swallowed hard. She didn't feel bad being on the receiving end of this conversation. She got it. Kate was making sure she didn't have any underhanded plans for her son.

Only she didn't think Trevor was the type to let his mom make his decisions for him. She hadn't done anything wrong, and Trevor was a grownup.

In some ways, though, Becky was a little jealous she didn't have anyone in her life keeping an eye out for her like Kate was watching out for her son.

This conversation was going under the heading of things she simply wasn't going to think about too hard, or dwell on.

Good thing she had a lot of experience with

151

changing topics when there were things she didn't want to discuss anymore. "Trevor doesn't want to give the shirt off his back," Becky said with a completely straight face. "He just wants to give his truck to everybody."

Kate jerked her coffee cup back from her lips, covering her mouth with her hand as she caught a laugh. "I guess you do know him well enough if you're making that kind of comment." She offered a smile that seemed a lot more welcoming. "Trevor went riding with his father this morning, and he parked the big beast blocking the garage. Either I did a vehicle shuffle, or took his."

"Obviously Trevor doesn't mind other people driving his truck." Becky focused forward. "When I come over, will we be cleaning or cooking?"

"A bit of both? We'll play it by ear. You know how to get to our place?"

She shook her head. Kate gave directions, and Becky paused, her thoughts whirling.

Trevor's place was to the north of her, and there were a few other Coleman homes accessible from that direction, but not his parents' house. The Moonshine Coleman place was nowhere on the road that it made sense for Kate to be *casually* driving past Becky's. "You went out of your way to pick me up this morning."

Kate nodded cheerfully as she got the truck into gear and headed toward the quilt shop. "I wanted to meet you."

Oh boy. Becky took the bull by the reins, not sure where she was finding all this attitude. "And? Do I pass muster?"

Laughter rang out, then Kate reached over and patted her shoulder. "You'll do fine, Becky. The interrogation is over. I can see why Trevor likes you."

Maybe the conversation should have been

152

uncomfortable or awkward, but in some ways it felt very freeing. "Thank you."

"By the way," Kate added, "I expect you to come to the party, as well. On Canada Day."

Becky didn't get a chance to say if she could or not. Kate didn't give her an opening, just assumed her answer was yes.

"Here we are," Kate announced, parking outside the Stitching Post.

"Are you coming into the shop?" Becky asked, not sure if that part had been an excuse to give her a ride.

"I am most definitely coming in," Kate answered, joining her on the sidewalk. "I haven't seen Hope for a while, and even with her visiting next week, I find we can never have a really good conversation with everybody else around."

Hope answered Becky's knock at the door with a smile, and she seemed pleased that her aunt-in-law had stopped in to visit in the brief time before the store opened.

Kate exclaimed over the growing size of Hope's belly. "You've popped since the last time I saw you," she teased.

"Ultrasound last week said there's only one kid in there," Hope assured her. "I double-checked, because that would've been just my luck that Matt would get the Coleman genes as well." She glanced at Becky to explain. "There's been a set of twins every generation. Matt's got twin brothers, and his oldest brother and his wife have twins. I wasn't looking to add to the legacy."

"My sister married into a family with twins," Kate said. "She wanted so badly to have two at once. I think one at a time was more than enough."

"One will be enough for me to start with." Hope

153

led her aunt toward the notions she needed, leaving Becky to deal with another wave of nostalgia and sadness.

Talk of babies and family made her sister's absence worse. She wondered what Sarah was doing, and how the children were. Becky missed being around them, finding ways to make them smile.

Everything else she didn't miss still tipped the scales way over in favour of her new life. Lingering sadness was worth the intoxicating freedom she had now, especially the positive things she'd gained by making friends with the Colemans, and Trevor.

But some day...

"I've got what I need, so I'll head out and let you girls get to work." Kate turned to Becky. "I'll send word with Trevor if things change. Otherwise, I'll see you tomorrow night at six."

Hope waited until the bell had finished swaying as the door closed behind Kate before whirling on Becky. "Holy moly, you had to do the meet-the-parents thing already?"

"She didn't ask what my intentions were," Becky said with a laugh, although Kate had come pretty close.

"Kate is cool, although I love my mother-in-law even more. All of the moms in the Coleman family are great."

"I'll get to meet them next week," Becky shared, suddenly feeling a little awkward. "Is it okay with you that Mrs. Coleman invited me to the family thing on Canada Day?"

Hope looked confused. "Why would it not be okay?"

Becky shrugged. "Just wasn't sure if you minded mixing work with non-work company."

Her boss came over and laid both hands on her shoulders, looking Becky straight in the eye. "Trust me, I have no objections to spending time with you here at work, or out there when it's play time. So stop that nonsense."

It was good to know. "I feel the same."

"You know, if you get a ride with a different member of the family every day, you really won't need a car," Hope teased.

"I should post a sign-up schedule," Becky said with mock brightness.

The other woman laughed. "Don't do it unless you honestly want all of us up in your business all the time."

"Colemans? Into other people's business? *Really?*"

Hope snickered, and they both headed off to their tasks. Something very satisfying glowed inside as Becky moved through her day.

No, she might miss her sister and the kids, but this was all being done with the intention that someday she could offer them freedom as well. Until then, there was nothing about her current situation that wasn't amazing.

She took down another bolt of fabric and went to work.

IT WASN'T until after lunch Trevor felt the time was right to lead the conversation where it needed to go.

They'd had a glorious morning, from the fresh sunrise slowly breaking over the dew-drenched land to the slow easy stride of the horses as they'd worked their way toward the northeast corner of the Moonshine land.

155

All their fences butted up against other Coleman land, but it was still important to make sure none of the cattle could dance from range to range unsupervised.

There was something satisfying about tugging wires into place, or pounding a post a little straighter. Years ago when he'd done this task with his father, Randy had been the one to do the heavy labour while Trevor braced the post, determined not to flinch as the heavy sledge whistled by, far too close.

He'd trusted his dad, but it'd still been an exercise in restraint to keep from fidgeting.

Now they'd turned it around, and Randy was the one bracing the post. Sometimes with an arm, sometimes a knee as Trevor lifted and swung, his motions sure and steady, just the way his father had taught him.

They hadn't talked much. They hadn't needed to as they'd let the horses move at a steady pace along the fence line, the shared tasks a sort of communication all of their own.

Randy finally broke the silence. "It's good to have this time with you," he said. "I think back to what I dreamed of when you boys were little tykes. About how nice it would be to have your help when that meant more than pretending to get things done while you were getting in the way."

Trevor laughed. "You never let on that we were a pain in the butt."

"Of course not," Randy said. "Because while you were, you were also so pleased to be out doing things with your old man, and there's something to be said for the ego-stroking that hero worship provides."

They grinned at each other before Trevor turned and led their horses in a shortcut around a pond. "I can't believe you and your brothers managed to ranch all the

Coleman land by yourselves back when you were young. There are so many more of us now, and at times it seems we can barely keep up."

"We weren't quite as ambitious back then," Randy pointed out. "Even with the six of us boys doing as much as we could, we weren't using all the land nearly as efficiently as we do today. Plus, your grandpa was a force of nature until he passed away." Randy's admiration was clear as he spoke of his father. "I swear that man put in twice as many hours as the rest of us even when we were young bucks."

"I wish I would've met him," Trevor said seriously.

"I wish you could've, too." Randy stared over the land, thoughtfulness drifting over his face. "It could be, though, that work ethic of his was what killed him in the end. As if he used up all the energy that was supposed to last a lifetime before he turned sixty. One minute he was there, and the next he was gone."

"Good reminder we need to take care of ourselves." Trevor waited for his father to respond to his blatant challenge.

Randy sighed heavily. "Did your mother put you up to this?"

"Totally my own idea," Trevor admitted. "I thought getting you out on a horse to do chores was inspired."

"It was a good move." Randy gave him a dirty look, before shaking his head. "Being sick is frustrating like nothing I've ever experienced," he confessed. "I might not have had as much energy as my dad, but I've never felt like a lazy fool before this past year."

"And yet, the Moonshine Colemans continue to do well."

His father looked disgusted. "It's the three of you

157

boys, plus Anna and Mitch, plus Melody, *plus* Kate, who's working harder than I ever intended her to when I asked her into my life."

"But this is why we're here. We're family," Trevor said firmly. "And Mom knew damn well what life was going to be like on a ranch, and she still signed up for it."

"So maybe she's not as smart as I always thought she was," Randy snapped.

Trevor pulled Tigger to a halt, eyeing his dad. "And maybe you need to accept that we all love you a hell of a lot, and it's not the extra chores that's gonna break us, it's worrying about you. Wondering if there's anything we could do to help you feel better."

"They can't figure it out—"

"Not when you throw up your hands and stop looking for a cure." Trevor leaned forward on the pommel of his saddle, his concern cutting through his manners. "You want to make Mom's life easier? You get your ass in to the doctor again, and if it means I have to haul you to Calgary or Edmonton, or even further to get some testing done, it'll be worth it."

Randy sat silently glowering at him.

"Maybe you're not out there at all hours dealing with the chores, or physically attacking all that needs to be done, but you're the heart and soul of this family. Not trying to get better is slacking off in your job, and I've never seen you be a slacker before this."

A dozen years ago his father's expression would have sent him hightailing it toward safety, but now Trevor stared him down, confident that nothing he'd said had been over the line.

Grasses swayed around them, a soft breeze brushing them as time slowed. A long while passed before his dad nodded, mouth set in a tight line.

"Stubborn bastard. *Fine.* I'll call the doctor when we get back today, and see what cockamamie thing he wants to try next." Randy snapped up a finger to point at him. "But I'm holding you to your promise. I don't need Kate spending any more time in those damn hospitals, so from here on, you're my ride. And if I want to tell you all the gory details, you have to listen."

"No problem." He'd accomplished what he'd set out to do. Anything else was bonus. "I have this great stereo system in my truck. I'll crank that baby up to maximum, and you can describe anything you want."

His dad rolled his eyes before grabbing his horse's reins and heading off to the next section they needed to check.

It still seemed as if something was on Randy's mind, but Trevor waited. Not so much because he had great patience, but because he'd begun daydreaming about Becky.

Another good reason to be out on the horses instead of the quads—the animals knew the route off by heart, walking slowly over the rough terrain, pausing as soon as he signaled them with his knees so he could dismount to tighten a line.

It gave him lots of time to think back to Becky's face as he'd touched her, the layer of bubbles a screen of innocence covering her while he'd done wicked things to her willing body. He could hardly wait to see her again. To touch her, and get to know her better.

His father interrupted a lovely daydream involving him, Becky and the sturdy kitchen table that was the right height that if he stripped her down, he could feast on her before sliding between her thighs and fucking them both senseless.

"We did get a lot done in the old days."

159

Trevor blinked himself back to the here and now, a trifle embarrassed by the direction his thoughts had drifted. Very glad his father couldn't read his mind.

Randy glanced at Trevor almost nervously before looking away. "Although we didn't always get along as good as you kids."

Okay, this was new. Trevor's curiosity rose rapidly. Conversation about the original six Coleman brothers was rare. He'd asked a lot of questions when he was young, but for the most part the answers had always been so boring that slowly he'd let it drop.

Maybe he shouldn't have.

"There were only three of us boys, and Anna. And all of us knew better than to push her around too much," Trevor admitted, trying to make an opening for his father to follow.

"Just like Mike," Randy returned. "He was the bossy big brother, but none of us minded because he was right so damn often. It was hard to argue with him when you knew you'd just end up looking a fool a few days later."

Mike Coleman was the head of the Six Pack clan—Jesse's father. And, yeah, Trevor had always minded his manners around the man, yet never really been afraid of him. Not the way he disliked Uncle Ben.

Randy held the reins loosely in his hands, the motion of his horse rocking him slowly.

"Mark was the one who reminds me most of you," his father confessed. "And I don't think anything like generations repeat themselves, but you've got the same giving spirit."

"I'm glad you can say that after I bullied you into seeing the doctor," Trevor muttered. "Is Mark the one who died?"

"That was John."

They'd reached the highest point of the Coleman land in the area. Too hilly for pastureland, it was used for grazing. Years ago Trevor used to come up here to stare out over the Coleman land, because from this vantage point, he could see in all directions almost to the borders.

A neat, orderly rectangle divided into...

Jesus Christ. He was a fool. He was a *fucking* fool. Six brothers.

He twisted in the saddle toward his father, pointing to the northwest at the different clan holdings in succession. Gathering frustration made his voice shake as he recited the names. "Angel. Whiskey Creek. Six Pack and the extra family holdings. Those were the bits that belonged to John, right?"

Randy nodded stiffly, his face tightening as Trevor continued to point around the circle.

"Moonshine land. And the land where the rental sits—which still belongs to Mark Coleman. Your brother who moved away. He never sold it, even though I thought he did."

His dad didn't answer. Didn't have to.

Trevor was torn between laughing and swearing. "You know I've been trying to find out who owns that parcel for nearly a year."

"I'm sorry to hear that. But you didn't ask me," Randy said quietly.

Fuck. "And this is the all-fired secret that everybody except me, Rafe and Jesse seems to know? That there's a chunk of land in the area that belongs to the brother who took off and has had nothing to do with the family for thirty years."

"Pretty much," his dad admitted. "I don't know

161

who knows and who doesn't at this point, actually."

"Damn stupid secret, if you ask me," Trevor snapped. "If he still owns it, but he's not using it, then there's no reason why we can't—"

"Drop it," his dad ordered. "Mark left for his own reasons, and I don't want you to go stirring up trouble."

"How is getting in touch going to cause trouble?" Trevor demanded. "You're not making any sense."

"And sometimes things don't make sense until you know all the details, and I'm not ready to tell you the rest of it. I just wanted you to know…" Randy dragged a hand through his hair before jamming his cowboy hat back on his head, frustration clear in his every move. "I should've kept my mouth shut, but maybe it's nearly time to try and do something, but it's not time yet. Trust me on this."

Crazy mixed-up…

From one extreme to the other, Trevor wasn't sure if the day had been a screaming success, or if he should go home and scream.

He shook his head. "And here I thought one of the reasons for living in a small town was that secrets couldn't last."

"Some things are better not talked about," Randy said quietly. "Look on the bright side. I promise I'll tell you everything, sometime soon."

Great. "I'm looking on the *brighter* side. When we get home today, you're going to call the doctor, and that means a lot more to me than missing brothers, or the fact I've been searching for information that's been under my nose for a hell of a long time."

Randy made a face. "You had to remind me of the damn testing, didn't you?"

"It's my giving spirit," Trevor taunted before

softening his tone. "I'm sorry, I'm being an ass. I won't poke for more information until you're ready to tell me, but I will keep you to your promise to be here for the family."

"Agreed." His dad rode close enough to pound him on the back briefly. "Now, if we want to finish this section before the sun goes down, we've got to stop chattering like old men on a porch with nothing to do but rock and chew."

Getting back to work was a good thing. It gave Trevor time to mull over all of the revelations he'd had tossed his direction.

Once again secrets hovered, but he'd told the truth. The best thing about the day was his father's promise to try to get healthy. The rest of it would be dealt with whenever.

The future might be filled with unanswered questions, but that was fine. Today, and tomorrow were enough to focus on.

Chapter Sixteen

THE FAMILY barbecue didn't start until midafternoon, which gave Trevor plenty of time to do the things he had to in the morning, including help his mom arrange far too many chairs into groups near the fire pit.

"You guys must be getting old, or something," he drawled. "I don't remember all these places to sit years ago."

Kate gave him a loving swat on the back of his head as she paced past him. "I never got to sit in those days because I was too busy running after you, you hoodlum."

"Should've raised me better," he teased.

They both knew she was pleased as punch with him.

Randy had cooperated without a single complaint, informing Trevor a couple days after their ride that he was on a waiting list with some fancy-schmancy doctor. He'd also told Trevor they'd be driving Randy's truck to any appointments, i.e., the one with nothing but a feeble am/fm radio, which Trevor promptly named the *Bitching Mobile*.

He escaped from the party preparations to zip over to Becky's house, pausing outside of his truck to straighten himself up.

A long, low wolf whistle snapped his attention up to the deck. Becky had caught him primping, and he didn't even care.

One glimpse her direction was enough to have his jaw dropping and eyes bulging. "I'm the one who should be whistling. Sweet mercy, Rodeo. You clean up nice."

She twirled, the pale pink skirt of her sundress flaring enough to give him a glimpse of her thighs, long and smooth, with a hint of a tan line where her shorts usually ended.

"You like it?" she asked. "Rachel came by the shop during my lunch break and took me to this place that's one step up from a thrift shop."

He was on the steps, approaching quickly. Her cheeks had a lovely dusting of colour to them as she showed herself off in her pretty packaging.

A pretty package he really wished he could unwrap. "You look beautiful," he said with complete sincerity, leaning down to give her the shortest kiss he could manage, which still meant they were both breathless at the end of it.

They grinned at each other for a moment before he offered his hand. "Come on. We have a party to get to." Moments later they were in the yard and headed for the main party area. He'd made sure they were there on the early side, before the masses descended. "Anytime you want to leave, you let me know."

Becky seemed to be searching for someone. "If I get tired, I can walk home."

"You could, or you could take my truck."

She waved into the distance, and he followed her line of sight to discover Rachel coming out from the house with an armload for the picnic.

165

Becky twirled, her eyes bright with excitement. "I'm going to help the girls. I'll find you in a little bit, okay?"

She was gone before he could answer, a whirlwind of pale pink, with pretty white sandals, and a lot more through-and-through happiness than he'd seen before.

Something strangely like pride rocked him, although the emotion made little sense. She was the one moving forward with her life, and making new friends, he noted happily as Rachel put down her load to envelop Becky in a big hug.

Nope, this was all Becky, and he was so pleased.

He wandered off to find his brothers as the rest of the family slowly arrived, cars and trucks lining up in the front yard, the number of bodies continuing to increase. Shouts from his cousin's children of various ages and stages filled the air, which he figured was his cue to go find the adults.

Of course, the instant he found them, he was ready to turn heel and walk away again.

Uncle Ben was pontificating. Rafe's dad looked old, his hair and beard gone gray-white, and a scowl that turned him into a very un-jovial Santa.

"No way we could've had everybody over at our place," Ben complained, looking around to see who was listening, which was everyone within earshot—he'd raised his voice over the conversation next to him and forced their attention. "Complete mess in the yard, and everything's torn up to hell everywhere."

Aunt Dana looked uncomfortable, as did the rest of the family who were gathered, coffee cups in hand. "It's only temporary," Dana said softly. "Just while we transition—"

"Stupidest thing I've ever heard of," he grumbled,

cutting off his wife as he glared into his cup as if the black liquid in it had somehow personally offended him. "Don't see any reason to build a new barn, or why it's got to be hell and gone at the other end of the property. Extra costs and extra labour, and all of it because *he* wants to rub it in my face."

Trevor sighed, recognizing the part of family get-togethers that was on his, and everyone else's, least enjoyable list.

Listening to Ben complaining about how Gabe had taken control of the Angel quarter and was slowly turning things around had become a regular event. Whatever stick he had up his ass, Trevor wished his uncle would keep it quiet and grumble to himself rather than trying to get the rest of the family stirred up.

Randy obviously thought the same way. "Things change. It's not always easy, but it's life," he said in a reasonable tone of voice to his brother.

"Did everyone get the notice about the renovations to the rec center?" Kate piped up. "It's going to be nice to have—"

"Going to cost us extra on our taxes. There's no reason for us to support a swimming pool and two hockey rinks." Ben again. "Kids these days are lazy, spoiled creatures."

His mom tossed a dirty look toward Ben, and another meaningful one at Randy as Ben went off on a long-winded tirade about everything that was wrong with the community project that he'd decided was being done to annoy *him*.

Trevor could tell his father wasn't feeling well today, but he still leaned forward, getting Ben's attention.

"I've got some new animals in the barn. Come

167

take a look with me."

Randy got ignored as Ben focused instead on his son who'd walked up to offer his mom a plate of goodies. Rafe handed it over with a smile, then silently laid a hand on her shoulder as he turned to go.

Ben made a rude noise. "Of course, you don't get anything for me."

Raphael blinked at his father in surprise. "Didn't want you to think I considered you incompetent to get yourself a snack."

Tension rose as Ben narrowed his gaze, standing to approach Rafe.

Trevor glanced around, wondering where his Uncle Mike was—Ben didn't act up nearly as much when Mike was there.

He'd just decided he'd have to step in and offer a distraction when Randy pushed himself into the middle, catching his brother by the arm to pull him away from the gathering. "Breath of fresh air, Ben. This way."

Ben shook off Randy's grasp, stepping closer to glower at Rafe. "Don't sass me, boy. Or think you're too good for me. You'd be out on the street if it weren't for me, so mind your manners, or you'll find yourself in a heap of trouble."

Raphael stared him down, not flinching as his father roared in his face.

"Enough." Randy caught Ben again, more firmly this time, jerking his brother hard enough to rock him off his feet and get him moving in the direction of the barn. "This isn't the time or the place. Come on."

There was silence as he manhandled Ben until his brother shook off his hand and marched stiffly away.

Then Rafe turned toward Trevor's mom, putting on a happy face and pretending as if his father wasn't the world's biggest ass. "Thanks for making gingersnaps, Aunt Kate. I know it's not Christmas, but they're my favourite, anytime of the year."

She offered a shaky smile. "I'd like to say I made them for you, but I can't take credit. They were Becky's contribution."

Rafe must have spotted Trevor standing at the edge of the gathering because he smirked. "I'll offer her my *personal* thanks."

He gave his mom another quick kiss on the cheek before heading away from the group.

Trevor sauntered casually after his cousin, waiting until they were out of earshot. "Don't you dare flash that Angel smile at my girl," he warned.

Rafe tossed a grin over his shoulder. "So, she *is* your girl. Good to know. I like a challenge."

Trevor ignored what he knew was a tease, focusing instead on a more important issue. "What the hell's wrong with your dad?"

"Other than the usual?"

Raphael waited for Trevor to catch up as they headed toward where the girls had gathered near the horseshoe pits. They walked in silence for a moment before Rafe pulled to a stop, shaking his head in frustration.

"My father is pissed off that Gabe and Allison have made a lot of smart changes to the ranch, including setting up operations closer to their house. And he's pissed off that I agree with Gabe, and he's just...fucking pissed off all the time." He turned haunted eyes toward Trevor. "I used to hate him, but I don't care enough anymore to do that. I wish there was some way to get him out of our hair."

Which was impossible. The Angel Colemans were

169

finally getting their feet under them again financially because of Gabe and Allison, but there was no way they could afford to buy Ben out.

"I'm sorry he's... *him*." Trevor laid a hand on Rafe's shoulder. "If there's anything I can do, *ever*, let me know."

His cousin paused. "I'll be moving back to the ranch house at the end of the month, or at least into the loft over the garage. You can help me haul my shit."

Trevor's jaw bounced off the ground. "You're moving back... What the *fuck*? You moved out to get away from Ben. Moving back isn't going to make dealing with him any easier."

"No, but it'll make Mom's life easier..."

Shit. *Double shit*. "He's not doing anything stupid, is he?" Being an asshole was one thing. Stepping over the line and hurting Aunt Dana would have the entire family stomping down hard on Ben.

Rafe's face tightened. "The day he hits her is the day I put him in the fucking ground. No, he's just a mean old bastard, but if I'm around he'll mind his manners more."

Jesus. This was not typical Coleman party conversation, at least not for Trevor. "Offer stands. You need me for anything, you shout. Day or night."

"Appreciate that." In a surprise move, Rafe hauled him in for a rib-creaking, back-pounding moment before shoving them apart and tilting his head toward the girls. "I have to go thank Becky for my cookies."

"You're going to find those cookies shoved where the sun don't shine," Trevor warned, before thinking of another concern. "You do know moving home is going to wreak havoc on your dating life."

His cousin made a rude noise. "What dating life?

Don't worry about me. I'll live vicariously while watching you make a fool of yourself over the sweet young thing next door."

They were steps away from the girls so Trevor didn't ask about Laurel, but he made a mental note to bring it up later.

He was too distracted by the welcome greeting they got from the gathering of ladies, accompanied by teasing and feminine laughter. Becky looked like a pretty pink flower, her eyes dancing with happiness as he made a beeline toward her.

IT WAS the second most wonderful day Becky had enjoyed recently, out of a surprising lot of wonderful days.

Like earlier in the week when Rachel had stopped in at the shop during lunch break, not only to take her to find pretty clothes, but to give her a used ebook reader filled with all sorts of books. The lesson in how to use the device had gone smoothly, and even though she was still a little worried she would break it, having an entire library at her fingertips was giddy making.

Becky'd stayed up far too late reading that first night before paying for it the following day at work.

And there'd been the evening she'd spent at the Moonshine Colemans, helping clean and tidy and cook for today's party. Trevor's mom had shuffled off the men so it was ladies only. Rachel had been there. So had Melody who promised to bring by her horses sometime, with or without the cart, and take Becky for a ride.

Still, nothing could top the afternoon she'd gone to

the river with Trevor, or how often she thought back to the pleasure she'd experienced at his touch.

"That's a sweet smile," Trevor teased as he slipped next to her and settled his arm around her waist. Yup, she was daydreaming again. About his strong arms and firm grip, and all the *lovely* sensations he'd caused.

Becky leaned into him, lifting her mouth toward his ear to whisper quietly, "I'm having a good time. Your family is really nice."

He made a face. "Most of them."

She'd obviously missed something, but he didn't give her time to ask. Instead, he whisked her away from the horseshoe game to take her on a tour of the ranch, slipping back to steal tidbits from the table where the snack food had been laid out. The two women safeguarding the table smiled at them tolerantly while in the background, three nearly teenage boys and a couple cute little girls wove at high speed in and out of the family, miraculously not running into anything. Or at least not often.

There was a crowd, but not nearly as many kids as she'd been used to. Another shot of sadness mixed with the joy of the day, but this time she accepted the emotion. There was nothing she could do about missing her sister and the kids—not yet.

Trevor tugged her around the corner to where a hay barn stood next to a straight-as-an-arrow corral fence off the horse barn. He twisted her against the wall of hay then leaned in, resting his forearm beside her head. "You look delicious. I need another taste," he rumbled as he slipped his finger over her lips.

"You're going to spoil your appetite." Becky was as hungry for him, although she didn't want to say so.

"Too bad."

And then he was kissing her, and she didn't care that anyone could be watching. Focusing on the here and now was far more important than worrying about anything else.

Sweet and seductive. He nibbled on her lips before biting down more firmly. A zing of excitement shot through her as he stepped closer, inserting one leg between hers and pressing his thigh forward to make contact.

Now she had multiple points of pleasure to focus on, resting her hands on his waist to feel the firm muscles move as he rocked slowly against her. Time stopped as desire grew, with only a faint voice in the back of her mind cheering as it pointed out how impossible this whole situation was.

She didn't care. Impossible or not, she was grabbing on with both hands and holding on tight.

With a groan, he pulled away. Staring into her eyes with a heated expression. "And that's where we'd better stop."

Her heart rate raced, but she agreed. "Maybe when you take me home, we can pick this up again."

Trevor chuckled. "Oh, Rodeo, there's no *maybe* about it." His strong fingers stroked along her neckline. "I guess the next part of the tour should involve dinner."

He escorted her back to the family and took care of her. Helping her fill a plate then carrying it to empty chairs by where Hope and Matt had settled next to another couple.

"Becky, meet Beth and Daniel." Trevor pointed to them in turn.

"The parents of the whirling dervishes masquerading as boys," Beth informed her.

"You're...Six Pack?" Becky asked.

Daniel laughed. "You're a fast learner. Yup, although I don't ranch anymore. I just call and taunt my brothers the night before they have early chores."

She visited for a while, enjoying soft-spoken Beth's company, and the way the young boys continually checked in with their parents. There was mischief in their eyes, but they listened when Daniel offered a stern warning, and sounds of family lingered on the air as she excused herself to use the bathroom.

Becky was coming out of the house when movement caught her attention. Just like she and Trevor had snuck away earlier for a little private time, there was a couple in the shadows by the trail leading to the barns.

It was a bit strange to stand and watch, but a heated sensation rose in her gut as the man kissed the woman, his hand cradling her face tenderly. Neither of them showed the darker colouring of the Coleman family—him a dirty blond, and her a gorgeous, sundrenched nearly white blonde—and Becky wondered if they were like her, invited friends and guests.

A moment later she wasn't wondering anything. She was fighting to keep from bolting.

Another man had joined them, slipping up with a smile to capture the long-haired blonde between him and the other man before the two of them dipped their heads to kiss her.

The woman didn't complain. In fact, her hands rose so she could catch hold of their necks, but by that point Becky was done. Her feet were moving of their own accord, headed past the vehicles in the private yard toward the gravel road.

Her sandals were thin enough the sharp stones underfoot bit through the leather into her tender flesh, but she didn't mind the pain. Each stab was a wonderful distraction from the agonizing coldness that had wrapped around her heart all over again. Horrid memories rushed in so hard she tasted bile.

Each step away from the Moonshine Coleman house was a step closer to the rental where she could hide away and deal with the pain. Running was totally rude. Not only toward Kate, Rachel and Trevor, but she'd left Hope without a word. Not a great way to deal with the woman who provided her precarious income.

Right now, she didn't care.

She made it around the corner, a mile on foot, before Trevor's truck appeared beside her, his concern clear as he stared out the open passenger window. "Hey, Rodeo. What's up?"

She shook her head and kept marching, afraid if she spoke the only thing that would come out would be a cry of pain.

He pulled over to the side of the road behind her, his voice rising in volume as he chased her down. "Becky. *Stop.*"

Trevor stepped in front of her and she broke, jerking to the right and off the road into the field behind her house. Racing not from him, but from everything she feared she couldn't ever have.

She shouldn't have even tried.

Chapter Seventeen

THE URGE to chase after her was there, but whatever was wrong, he didn't want to compound it by doing something stupid like tackling her to the ground and demanding answers.

He *would* demand answers, but he knew where to find her.

Trevor raced back to his truck, spinning wheels on the gravel as he gunned the engine and shot forward, screaming into her yard in under a minute. He dropped from the cab and sprinted for the backdoor, making it there seconds after the heavy door slammed on her retreating back.

"Becky, talk to me," he begged, slipping inside before slowing down—he didn't want to scare her, but damn if he'd let this drop before she'd shared what was wrong.

He rounded the corner and found her curled up on the couch, the once crowded and junk-filled room now shades of green and white as she'd taken it and begun to make it her own.

Becky refused to meet his gaze. "I'm a fool."

Trevor approached gingerly, watching carefully as he lowered himself onto the opposite corner of the couch.

"We all get foolish at times."

She made this noise halfway between a laugh and cry, and his heart damn near broke. He reached around her and tugged her in close, satisfaction rising as she accepted his hug, curling up against him as if she were hunkering down for a storm.

"What happened at the party that scared you into bolting?"

Her face was still buried against his chest as she responded. The words were mumbled, but he finally figured out "two men with a woman" in the middle of the clutter.

For fuck's sake.

His cousin's unusual *two for the price of one* relationship had caused all sorts of amusement and scandal in Rocky over the past year, but it was a lot less entertaining now that it was innocent Becky who was upset. Only he needed to tread carefully, because even if she was shocked, the threesome's situation wasn't wrong.

"I think I get it. One of them was my cousin, Travis—he's a bit of an ass, but he's also got a huge heart. When he fell in love he didn't find a nice girl to settle down with. He found a nice girl *and* a nice guy."

Becky stiffened, sliding back far enough to blink wide eyes at him. "Wait. The *three* of them are together? You mean the guys are—?"

"The guys are lovers too, yes." Might as well speak bluntly. They were family, and Trevor wasn't about to apologize for them. "Travis, Ashley and Cassidy are all in love with each other, and it's not typical, I know that. But for them, it works. There's no doubt they are completely into each other, and care for each other like any couple, only with three. Heck, if anything they have to work harder than a couple to keep that extra person happy, but they're doing it. They've been together for well over a year."

"Wow."

There was surprise in her eyes, but not disgust. That was good.

"I'll introduce you to them sometime, but honest, they aren't that scary." He stoked his thumb over her cheek. "I'm sorry you were upset."

She shook her head, her expression tightening. "I'm not upset about them. I mean...if you say they're happy, I guess that's okay." Becky spoke quieter, her lashes dropping to hide her eyes from him. "But I saw them, and it made me remember...something. I thought because I ran away from my past, I could pretend none of it ever happened. But it did."

"Bad things?" So there was more. Trevor carefully linked his fingers with hers, thankful when she didn't jerk away.

"Some," she admitted, "but mostly things that will make a difference to how people will see me. How *you'll* see me, and I can't pretend that all away."

He stroked the back of her hand gently. "Then tell me everything. I can pretty much promise I won't think less of you for anything you can tell me."

She shook her head. "You can't promise that."

"Of course I can. I'm complicated, remember?"

His mind raced, wondering what she possibly thought was so bad. And what she could have been reminded of after seeing Trevor fooling around with his lovers.

He could think of things he didn't *want* to think of— Abuse? Prostitution?

Nothing his imagination came up with could have prepared him.

"I'm married."

What the fuck? "You're *what?*"

Becky scrambled for words. "Only it's not real, but it is. Wait, that's wrong, but—" She retreated to her corner of the couch, wrapping her arms around her thighs, sheer misery on her face. "It's not real. It was a sham, and I know that, and I'm saying this wrong."

Trevor locked down his emotions. Put a temporary lid on his questions and his rising anger—not at her, but at this situation that had left his sweet Becky floundering so hard. "Just say it, in whatever order you want. Talk until it's all out, and we'll figure out if you missed anything later."

She nodded slowly. "Where I grew up in Manitoba wasn't so bad. I mean, the rules *were* very strict. The pastor and my father talked a lot about how we were evil and headed for hell, but my mom was nice, and my sister, who's four years older than me, and I were close. Then our church joined with another. Sarah married their leader and moved away, and all we got for nearly two years were letters. And our church turned even more... *intense.* There were rumours that the government was conspiring to take control of us—crazy things like that."

He was still stuck on the *I'm married* bit, but he waited as patiently as he could.

Becky stared straight at the wall behind his shoulder. "Sarah said she missed me lots, and hoped that someday I could come live closer. Then she wrote all excited to say she'd had a baby boy, and now she was senior wife, and she'd asked if I could join the family. My dad—"

"Wait," Trevor interrupted, not sure he'd heard right. "*Senior* wife? What the hell is that? Are you

179

saying...?"

Dull eyes full of sorrow instead of her usual snapping, lively ones met his. "The man my sister married was the leader of what I've since been told is a religious cult. Abel already had three wives, but she was the first to give him a son, which made her more blessed than the others. So when she asked for me, he agreed."

"Your sister brought you into a religious cult." *Goddamn it.* He was working hard to keep from shouting, and his words still came out at a dull roar. "And what the hell is going on? Polygamy is illegal in Canada."

"Still happens," she said lifelessly. "Legally he married his first wife, and the rest were religious ceremonies only, but that didn't matter to them. And that's what happened to me. Sarah asked, Abel arranged it, and my father said yes. I got sent to Paradise Settlement for my sixteenth birthday to be married to Abel as well."

He was ready to puke just thinking of what had happened to her.

"I know you're shocked," she whispered. "It's not real—that marriage. I never would have kissed you if—"

"Of course it's not real." *Jesus.* He wanted to tear something apart. Someone. A whole lot of someones, but he had to hold it together and not make this worse for Becky. "I'm not judging you, sweetie. I'm sick to my stomach that you had to deal with any of this, because it's not only wrong, it's fucked up and wrong."

"I didn't want to. I didn't love him. I mean, things were getting scary at home, so I thought it would be better to leave. There was no place for me with my parents anymore, and Sarah *said* he was a good man, but—"

"Good men don't take more than one wife," Trevor

180

snapped, instantly feeling the need to qualify his remark. "Okay, there are exceptions like my cousin's situation, but that's not what you're talking about. And no sixteen-year-old should be a fourth or fifth wife to a man."

"I know." She refused to meet his eyes again. "I also wasn't a very good wife, according to the family. A good wife would have gotten pregnant. I didn't, not even when he gave me to the other leaders of the family."

Goddamn bastards. Old men with stupid religious rules that did nothing but hurt the innocent. Becky's voice had gone monotone, and Trevor's heart was breaking apart while he burned with fury at mankind's cruelty and full-out evil.

He'd been so blown away that he'd nearly missed it. "Wait. *Gave* you to other...?"

A hollow scream echoed in his brain, numbness setting in. He was past fury. Past trying to comprehend. It was too much, and he didn't want this conversation to continue. Not because he'd heard enough, but because he didn't want Becky to have to relive any of the indecent things that had been done to her.

Trevor Coleman might not be the brightest bulb in the pack, but he knew one thing. Becky deserved far more than what she'd been given. He couldn't fix it, but he'd be damned if he'd let her ever doubt or worry about her worth again.

———————⟶⟨∽⟩⟵———————

TREVOR HAULED himself off the couch so rapidly it was as if he'd exploded.

Becky had figured what she had to share would upset him, and obviously she'd been right, but the way he stomped across the room away from her, dragging a hand through his hair, spoke of anger and frustration for her, not with her.

He stood with his back to the room, every muscle bunched up tight. Rock solid and granite hard. Out of nowhere, he swung his fist at the wall and smashed it though the drywall, and she shrieked in surprise.

"*Trevor*. What—?"

He spun on his heels, barely two feet from the couch, breathing hard, eyes gone to ice. "You asked me to get naked for you. I'm going to do it. Right now."

Becky hauled her jaw back into position. "Um, okay…?"

He stood with legs spread wide, a solid hunk of one hundred percent prime masculinity "I have to say it. You have had one hell of a life, sweetheart. I'm so fucking mad that I can't change what happened. If I could, I would go back and tear those bastards apart limb from limb, because what they did to you wasn't right, none of it. For so many reasons."

His voice was grim. Powerful, begging her to picture him storming into the family hall and causing chaos on her behalf. It was a sweet thought for a few, brief seconds before reality kicked in.

She didn't want him to get in trouble for her. She didn't want him anywhere near her past.

Besides, what he'd suggested sounded more interesting and it was here and now. The mere suggestion was amusing. She was tired of crying, and it made more sense to laugh.

Somehow Trevor always said things that made her laugh.

"So instead of ripping people's arms off, you're going to strip. I don't know how your brain works

182

sometimes, Trevor, but I like it."

He stooped and caught her fingers in his, squeezing them tight. "Yeah, my brain is a special and sparkly unicorn. But what you are is an amazing, gorgeous, unique woman, and any man who couldn't see that you deserved to be treated with care and respect, they're fucking not real men."

"You want to show me what a real man looks like?"

Fire flashed in his eyes. "I guess I do."

So much emotion churned inside that it threatened to rip her apart as it escaped. Laughter bubbled up, and hope, and an unstoppable thread of rising attraction and passion.

Becky liked the way her day had changed so completely, from bitter memories to something deliciously distracting. She lifted his hand to her mouth, kissing his poor, bruised knuckles. "Don't let me stop you. I've got the best view in the house."

Trevor stepped back and undid the button on his jeans, lowering the zipper the slightest bit before reaching over his head and grabbing hold of his flannel shirt. He jerked it forward over his head, ripping it from his body.

A harsh move—desperate. As if he were frantic to break free of what he was trapped in as rapidly as possible. He did the same thing to the T-shirt underneath it, staring her in the eyes as he flung the black fabric to one side as if he didn't care what happened to it.

As if she was the only important thing in the room.

And then he spoke, and her world shuffled three feet to the left, taking a brand new path.

"You're in charge, Rodeo. Not only today, but I promise you right now that whatever you want, *whenever* you want, I'm going to give it to you. You want me on my knees next to you planting in the garden? I'm there. You need driving lessons? No problem."

He didn't need to offer his truck—she knew that was a given.

"You want me naked? I'm yours. No questions asked."

It was more than she'd ever dreamed of when this day had begun. "I don't want you to be anything other than yourself," she insisted.

His dark eyes flashed again—deep burning fire and tender caring at the same time. "You need to know there's one man out there who will never take more than you're willing to give."

"Oh, *Trevor*." She refused to let the tears come. "I'm so glad I met you. I'm so glad I'm free of Paradise and came here to start a new life."

Becky bolted off the couch and into his arms, throwing herself the final few feet and trusting that he'd catch her.

He was warm and protective and wrapped himself around her as much as she curled herself around him and hung on tight. She had his neck in a chokehold, her legs over his hipbones as he pulled her to him and stood immobile, supporting her like a rock.

Her rock.

Her *half-naked* rock, with smooth skin that was flaming hot under her fingertips. She took in the scent of him—clean and masculine as she dipped her nose to his shoulder and breathed him in.

He stood there for at least a minute before lowering her feet carefully to the ground. She stayed close, hands stroking the firm muscles of his chest. "I know you said you needed no explanations, but I want to give them."

"I'm all ears." His tone wasn't quite back to normal, but he was trying to lighten up, and she appreciated that.

She planted one hand firmly against his chest, fingers spread wide. The steady thud of his heartbeat connected with her palm, and her own heart skipped a beat. "Whenever they did things to me that weren't my choice, I shut myself down and pretended it wasn't real. That I wasn't really there. That's how I've dealt with life, but it means there's so much I haven't gotten to experience. I've told you that before, and that's why *this* is so amazing."

She stroked his skin, fingertips trailing gently over his nipple. The flat disk tightened under her touch, his already solid muscles flexing harder.

"Touch me all you want." He sucked in a gasp as she leaned closer and pressed her lips to his chest. More of his typical amusement had returned to his voice as he continued. "I'll be your real-life mannequin."

"You're my *friend*," she corrected in a whisper. "That's what I need. That's all I want."

They were in the eye of the storm. Everything she'd shared in the past moments had turned their relationship upside down and sideways, and they still had more to talk about in the days to come. It wasn't as if her world had been swept clean in under thirty minutes.

But right now there was only them. Only this intimate, strangely peaceful togetherness.

And like she'd been doing for the past couple months, she ignored the past and looked to the future. Taking life by both hands and riding it as hard as she could.

Although not quite *riding it*. More like barely containing it. Molding power and strength and iron-will under her fingertips as if she were harnessing a wild stallion.

Trevor stood stock-still while she touched him, and slowly the tension in his body changed. Sliding from fury to raw passion. His eyes no longer held the urge to kill, but desire and arousal.

She stroked her fingertips down the faint trail of hair leading toward the open button on his jeans. Under her caress his muscles formed a grid, and she laughed.

It came out rather breathlessly.

"Six-pack, right?"

He curled his hand around the back of her neck and tugged her close again, his hot breath pressing over her cheek. "Kiss me," he demanded.

She was more than willing to oblige. His mouth settled over hers like a benediction—a blessing for what was about to happen between them. Like her history was scrubbed clean and this was all that remained. Passionate need. Fierce want.

Heat dragged up her spine, melting it rapidly as his tongue stroked into her mouth and he owned her completely.

Trevor had threaded his fingers into the hair at the back of her head, but he cradled her even as they feasted hungrily. Becky's eyes were closed, hands exploring without the aid of sight.

He twitched as she skimmed her palm lower over his jeans, over the ridge of his thick erection that lay under the taut fabric. He moaned as she scooped farther, both hands going to his butt so she could squeeze the muscle there.

The new position put her up against him, his arousal tight to her belly. It didn't scare her—the sign of his physical desire. Maybe she was supposed to be more broken, or fearful, but she was tired of being told how she should behave.

She was turned on, and Trevor did that to her. Maybe she'd never been there before because of life and circumstance, but he did it for her. Left her aching, a deep need in her core and a tingling sensation all over her skin that made her want more, not less.

Telling her she was sinful and damned, and whatever the rest of the warnings she'd been threatened with, didn't make it real. This was real. The heat washing over her as she snuck her hands under his jeans to touch skin.

Trevor jerked them apart—still careful. Still caring.

But even as they dragged in gasps of air, he was ripping off the rest of his clothes until, as promised earlier, he stood fully naked in the evening sunshine streaming into her living room.

She'd seen pictures once of statues without clothes, and the images had never gone away. Yet they weren't anything nearly as titillating or exciting as the real thing.

Maybe it was terrible, but the first thing curiosity focused her attention on was his erection. It stood upright, dark black hair at the base, and when he wrapped a hand around the thick length and stroked, something inside her went fuzzy with need.

Becky glanced upward to see him smiling. Not cocky and flirtatious, but full-out male pride and pleasure.

"You look like a strutting rooster," she said,

surprised how rough and tight her throat had gone.

"It's tough to not feel a bit of pride right now. Jeez, Rodeo, you should see your eyes. They're on fire."

It made sense—her body was on fire, the rest of her should be too.

All of him was amazing. Lean muscles, firm stomach and backside. She stepped slowly behind him and touched again, unable to resist trailing her fingers over his butt.

"You having fun?" he asked, low and deep. "Anything you—*fuck*."

She'd slipped her hand past his hip and over his fingers where he held his erection. "Show me," she whispered. "Show me how you touch yourself. I want to make you feel good like you did for me the other day."

It was easier standing behind him, sneaking peeks past his torso as he immediately followed her directions than being out front and having to meet his eyes. At least this time, although she totally expected there to be a second and third go-round in the future, and then she'd see.

Trevor changed the game slightly, letting go and pressing her fingers around him before curling his fingers over hers. Now she was the one stroking skin, heat to her palm, a touch of wetness as he guided her over the top where his seed had gathered.

Becky's face was pressed to his side, his scent in her head as they stroked together, his breathing picking up in pace.

"Feel that? That's what you do to me," he growled. "You touching me, looking at me, *kissing* me—all of it makes me hard. Beautiful woman. So fucking beautiful."

She stroked more boldly, his grip surprisingly tight as he taught her, but once he let her take charge she worked him willingly. Bending over so she could watch closer as he brought one hand down to cup his balls. Groaning as she pressed her lips to his side. Her teeth, nipping his hipbone as she eyed what they were doing.

Trevor's head tilted back and a low moan escaped his lips. A cry of pleasure broke free as he brought his free hand over the top of his shaft, moisture and seed spurting over his fingers, over hers, as she continued to work him.

"Easy, sweetheart," he gasped, guiding her to move slower. To adjust her grip to let the final pulses escape, his erection still impossibly hard.

A delicious stickiness covered her hand, and an ache pounded between her legs, but she wasn't in want, she was glad. Satisfied at giving back to this man who'd made her so happy.

Trevor stooped and grabbed his T-shirt. After wiping their hands with it, he kissed her, a wall of male contentment.

His lips curled into a smile and she felt it during the kiss. A moment later a laugh escaped her, sheer joy making her break away to stare at him in amazement.

She shook her head. "You're beautiful. Thank you for indulging me. Thank you for being so amazing."

Trevor's smile shone like a beam of sunshine, or bubbles in a fizzy drink. He stood buck naked in her living room, bold and shameless in all the right ways. "We sparkly unicorns *are* amazing."

Quiet hovered—would he turn the conversation back to what she'd shared? In a way, she hoped not. This moment was flawless how it was, and she didn't need more time spent on bad memories.

Fortunately Trevor was his perfectly wonderful

self, stroking her arm slowly as his grin turned wider. "If you want some ice cream for dessert, I should put my clothes back on."

Becky laughed again then offered his clothes, watching as he pulled on everything but the T-shirt. "Do you mind if we don't go back to the party?"

"Not at all." He tucked his fingers under her chin and tilted her head back. "This is a party made for two, and I'm fine sticking around for a while."

It hadn't been the day she'd expected—it had ended up so much more. And the reason was very clear.

The man now pacing toward her kitchen to raid her freezer.

Chapter Eighteen

THEY TALKED for a long time that night over ice cream. She shared more about Paradise Settlement, and about how her rescuer had taken her home and treated her like a long-lost daughter.

His Uncle Mark—there was no stepping around the connection now—had been the one to help her get the paperwork started to replace her missing ID.

"I didn't have much," Becky admitted. "My mom had us girls at home with a midwife, and the church was very insistent it was important to stay off the government records. And with how paranoid they'd become before I left, I don't plan on ever contacting them."

Trevor nodded, listening without comment as she shared. He breathed a sigh when she mentioned that during the weeks she'd stayed with him, Mark had found her a doctor to visit—a *lady* doctor. The woman had not only listened to Becky as she explained her background, her cheeks on fire with shame, the doctor had done all sorts of tests that eventually came back to say Becky was healthy. The doctor also reassured her none of it was her fault, along with suggesting the name of a counselor if Becky ever wanted it.

"It *wasn't* your fault," Trevor agreed vehemently, before praising her rescuer again. "It sounds as if Uncle Mark did everything he could to make a difference."

"I trusted him, and he saved my life," Becky said simply. "And he trusted me, I guess, because he wasn't there the whole time—he was off driving. I think I slept for most of a week. Like my body wanted to restock energy that had been drained away over the years."

"And he brought you here."

She heard the question in Trevor's voice. "He said he owned a place he would never use, and that I'd be helping him out by taking care of it. He dropped me off late one night. Barely even stopped in the yard other than to make sure I got into the house safely."

Trevor shook his head slowly. "You never mentioned him when I was talking about my family."

"He didn't want me to talk about him. I felt like I was imposing all over again when I had to bother him again to write a letter to Hope and Matt."

By the time Trevor left, Becky felt as if a huge weight had been taken off her shoulders, and she fell into bed exhausted, yet relieved. She hadn't realized how hard it had been on her to keep the secrets she'd been hiding from everyone, including Trevor.

She was glad everything in her past wasn't common knowledge, but over the coming days as she spent time at work, and with her new friends, it was good to know that whenever Trevor dropped in, he was the one person who knew everything about her and *still* liked her.

More than *liked*, she hoped, but she wasn't going to get ahead of herself. Right now it was enough he was willing to teach her, and while he didn't make her feel as if she was somehow broken, his care and concern hovered on the right side of a fine line.

She enjoyed having someone looking after her for once in her life.

Hope jabbed her in the arm with an envelope. "You're daydreaming again," she teased.

Becky couldn't stop the heat flushing her cheeks as she accepted the cash. "I'm not the only one," she said, trying to sound scandalized. "I saw you after *that man* called earlier today."

"What man?" Hope pretended innocence. Matt had phoned, and whatever he'd said had left her boss flustered and smiling with secrets.

She replied as deadpan as possible. "The tall, good-looking guy with a beard who forgot I was working here. I'm still blushing from what he said before I could—"

"He did not!" Hope slapped a hand over her mouth before looking totally embarrassed. "I'm sorry. He should know better."

Nope. No matter how hard Becky tried she couldn't keep a straight face. "I'm kidding. Matt didn't say anything other than ask if he could talk to you."

Hope planted her fists on her hips and mock-glared, a smile twisting her lips. "You've been hanging out with Trevor too long. He's the biggest tease, and you're learning bad habits."

"Trevor's amazing," Becky said, shocked at how breathlessly satisfied she sounded. "And so are you, thank you for this." She waved the envelope containing her salary in the air for a moment before tucking it into her purse.

"You've been a big help. I'm glad you're working here, and I'll be even more glad in the months to come." Hope lowered her feet from the stool where she'd had them propped up, rising slowly to vertical and stretching her lower back. "I don't feel bad, but I do feel pregnant. I can't imagine what it's going to be like once my stomach is bigger than muffin-top size."

"My sister said for her the biggest challenge in the last trimester was to try not to get overtired. It's harder to get caught up, if that makes sense."

Hope nodded thoughtfully. "I don't have any family to ask what my mom's pregnancies were like, so I'm going in blind here."

Over the past couple of days Becky had begun to talk about Sarah more, which was wonderful, but made missing her all the stronger. "If I ever have kids, I'd probably get frustrated if my pregnancies are way different than hers, so I figure generalities are best. For the rest, see what happens."

"That's a good way to look at it," Hope agreed, "It's nice that you're close to your sister. I wish I was closer to mine, but that's never going to be possible."

"People change," Becky said letting optimism and hope colour her voice. "Who knows what might happen?" She got up to greet a customer who'd come in the door, and the conversation faded.

Concern struck briefly at the end of the day when she looked up to find an RCMP officer striding though the door, at least until she recognized the woman.

"Anna." Hope moved forward. "Tell me you want to learn how to quilt and blow my mind."

Trevor's sister made a rude noise. "Sorry, sweetie. I know you've seduced most of the clan over to your evil side, but the domestic arts and me stopped getting along sometime back in the tenth grade. If I can't fix it with duct tape or a stapler, it's not worth fixing."

Hope held up her fingers in the shape of a cross as

if warding off evil. "You just wait. You gonna wake up one morning and the nesting instinct will kick in. The next thing you know, you'll be wearing prairie dresses and canning pickles."

"When pigs fly in space ships," Anna said sweetly before turning to Becky. "I'm here with something for you."

"For me?"

Anna pulled a legal-sized envelope from under her coat and held it forward. "Whoever you got to help you was damn smart. I'm very pleased to present you with an official copy of your birth certificate."

It was suddenly hard to breathe. Becky reached to accept the envelope, her hand shaking and her knees unsteady. She used her free hand to clutch the cutting-board counter next to her for support. "What—?"

"You got your new ID," Hope said excitedly. "That's great news."

It was hard to believe, but it was true. Becky opened the envelope and peeked inside, pulling out a large rectangular paper to stare at the names in shocked disbelief.

Rebekah Hall. Born: Joyful, Manitoba. Her parents' names. Her birthday.

Hope leaned over her shoulder to read as well. "Rebekah. That's a pretty way to spell it, but I like calling you Becky more."

"I like being Becky," she confessed, turning back to Anna. "I didn't expect anything to come to the RCMP. Thank you for bringing it to me."

Anna nodded. "It's one of the safest channels, and I'd guess the lawyer you used wanted to make sure everything arrived properly."

"This doesn't mean you have her on a police file,

or anything?" Hope asked.

"Oh, no. Just means at some point the RCMP
were used as a step in gathering the information to prove
that you exist, which you obviously do." Anna hesitated
before admitting, "I vouched for you. That you're living
here, and a productive member of the community."

The sensation of intense gratitude was easy to
diagnose. "Thank you for that, and yet I'm sorry I got you
involved. I hope it wasn't a bother."

"Not at all. If you need help, I'm available," Anna
offered. "Now, the next steps are for you to take that and
get the rest of the resources you need. Health card, photo
ID, driver's license, social insurance number."

"Library card," Hope teased.

Her mind was spinning. Becky clutched the
envelope to her chest. "Thank you," she said again.

"You're the one who has to fill in all the
government forms." Anna adjusted her coat, preparing to
leave. "You may not be thanking me after the first hour
or two of that."

Becky didn't care how much work it was. This was
as good as a miracle.

Hope glanced at the clock. "You're not going to get
any work done this afternoon. Why don't you go and start
some of that paperwork? You can apply for photo ID at
the insurance office. If you go now, you might have it
before the end of the week."

"I'll give you a ride over," Anna offered.

Which was how Becky found herself filling out
paperwork and shoved in front of a camera and told not
to smile. Before the flashbulb glare had faded completely
from her vision, she was handed a plastic card with her
picture and birthdate.

She damn near danced home.

A heavy knock sounded on the back door an instant before Trevor's voice echoed through the house. "Can I come in?"

Becky met him in the kitchen. "Usually people wait for an answer before—"

—and then she was squealing because he'd snatched her off her feet and was twirling them both in a circle. His arms strong and confident around her as he laughed, settling her on the floor and giving her a brief kiss before looking into her eyes expectantly.

"So? Where's this shiny thing that happened to you today?"

She reached into her pocket and pulled out her ID. "How did you know?"

Trevor held her hand in his as they looked the card over. "You're kidding me, right? The Coleman gossip chain carries news at one notch past the speed of light."

Didn't even matter that she hadn't been the one to tell him. "I can't believe it."

He squeezed his fingers, pressing hers to the hard plastic. "That's real, Rodeo. It's right there in black and white and bad government photo, although you look a hell of a lot cuter than anyone else I know."

"I still have a lot to do. I had to get all the things that Hope needs for work, and I want to practice before I try taking the driver's test, and then I need—"

"But first," Trevor said, tugging her toward the stairs, "we celebrate. Because that's what we do when good things happen."

She wasn't sure where this was leading. "What kind of celebrating we going to do, Trevor Coleman?"

Trevor patted her on the butt then sent her up the stairs alone. "Why Becky Hall, I'm shocked. Did you think I was suggesting we go get into some wild and unruly shenanigans?"

Shenanigans sounded fine to her. She paused mid-flight, hand on the railing. "You aren't?"

"I meant, you need to go put on a pretty dress so I can take you out." He leaned forward and glanced up at her, temptation and mischief mixed together on his face. "We'll grab some supper then go to Traders Pub, now that you have a shiny ID saying that you're legal."

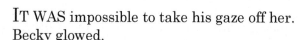

IT WAS impossible to take his gaze off her.

Becky glowed.

Instead of a dress she'd pulled on jeans and a blouse that showed off her curves and gave him all sorts of ideas. They'd grabbed burgers and fries at the café before making the short trip over to Traders. She stood next to him at the pub entrance, her smile stretching from ear to ear.

"I've never been to a pub," she confessed.

"I figured. Traders is a good one. Bunch of the family will be here since it's Friday night. Less than a few years ago—some don't come out every week anymore. But for the most part, this is where anyone in the clan who's single can be found most Friday nights."

They were there, in the midst of the noise and bustle, but it was easy to see where Becky wanted to head. Familiar faces turned toward them in the crowd, Rachel waving excitedly, Lee rising to his feet to pull in another couple chairs on the side of the long table away from the rest of the clan.

"It's noisy in here," Becky noted as he guided her forward.

He settled in the chair next to her, grabbing two glasses and filling them with beer from the nearest pitcher. "A few weeks from now we can have a bonfire," he promised. "Steve plays his guitar, but otherwise it's a lot less chaos. You'll enjoy that too."

"Hope and Matt told me they needed some deadfall moved," Lee mentioned. "We could spend a few hours cleaning up around their place then have a hot dog roast."

"Sounds good." Trevor watched with amusement as Becky took the first sip of her drink, her face twisting and nose wrinkling up. "I forgot. Is that your first beer?"

She shook her head as she placed the glass carefully back on the table surface. "I tried some about a month ago, but this tastes different."

"It's a local brew." He laid an arm along the back of her chair, moving in close enough that their thighs touched. "You want something else? You don't have to drink if you don't want to."

"Maybe just a pop," she admitted, pushing the glass away.

Rachel had overheard. "I have an idea. One sec."

She popped up from her chair and headed to the bar, coming back with a can of Sprite and a clean glass. She poured the glass half-full with Becky's beer, then topped it up the rest of the way with Sprite.

Becky took the drink cautiously, but she seemed willing. And after the first taste she nodded. "That's much better."

"That's called a Shandy." Rachel leaned around her to offer a snarky grin to Trevor. "Sad for you. She likes my drinks better than yours."

"Yeah? I bet she'll like the way I dance better than the way you do," he teased back.

"Hey, I know how to lead." Beside her, Lee snickered, glancing away innocently when Rachel twirled on him, poking him in the stomach with her finger. "What's that noise supposed to mean, bucko?"

"I don't know how to dance," Becky admitted, interrupting Rachel's pretend assault on Lee, "but I'd like to learn." She turned trusting eyes on Trevor who felt about ten feet tall at that moment.

"Then dancing it is." He tipped his chin toward her drink. "Take that with you. We'll head to the dance floor and take a look."

He waved goodbye to the rest of the family, accepting with good humour the few teasing smirks that were tossed at them for leaving right after sitting down. They'd visit another time. Now? Becky wanted to dance.

Rachel and Lee grabbed their drinks as well, and the four of them made their way from the bar to the dance floor, volume rising as they rounded the corner.

It was early enough in the summer season the place was busy without being packed, and they found an empty table at the side of the dance floor. One of the tall ones without chairs, a place to stand and talk between time spent on the floor.

Trevor liked that it meant he could curl himself around Becky and stand close while he spoke in her ear. "For tonight's dance lesson, we'll focus on basic moves."

She wiggled against him, and he reacted instantly, the feeling of her all soft and warm against him setting off the sexual tension between them that never seemed to completely go away.

Becky leaned back against his chest, tilting her head so she could speak toward his ear and not shout to be heard over the music. "Doesn't look that hard, what they're doing on the floor right now."

"That's not dancing," Trevor whispered against her cheek. "That's standing around bouncing."

"Isn't that what Tiggers do?"

A laugh escaped. "Some of the time, but not when I've got a pretty girl I can hold in my arms. That's why dancing was invented in the first place, you know. It's a way to get close to someone you wanted to get close to without leaving the room."

She took another couple sips of her drink, and her cheeks were bright red as she turned toward him, slipping her arms up and threading her fingers into the hair at the back of his neck. "You're telling me it's like sex, but in public?"

Another deep shot of lust struck. "You're a live wire tonight, Rodeo."

She licked her lips, staring at his mouth. "I have no idea what you're talking about."

Lee was grinning at them, and Rachel as well. Probably planning already to harass him about how totally gone he was, but he didn't care. Guiding Becky out onto the dance floor and getting to curl his hands around her hips and bring their torsos together was worth any kind of teasing he might have to put up with.

"Dancing is about listening," he instructed her.

Becky dipped her head in agreement. "The music. Staying with the beat."

Trevor slipped a hand higher, pressing it to her lower back, slowing them down. "Forget the music."

She tipped her head back to look at him with confusion. "Really? But I thought music was important."

"Not as important as this." He caught her fingers of her right hand and lifted them in the air, tucking her in closer and swaying their bodies together. Their feet moving in time with the music, yes, but more

201

importantly, with the rising beat of his heart.

They weren't trying anything fancy. There was no footwork or hijinks to trip them up. Instead they had heat, bodies in alignment. Her lips close against his neck as he guided her back-and-forth in an easy rhythm that just *happened* to coincide with the beat of the music.

"This is nice," Becky said softly, barely a whisper compared to the singer in the music, but he heard every word.

He was so tuned in to the motion of their bodies, to the way that when he stepped forward, his leg rubbed between hers, his thigh settled tight against her softness. He turned his head and their lips met for a kiss. Sweet enough for public display, yet hot enough sweat ran down his spine, and anticipation took him from semi-hard to rock solid.

He'd only go the speed she wanted—he'd made that commitment and he was sticking to it, but the way she pushed forward eagerly, he wasn't taking things too fast for her.

Listening. It was easy to do when the sounds were there, even with the riot of noise around them. Arousal and desire sang loudly as needy noises escaped her throat, breathy exhales and tiny gasps as they danced. He kept her turned toward the back wall so that no one else could enjoy the expression of pleasure rising on her face. That was for him. His eyes only.

They stayed on the dance floor, rocking together. It was like she'd said—damn near foreplay in public— until the music changed again.

The heavy beat called for something more active, and he forced himself to drag them apart, putting them into a more *just friends* position and showing her how to two-step.

Because she needed to know more than how turned on she could make him.

The evening flew by. Trevor took Rachel for a spin when Lee demanded his chance to dance with Becky, and she agreed.

It was a strange sensation, watching someone else take her in his arms. The first sign of discomfort from Becky and Trevor would've been there in an instant to rescue her, but he trusted Lee implicitly, and it was good for her to know how to dance with other partners.

"She's not about to vanish," Rachel teased, letting him lead her across the dance floor. "She's having fun."

"I think so." He glanced down at the woman who would eventually be his sister-in-law. "She likes you. A lot, and I'm glad."

"Awww, well, I like her too." Rachel looked thoughtful. "I don't know all her secrets, and I don't need to, but if you guys ever need someone to talk to, we got your back. Lee and I."

Didn't need to be said, but he was glad that she had. "You're family. Of course you got my back."

"Except during girls' night out," Rachel qualified. "That night is free-for-all, and we are dirt-talking you boys so hard your ears will burn."

Jeez. The Coleman women on the loose—a disaster waiting to happen. "You're going to be careful, right? Don't get too wild."

Rachel widened her eyes in shock. "Look at you being all straight-laced and cautious. Don't worry, we won't play white rabbit, or make any prank phone calls."

"Those went out of style once people got call display." Trevor kept his face absolutely blank.

A deadly glare hit him hard. "That better not be some crack about how old I am, buster."

He gave her an extra-fast twirl, moving them toward where Lee and Becky were dancing. "I'm just as old as you," he said, "now go torment my baby brother. I'll take care of Becky."

They switched dance partners in the middle of the floor, Becky settling in against him like she belonged there.

"Did you have fun?"

She nodded. "You're right, though. Dancing is about listening. Lee is a good dancer, but I think we fit together better."

A dirty image of them *fitting together* intimately flashed through his brain, and he had to take a deep breath to regain control. "I think we're going to fit together *just* fine," he assured her, lips against her cheek.

They stayed for one more song before he brought her to the truck, and headed out of town with the stereo playing and the windows rolled down.

Becky curled her hands around his biceps. "Where are we going now?"

"For a drive."

She rested her head on his shoulder and snuggled in tight. "It's been a good night."

"It's not over." He turned up the music and sang along, Becky watching intently as he drove them past weathered old barns and alfalfa fields.

He slipped toward the ravine overlooking the river, backing the truck carefully into place so that the tailgate aimed toward a fine view of the Rocky Mountains.

"Come on." Anticipation made him grin as he guided Becky out of the truck, pausing to reach behind the seat for the thick blanket he kept there.

He dropped the tailgate, spreading the blanket with a snap before catching hold of Becky and lifting her to sit on the soft surface.

He hopped up beside her. "Want to watch the sunset with me?"

She was back against his side, her hand resting lightly on his thigh. "Is that all we're going to do?" she asked shyly.

"You think I have some ulterior motive in getting you all alone?"

"I hope so."

Hell, yeah. He slipped his arms around her, accepting the lips she'd raised toward him for a kiss. Sweet, soft. Everything about her called to him, and when she twisted closer, fingers catching hold of the front of his shirt, Trevor leaned over her and took her down to the blanket. Stretching them out full-length, his hips tight to hers, one leg pressing between hers.

He kept one hand on the bed of the truck to hold his body weight off her but they were still connected. Thighs and hips, and his chest against the soft swell of her breasts. Mouth-to-mouth, tongues tangling. Becky's fingers clutched his shoulders as she held him to her. Totally on board, no hesitation.

He undid the buttons at the top of her shirt, nibbling a path to her ear as she shivered under him. "Okay?"

"Uh-huh. Feels so good when you touch me," she confessed, her eyes bright as he checked to make sure she was still having fun.

His gaze drifted downward, the creamy complexion of her skin glowing with the sunlight bathing them as he peeled back the sides of her shirt. Slowly exposing more of her pale bra and her rapidly shifting chest.

"You're breathing pretty hard there, Rodeo."

"I have never done anything like this," she confessed. "Outdoors, where I can see you, and you can see me."

"That's one of the best parts of it." Trevor ran his finger along the edge of her bra, loving how her nipples stabbed upward against the soft fabric. "I like seeing all of you. It turns me on."

She pushed at fabric of his shirt. "Take yours off too."

He didn't really want to stop what he was doing, but he'd want to stop even less a few moments from now, so he pulled back obediently and stripped off his shirt. "Your turn," he teased.

Becky wiggled out from under him, or at least partially. She was close enough that as she pushed the shirt from her shoulders, the warmth of her skin brushed his a half-dozen times before she laid the fabric on top of where his rested.

She paused, wearing nothing up top but her bra and glanced at him from under her lashes. "Oh, boy."

Trevor caressed her waist, sliding up the side of her body until he cupped one beautiful breast. "You have no idea how much you are turning me on."

He rubbed his thumb over her nipple, and she arched against him, a soft sigh of pleasure escaping. "I want more."

Not a fucking problem. Trevor pressed his lips to the curve of her neck. He licked a trail up to her ear and drove her wild as he reached around and undid her bra one-handedly. He kept kissing her as he smoothed the straps from her shoulders, their bodies tight enough that the cups stayed in place until he pulled back.

Neither of them moved as the material fell away and she sat there, finally naked from the waist up. So intensely provocative and innocent at the same time Trevor's brain was having trouble functioning.

He knew he was staring but he couldn't stop.

He lifted his hand back to where it had been before, only now there was no barrier between them, and the warmth and weight of her breast made him groan with need.

Trevor put his mouth over her nipple, licking first before pursing his lips and sucking lightly.

"Oh. *Oh*, that's good." Becky held his head and curved her body toward him, her response a reassurance she was enjoying this as much as he was.

She tasted amazing, so he licked a trail from one breast to the other, teasing gently with his teeth until she gasped with delight. He got lost for a while—they both did—because by the time he pushed her to the blanket again the sun had vanished behind the mountain, leaving nothing but fading sunset streaks to light the sky.

More than enough light to see, though, especially when he used his hands, trickling them down her body to unsnap her jeans and slide his fingers into her underwear.

"Let me touch you," Becky whispered.

"Not this time," Trevor murmured. "This time, I'm in charge of what we're playing. Trust me, you'll enjoy it."

There was nothing he would've liked more than to strip them both down and take this to its natural conclusion, but it was too soon. Far too soon, no matter how hard Becky was writhing under his touch, little gasps escaping her lips, teasing noises rumbling up as he returned to her breasts, his fingers sliding through her folds to tease her clit.

"You're so wet, Rodeo. Your body likes it when I touch you. You were made for passion and pleasure. Made to enjoy this."

"I am," she agreed. "I like everything you're doing to me. Oh *yes*, right *there...*"

Her hips rose against his hand as she rocked into his touch. Trevor's jeans were far too tight, his erection pressed hard to her hip.

So much pleasure was contained in the back of the four-by-six truck bed. The blanket could've been a luxurious mattress. Hell, they could have been lying in the most expensive suite in some fancy hotel, and it still would've come back to the sensations of sex. The outpouring of physical desire.

"You're going to come. Right here, outdoors, with me watching you." Trevor pressed his forehead to hers and increased the tempo of his fingers. He couldn't resist rocking against her, trying to ease the pressure in his cock as his body screamed for release.

Her lashes fluttered, but she looked him in the eye. Kept with him one hundred percent as her breath escaped in tight pants, tongue sneaking out to wet her lips a second before she quivered under him. Her eyes went out of focus as a cry of satisfaction rushed to greet him.

He rocked again, the tightness in his balls and the tingling at the base of his spine signaling the beginning of the end. A moment later he was gone, taking her lips and kissing her madly as he lost control.

Didn't care one bit that he'd gone and messed in his clothes. Didn't matter. What did matter was the woman under him looking satisfied and spent, wisps of hair around her face framing eyes that glowed with happiness.

Trevor rolled her on top of him, still skin to skin, her breasts pressing against him tightly and getting him riled up far sooner than he thought possible.

"And that's the best part about dancing," he said with a smile. "When you're listening, you can always hear the music."

Chapter Nineteen

IT TOOK another couple of weeks for Becky to finish filling out all the paperwork she needed to become an official part of society.

Anna Coleman helped her a few times when things got tricky, the patient RCMP officer going through each form one at a time. It had to be a foreign language because it wasn't English, at least not to Becky.

Not to Trevor either who'd taken one look at the mass of papers she'd brought home one night and shook his head, reaching into his pocket for his phone to contact Anna once again.

"I'll help you however I can," he apologized, "but that's a kind of puzzle I can't get my head around."

Not that she cared. Having Trevor there for all the other things he was teaching her was more than enough. He brought over music and books. Showed her TV shows and movies, some of which she watched for five minutes through her fingers before refusing to look any longer.

He took her out to the fanciest restaurant in town, which happened to be run by another Coleman, and made her try a whole bunch of different foods that she'd never had before.

Most of the time, though, they ended up laughing so hard her stomach would hurt by the end of the evening. And then he would take his time and offer sweet, drugging kisses that made her ache for more, which he always willingly provided.

They were fooling around an awful lot, and none of it scared her. All of it just made her want to try the next thing.

She figured that might be the idea, but she wasn't about to complain. He was setting the speed, and that was fine by her.

He'd showed up today after work, fresh scrubbed from a shower with a piping-hot casserole in hand. They demolished it while sitting at the table and talking about their days, and things were just about perfect.

Just about.

He wrapped his fingers around hers after they'd cleared away the plates. "That's a sad expression. Are you tired?"

Becky shook her head. "Thinking about Sarah and the kids."

He stiffened slightly like he always did when she mentioned Paradise, but he didn't pull away. He guided her back to the table and sat her down, pulling his chair next to hers so he could sit with an arm resting along the back. As if he was holding her in an embrace. "Are you thinking about contacting her?"

Wariness in his voice. Concern.

"She's not bad," Becky insisted. "She's as much a victim as I was."

Trevor nodded slowly. "I won't argue with you, because I have no idea what it's like to be in that kind of hell, but I also don't know her. I know you." He tucked his free hand under her chin and tilted her head so he could kiss her, a brief, sweet connection that softened his words. "I don't want you to hurt anymore, and talking about Paradise and the past makes me afraid for you."

She curled her fingers around the back of his neck and pulled him in, resting their foreheads together.

It'd become something of a habit, and she really liked it. The position was warm and intimate, but if it got too much, she could close her eyes and still feel him there without him looking into her soul.

"Sarah's got three kids." Becky spoke softly, but she wanted to share this. "Isaac is her firstborn, and I think after he arrived, her life got a lot better. She was always kind to me, even when it was clear I didn't really fit into the community very well."

Tension stiffened his body and voice, but he was listening. Sharing. "And two little girls. Hannah and Mary?"

Becky nodded. She could picture the girls running up to her and crawling into her lap. She'd always tried to have time for them, especially after it seemed she wasn't going to have any kids of her own. *Someday I'll get in touch*, she'd promised herself. Promised *them*.

It was part of why she'd found the courage to run away in the first place. So she could offer them a different future as well.

But it was time for other distractions. She kissed Trevor on the cheek then reached past him to the top of the bookcase for a deck of cards. "Next lesson. You get to help me practice."

A soft chuckle escaped him. "I heard you got tromped the other day."

"They *cheated*." Becky pulled out the deck and began shuffling awkwardly, the cards uncomfortable in her fingers as she learned how to handle them better.

"Those little girls of Jaxi's are mind readers. I swear every time I pulled a card, they asked for it on the next hand."

"Cheating at *Go Fish*. That's just wrong." Trevor winked as he slipped the deck from her fingers and gave it an extra shuffle, bending the cards and sliding them together far faster than she could.

"I need to win the next time," she insisted.

"Hmm, that's going to take a lot more practice. You've got *tells*," he said. "Little things you do that give away clues to what your hand holds."

Playing cards with four-year-olds, and they could read her. "Great. I'm not going to a casino with *anybody*, not any time soon."

Trevor laughed as he dealt the cards for a game of rummy, patiently going over the rules again, but this one she'd begun to master.

After she laid down on the table ahead of him three times in a row, he gave her an evil eye. "Now who's cheating?"

She leaned her elbows forward on the table, close enough she could smell his fresh scent. "Not cheating. I just know how to read you," she teased.

Trevor raised a brow. "I guess that means it's time to raise the stakes."

Ha. "How do you bet on rummy?"

Trevor leaned back in his chair and stretched his long legs out in front of him. "Well, if you want to combine a couple of lessons here all at once, I suggest we play strip rummy."

"Strip..." Becky swallowed hard as a sudden vision of Trevor in the exact position he was currently in, but with no clothes on, made her mouth go dry. "Okay."

He leaned forward with a laugh, shuffling the

213

deck once more before lifting the top off to show a card. "Then cut for deal, Rodeo. Play your hand the best you can, and instead of counting points, loser strips off one piece of clothing."

Becky couldn't wait. She concentrated hard on the cards, thrilled when her luck continued, at least for the first couple hands. Trevor pulled off his shirt, then his jeans, sitting at the table in a pair of boxer briefs and black socks.

She wasn't sure she needed to play the game anymore. "How about I just sit here and stare at you? I'm happy."

Trevor dealt the cards again, flipping up a wildcard for her and groaning in disgust. "At some point, one of us is going to be completely naked—"

"Or both of us." Becky picked up the wildcard and tried desperately to rearrange the sets she held, but she couldn't quite go out.

The next three hands found her losing her shirt, her jeans and her socks. She sat at the table with not much on, squirming as Trevor spent more time looking her over than looking at his cards.

He reached into his hand blindly and tossed a card on the pile, and she snatched it up eagerly. "I don't think you meant to do that," she teased, laying down her hand with the help of the wildcard he'd accidentally discarded.

Trevor sat back in his chair with a filthy satisfied smile on his face. "Gotta love this game," he said. "The only time that when you lose, you win."

She wasn't the best of dealers regularly, but now that she had him in front of her, naked, it was even worse. Every inch of his body was highlighted by the sun shining into her kitchen. His muscles were relaxed but the outline of the six-pack was clear. His cock stood upright, tapping toward his belly.

She picked her cards off the table and tried to put them in order.

Another card flicked across to land in front of her. "Looks like you're a little distracted, Rodeo," he teased. "Having trouble counting?"

"Yes," she admitted. She met his eyes straight on. "Now that you have no clothes on, what do you forfeit when I win?"

Trevor looked thoughtful. "Winner's choice, I suppose, but I wouldn't get my hopes up if I were you." He eyed her bra and panties, licking his lips as if he were preparing for dessert. "I have a feeling your luck is about change.

He won the next two hands, and Becky stood up to slowly slip off her panties, both of them naked in broad daylight.

Her heart was pounding so hard she could taste the rhythm.

"Next victory is winner's choice."

Opening her hand, it didn't take long for Becky to realize she was outgunned. The cards held absolutely nothing that matched.

But when she glanced at Trevor, he was frowning, concern on his face as they both took turn after turn until finally she was one card away from winning.

He tossed down a seven, and she snatched it up, fanning her cards on the table with a racing pulse. "I win."

He nodded, folding his cards and laying them aside before leaning his elbows on the table and offering her a heated stare. "So, what do I have to do?"

Becky was sure. She was one hundred percent

sure. "Take me to bed."

Trevor stilled, a pulse beating hard in his throat. Then he held out a hand, bringing her to her feet as well. They stepped together, skin to skin in her kitchen, the old worn linoleum cool under their feet. A nice contrast to the steaming sensation between their bodies.

He pulled her with him, almost dancing as they moved toward the stairs. One hand cradled her head as he kissed her, the other on her back, his fingers splayed downward, trailing over her naked butt. His erection trapped between them, thick length of it unmistakable—unavoidable.

He guided her blindly to the foot of the stairs, kissing and caressing the entire way. She'd been turned on before, but now a fever had her tight in its grip. She stroked her hands over his ribs, swooping down to boldly catch hold of his naked butt. Firm muscles and soft skin, and a deep need pulsed in her core.

They broke apart for long enough to get to the top of the stairs, and then he was back, caressing her the entire way to her bedroom.

Trevor picked her up and laid her on the quilt, stepping back to offer a smile that had all kinds of mischief tied up in it as he glanced around. "I knew you had a thing for frills, Rodeo."

She'd begun to decorate the room, each soft feminine touch making the house a bit more her own. "It's nice to look around when I wake up and see things that make me happy."

Becky curled herself up and caught his hand, tugging him toward her. Trevor crawled onto the mattress over her. His elbows supporting his weight, he leaned down and kissed her tenderly.

Every inch of her was covered by him, a weight

pressing her to the mattress, and a flicker of unease struck, passing so fast she wasn't sure it had really happened.

Not when he moved downward, his mouth on her breasts, hands holding her as his hips settled between her legs. Becky stroked her fingers through his hair and closed her eyes, soaking in the perfect sensation of his tongue stroking her nipples.

She was breathing hard by the time he made a reluctant noise and moved farther down the bed, pressing her legs apart as he went. Kisses to her abdomen, to her belly button. To the very top of her mound.

She met his gaze. "You look hungry," she whispered.

"Starving."

Trevor slipped a finger through her folds, the soft caress sending a ripple through her entire body. Then he lowered his head, and his tongue that had teased her so deliciously before made contact with her clitoris, and her hips rose off the bed of their own accord. "Oh, my goodness."

He hummed happily and did it again. "It is good. Not only are you delicious, I love the noises you make. Let's me know what you like."

He licked her again, circling his finger at the very entrance to her body even as he focused on the tight bundle of nerves that seemed to be a trigger for every one of her pleasure sensors. "I like it all. Everything you do to me. I can't believe we're here."

"We're here all right, and the next thing that's going to happen is you're going to come."

He wasn't gentle anymore. He'd said he was starving, and he moved as if he were. Pressing his hands under her butt and lifting her to his mouth, he ate hungrily. Licking and thrusting, driving her wild. Trying to get air into her lungs didn't seem as important as it had been before. Her only focus was how amazing what he was doing to her felt. A tight spiral of excitement kept closing in. Nearer and nearer until the shockwave of it set her off, shaking her body as his name escaped her lips.

Her core squeezed tight, clamping down on the fingers he'd slipped into her. When she reached to pull him up, he pulled a rock imitation, locking in place to start all over.

"I *can't*. Oh, Trevor, it's too much."

"Not too much," he insisted, nuzzling his nose against her curls and breathing deeply, sexual tension in his voice, but that mesmerizing smile on his face. "I want to see that again. I want to taste you some more. I haven't had *nearly* enough."

He pulled her to him, thrusting his tongue deep. Becky wrapped her legs around his shoulders, her fingers clutching the bed sheets in the hopes that would keep her anchored to the ground instead of floating off.

A second climax hit, and as if oxygen had been denied to most of her body and was now rushing in, tingles hit, sparks struck and stars danced in front of her eyes. She moaned, a high wavering sound of happiness and satisfaction.

Trevor moved quickly, grabbing a condom from— she wasn't sure where it had come from. Becky lay sprawled on her bed, relaxed and satisfied, but the sight of him touching his heavy shaft to roll down the condom made something tingle all over again.

She wiggled upward, reaching for him as he moved back between her legs, his hips settling over hers.

Trevor kissed her, teasing with his tongue as the hot hard head of his cock nudged between her folds.

She curled her hands around his shoulders, lightheaded and eager, as he pushed his way inside. His cock opening her, the length thicker and hotter than his fingers had been.

Out of nowhere an icy wind blew into the room. Fear curled its way up her spine and took control of her body. She tensed, her hands falling from his shoulders, heart rate tripling, not from desire. Terror locked her throat and she couldn't breathe.

Trevor pushed himself up, staring into her face with concern, "Becky?"

She couldn't move. Couldn't get enough air in to say anything at first, and then the words shot out of her. Barely a whisper, if she even got the words out. "No. My God, *no.*"

Becky squeezed her eyes tight, trying to force away the horror riding her that made no sense. It was nothing Trevor was doing. She wanted this...

...but some part of her body didn't.

Without her saying another word, Trevor rolled away, slipping from her body to lie beside her on the mattress. He cupped her face carefully. "Are you okay? What happened? Did I hurt you?"

She shook her head. "It's not you. Really. Oh my God, what's *wrong* with me?"

She pressed her face to his chest and hid, the icy-cold sensation of fear still tangled around her as she turned to Trevor for protection.

He held her tightly and made soothing noises as he stroked her back. His erection made contact with her hip, leaving a stickiness on her skin as his desire slowly deflated. They lay there in silence but for the pounding of her terrified heartbeat.

"I'm so sorry," she managed to whisper against his chest.

Trevor swore softly. "Don't you do that. You haven't done anything wrong."

"I feel like—" She wasn't sure how to define it. Like she'd failed him? "I enjoy everything I do with you. I don't understand why this happened."

He pressed his lips to the forehead. "Did you have fun up until I went inside you?"

She nodded.

Trevor chuckled. "Good. Because I had a hell of a good time going down on you, and I have this thing about your tits. I'm not done with them, just so you know."

It was so him, trying to make her feel better. "I want to have sex with you. I really do."

He shrugged, settling her tight against his warm body. "We went a little fast, I suppose. Don't worry. We'll try again another time. Maybe a different position will make it better."

There was no way she'd get out the words apologizing for him not having come. She felt guilty, but she couldn't bear to offer anything else in return. Not right now.

The muscles of the back of her neck ached, and terror still rolled through her even though she knew she had nothing to fear. "I don't like me very much right now," she murmured.

"Going to spank you if you don't stop that," Trevor warned. "You didn't do anything wrong." He tilted her chin up so she had to meet his eyes. There was no reproach there for being inadequate as a woman. The warm depths held nothing but concern. "You are one of the strongest people I know, Rodeo. You're making a brand-new life in a world you didn't grow up in, you've lived through hell, and as far as I know this is the first time you've hit a brick wall. Don't you *dare* put yourself down for having to take a deep breath and pause."

"I don't want this," she insisted. "This horrid fear."

"It won't always be there," he promised. Trevor kissed her. A brief, dancing touch on her lips as he lowered his voice and spoke with confidence. "I know you'll eventually accomplish every damn thing you want to, including sex, but if it takes a little while to get there, so what? We've got other things to have fun with along the way."

He blocked her response with another kiss, stroking and petting her until there was no way for the tension in her body to remain.

They crawled out of bed, and she got dressed while he snuck downstairs to where he'd left his clothes.

"You want to go for a drive?" he asked as she joined him in the kitchen.

Becky shook her head. "I think I'll have an early evening. I'm exhausted."

Trevor held her again, squeezing her tight as if that alone could get rid of the web of misery tangled around her body and brain. "I'll see you tomorrow?"

She nodded, staring out the window as he left. Wondering at the injustice of being trapped by the actions of others. Over the past months she'd gone though a lot of emotions regarding her life. Fear, confusion...

This was the first time she'd actually felt something close to hatred toward the men and women who had been involved in her past, whether directly or by complacency. It *hadn't* been her fault—Trevor was right.

But she still had to deal with the fallout.

And for all tears she'd already cried, and all the times that she'd said she was done crying, she had nothing left in her except to drop into a chair at the table, put her head down and let them fall once more.

She was finished far sooner than she'd expected, maybe because anger gave her something to burn away the tears.

Trevor was right about something else. She would get through this. She *would* find a way to take back everything that had been stolen from her. It was going to take time, and knowing that fed another load of fuel onto the flames of her anger.

She wiped her eyes dry and took a deep breath, trying to steady her breathing.

Trevor's discarded final hand sat by her elbow, and she picked it up absently, intending to put the cards away. Confusion struck as she focused on what she was seeing. That last hand that had taken so long to play—Trevor had held three wildcards and a set of pairs. Enough that he should have laid on the table and declared a win.

He'd cheated. He'd deliberately let her take the game, and make the decision, and all over again her throat was tight.

He was a good man. Far *far* better than the ones who had taken her unwilling body and left her broken. She didn't know what she had done to deserve having Trevor walk into her life, but she was going to do her utmost to make sure he knew she appreciated it. Every single thing he did for her.

Somehow she was going to get to the other side of that brick wall, and when she did, she sure hoped Trevor would still be waiting for her.

Chapter Twenty

TREVOR DIPPED his head toward the phone, fighting to see who was calling him at seven a.m.

"Dad?" He'd seen Randy not even thirty minutes ago back at the barns.

"There's been a cancellation, so if we can get to Calgary by ten o'clock, they're gonna do more tests on me." Randy hesitated. "Part of me wants to say to hell with it, but I promised you and your mother, so I'm ready to go. You drive your truck, though, so if we get stopped for speeding, the ticket goes on your record, not mine."

Trevor snickered as he hit the brakes and pulled a U-turn, gravel flying up from under the wheels, a cloud of dust rising as he changed direction and moved back toward the main house. "Let Steve know we'll be gone today?"

"I'll do that now," Randy promised.

The trip to Calgary took less than the three hours it should have, but the rest of the traffic on Highway 2 was also traveling well above the limit. Randy stayed pretty quiet the entire trip, and Trevor didn't want to push.

Besides, he had enough on his mind to keep him occupied all on his own.

Becky's terror the previous night had scared the beejeezus out of him at the time. She'd been so on board with everything they'd done along the way he'd...not *forgotten*—there was no way on earth he'd ever forget what had happened to her—but more like *assumed* she'd ended up with no long-term trauma.

He was a fucking ass for pushing too hard, too soon. He was going to keep it in his pants from now on until she was good and ready.

They pulled into the clinic with plenty of time to spare. Randy got called nearly right away while Trevor sat in the chair he was directed to, flipping halfheartedly through a magazine and wishing he had something else to entertain him.

Stupid. Of course—they were on the north end of town, with plenty of stores around. He double-checked at the nurse's station to find out how long his dad was supposed to be, then took off to do a little shopping.

Summertime, and the mall was full of teenagers and moms with strollers. He waited at a set of doors, holding it open for a frazzled woman who was corralling along four kids. He felt sorry for her up until one of the kids slipped a hand into hers, and she looked down with a smile that wiped away a lot of the tiredness from her eyes.

It was enough to set Trevor pondering. Maybe he didn't get the rug-rat thing, but obviously *other* people did.

...which made him think about Becky and her concern for her sister.

Did he want Sarah and her kids trapped in the hell that was Paradise Settlement? No, especially not after he'd done a Google search and found out more about the place, way back when Becky had mentioned it the

224

first time.

He wouldn't want a dog raised in that setting.

An ugly, barely contained anger simmered in his gut. Sarah had dragged her sister into danger knowing what might happen. He'd never tell Becky that, or tear down her sister in front of her, but the whole shit-storm made him ultra-wary.

He honestly ached for the innocent kids stuck where they didn't belong, the sensation strange and new, but he didn't see any way for him to change things. If the government couldn't shut the cult down, how was a simple rancher from nowhere supposed to make a difference?

Right now the only person he could make a difference to was Becky.

He walked past a shop window filled with pretty little knickknacks, his feet jerking to a stop. He slipped in the door to look around in the hopes of finding something that would put a smile on her face. He made his way back to the clinic with a few minutes to spare, dropping into one of the uncomfortable waiting room chairs and trying to distract himself with a magazine.

His dad escaped the back room the instant the nurse opened it for him, heading out of the clinic like his ass was on fire.

Trevor rushed ahead to open the door. "You need us to stop anywhere?"

His dad shook his head. "Just get me home."

It was a quiet ride for the first hour before Trevor thought it was time to break the silence. "You were going to torment me with descriptions of everything that they did to you."

Randy made a rude noise. "Trust me, even I'm not that mean. But they're done, and hopefully this time we

225

find out something more than I'm getting old."

"You're not old," Trevor assured him. "Other than this stupid illness, you're probably in the best shape out of all your brothers."

"You're buttering me up for some reason," Randy accused, but he smiled. "Mike's got an excuse. He is a good bit older than the rest of us."

"Mike, and then Ben?"

"George, me, then John and Mark."

Another cold sensation hit his gut. Sadness at the loss, and the missed opportunities death brought. "They were twins, right?"

Randy grunted. "That's not a secret."

"No, I guess, not." He'd been too wrapped up in his own head to care. "Did Mark leave because his twin died?"

For the longest time his dad sat in silence before sighing. "Fine. You want all the dirty laundry, it's yours. Maybe it's time anyway. Hell, who knows how much longer I've got—"

"Don't," Trevor snapped. "Don't you fucking go and put yourself on your deathbed before your time."

So much for being reassuring and gentle. Trevor gave himself a mental slap upside the head.

But all he got from his father for his rudeness was a chuckle. "You sounded like your mother just then."

"She's a smart woman."

Randy nodded. "Damn right she is. But this is something you should know about, and I'd prefer to be the one to tell you than have you get rumours or bullshit down the road. Mark didn't want to ranch. He was a bit like your cousin Daniel in that way. Had other things that he was interested in, but we needed him, so he stuck around longer than he wanted. And he stuck around because John needed him."

Trevor felt like he had to move cautiously or the conversation would come to an end before it'd begun. "Was there something wrong with John?"

A soft shrug lifted his father's shoulders. "Nothing that you could come right out and say, but he was moody. He'd get lost in what he was doing, and was easily distracted. Mark could always pull him out of it. Just like you're always able to lighten up any situation. Sometimes you do it by making people laugh, even if that means they're laughing at you." Randy stared out the front window, drumming his fingers on the armrest. "Mark was like that, and we all relied on him. Our folks were gone by then, and it was just us boys. Mike in charge, Ben complaining about things. George with stars in his eyes, and dreams about horses."

"And you, if memory serves me from what Uncle Mike shared, you were the family peacemaker." Trevor heard the admiration in his voice, and he hadn't had to try to put it there.

His father laughed. "Peacemaker, *ha*. I was the one most willing to mix it up and get in people's faces. Or use my fists, if need be." He shook his head. "And maybe that is a peacemaker in this crazy clan of ours. But Mark held a special place, only it was slowly killing him, and we didn't even notice."

"What happened?"

Their eyes met for a second before Trevor had to focus back on the highway. "Mark had enough. He told us he was leaving in the fall, after he'd helped with one more harvest. It was strange to think of him being gone, but when the time rolled around, we mostly accepted it."

"Then he left?" It didn't sound that terrible. It didn't sound like a secret that needed to be kept for thirty years.

"He left, and John went quiet. We thought they were just missing each other—you know that weird connection some twins seem to have? But John faded away more and more, until the morning he didn't show up for chores." Randy's knuckles were white on the armrest where he clutched it. "We found him later that day. In the dugout beside the barn."

Jesus Christ. The truck lurched as Trevor snapped it back into the proper lane on the highway, his heart in his stomach. "You think he killed himself?"

Randy made a noise of pain. "God, this isn't the time to be telling you this—"

Trevor pulled off the side of the road into the next rest stop, hitting the brakes and jerking the truck to a halt as soon as he could. He twisted toward his father. "What the hell happened?"

His dad took a deep breath. "Yeah, I think John killed himself. I bet now he would've been diagnosed with depression or something, and it'd only been Mark who'd pulled him through for so long. Once that buffer was gone, he got worse and worse until he didn't think there was any other way out."

Heart wrenching and stupid. "It was nobody's fault," Trevor said.

"I know that now, but in those days it was a lot harder to understand. And then we couldn't get hold of Mark to let him know—he'd fallen off the face of the earth as if he didn't give a damn what had happened. So we got angry, and we set blame. Ben and George, and me. Mike, he tried his best to make us see reason, but we weren't having any of it."

"How come the rumour mill doesn't know how John died?" Small towns, with their long memories never

forgot a scandal or a painful falling-out amongst family.
"Because it could have been an accident." Randy
turned toward him, face drawn with sorrow. "The doc
called it an accident, and hell, maybe it was. John wasn't
healthy. Maybe he'd fallen in and couldn't get out, and
that was the end. But it wasn't suspicious, not to anyone
else."

"Just to you, because you knew what John had
been acting like."

"*God.*"

The pain in his dad's voice made Trevor reach
over and give his arm a tight squeeze.

"I found him," Randy confessed, his strong voice
weak and shaking. "I pray I never have to deal with
another moment like that in my entire life. It breaks
something in you. To know you're too late. To know you
didn't do enough."

Trevor waited in silence, the faint click of the
engine fan the only noise as Randy pulled himself
together.

"All three of us brothers who were married at the
time had kids on the way—you, and Daniel, and Ben's
son Michael, and it was hard enough to have John gone,
and Mark missing in action. That was one hell of a
mixed-up year."

"It would've been brutal. I can see that."

Randy laid a hand on his shoulder. "You were a
gift. All three of you boys born that year seemed to have
a special ability to make other people happy. But at the
same time, there was a deep bitterness that grew, and
when Mark finally did show up months later, none of us
were very welcoming. Mike was okay, and he's always
had an open-door policy toward Mark, but the rest of us?
We weren't big enough, even once we realized it was no

one's fault."

One hell of a story. "So where do things sit now? I mean obviously Mark still owns the land—that's the rental where Becky lives."

"He never gave it up, but after that first time he came home and got doors slammed in his face, or worse, accusations and shouting, he's never been back." Randy leaned back in the chair. "I don't blame him."

"Is he welcome? If he wanted to come?" Trevor asked cautiously, even though it made no sense to him.

It took a long time before Randy answered him.

"There're a lot of years of bitterness built up. While I don't think it's his fault anymore, I feel guilty as hell for all of the wrongs that happened, and I don't know how we could possibly fix that, Trevor." Randy dipped his head. "Of course he'd be welcome to come, but I don't know that he likes us very much. I don't like us very much, and I think some mistakes can never be repaired. Like a bit of land that's been poisoned. Even if you try to put new healthy seed into the soil, it's never going to grow."

Trevor waited again, but Randy sat without saying any more, so he put the truck back in gear and aimed them toward Rocky Mountain House. Sitting silently and thinking over everything he'd learned.

Sadness settled in his soul.

His family had always seemed kind of untouchable. Oh, Uncle Ben was an ass, and there were fights and bickering among the cousins at times, including a lingering tension between his generation's twins, Jesse and Joel.

To learn there was a layer of rot deep in their history choked something inside him.

It didn't have to be there, his heart insisted.

But then he considered how he felt when Becky discussed her sister. How much she obviously wanted to be in touch with the woman, and how the mere idea sent streaks of disgust, and anger, and fear through him. He didn't want her having anything to do with the person who had caused such deep abiding pain, unintentional or not.

Trevor might be able to see the broader picture, in Becky's case, and in the case of his uncles. Didn't mean he knew how to navigate the dangerous emotional currents tangled up in both situations.

Didn't mean he wasn't going to try.

Chapter Twenty-One

RACHEL HAD done everything to try to convince Becky they needed a night on the town, but the whole idea of heading out in public with strange men around made her twitch.

Maybe Rachel was as good protection as anyone, and maybe they didn't have to worry, but Becky still wasn't comfortable going somewhere like Traders without Trevor along.

She wasn't going to apologize for that, either. "If we want to have a get-together, we can do it at my place," she suggested.

Rachel rolled her eyes. "Ah, *no*. The point of this is that *you* get to have some fun and not have to clean up after everybody when we're done. If you really don't want to go out, and I won't make you, we'll have the party here."

"Party?" Becky tried to keep the panic out of her voice, but it was tough. "How many people are we talking about?"

Her friend hesitated. "Okay, I'll cut down the invite list. Who do you want on it?"

"You."

A laugh escaped. "That's no longer a party, by any

stretch of the imagination."

Becky thought it over. "Anna? And Melody if she isn't working?"

"A Moonshine gathering. We can do that."

Which was how she ended up a couple nights later being escorted into Rachel and Lee's house by a very amused Trevor.

"I like that you like my family," he teased, the words whispering past her ear as they waited at the front door for someone to answer their knock.

She bumped him with her elbow. "They're good people. That's why I put up with you."

He hissed as if in pain. "Low blow."

The door swung open, and Rachel appeared, decked out in comfy leggings and an oversized flannel shirt. She welcomed Becky in then blocked the path. "Go away, Trevor," she ordered.

Trevor's laugh filled the room. "Awww, don't be like that. You need me around for entertainment."

A Nerf football flew across the room and smacked him in the side of the head. "You're more entertaining when you're not here," Anna taunted. "Now get out, this is my first night off in a long time, and Mitch is picking me up at midnight."

"A curfew? Poor girl."

Anna bounced up on the couch, grinning at him. "He's my designated driver, and that's when the party turns private and moves to our house. Now go away, you're harshing my buzz."

Becky peeked around Rachel, showing him shining eyes. "Are you going to pick me up later?"

"Since you're going to be drinking, for once I won't offer to leave my truck." He crooked a finger to motion her forward. "Give me a goodbye kiss then I'll be out of your hair."

Maybe she should've been more embarrassed to be the center of his attention while the other girls watched, but it didn't take long to totally forget they had an audience, because it was all about him, and how sweet it was to have his mouth on hers. His hands gentle on her hips even as his thumbs snuck under her top to brush the bare skin of her waist.

He tapped a finger on her nose before stepping back onto the porch. "See you later."

A promise that meant so much more than the words.

He hadn't said anything about their disastrous undertaking a few nights earlier. It was as if it hadn't happened. He'd still come around regularly to help in the garden, showing up whenever possible to give her a ride or to join her for a long walk on the gravel road in the evening.

She'd appreciated that he'd made her panic seem not nearly as big of a deal as it was. Now if her *body* would only figure out sex wasn't a big deal she'd have the solution to her problem.

Becky twisted on the spot, pushing aside thoughts of Trevor so she could enjoy her evening with the ladies.

The other three women were all lined up, ear-to-ear smiles as they stared back.

"What?"

Melody motioned her forward. "You're so adorable. Like a cuddly puppy who's fallen into a big box, and you're completely delighted by the surprise you don't even realize where you are."

Rachel patted the spot next to her on the couch. "Which isn't an insult, by the way. Anytime Melody breaks out puppy analogies, it's as good as her saying she loves you."

"Don't you think she's cute?" Melody asked, pulling her legs under her as she sat by the coffee table. "Becky, I'm teasing."

"It's okay," Becky responded. "I feel like a puppy at times, wandering around, not quite sure what's going on. But there are an awful lot of people giving me pats on the head and taking care of me. I can't complain about that."

She found herself getting an impulsive hug from Rachel before they all turned to the sound of Anna offering a cheer. She'd opened the box resting on the dining room table and was staring into it with delight.

"What'd you bring?" Rachel asked.

"Mitch went to town and promised to stock up on party supplies for us."

"We've already got food and drink." Melody pointed at the loaded table behind them.

Anna reached in and pulled out a handful of small bottles the size of a couple of fingers. "He grabbed samplers." She glanced at Becky. "I'm all about drinking responsibly, so if you're interested in trying some different things, now is the time."

"Drinks?" Becky joined Anna by the box. There were dozens of miniature liquor bottles of all sorts and shapes. "I don't want to get drunk, but it would be nice to know what I like."

"Not beer, right?"

She shook her head. "I've tried a few different types now and none of them work for me."

"It's not like you *have* to drink," Melody said. "Some people do, and some don't."

But the point was she didn't know if she wanted to because she'd never had the chance. And other than knowing beer was definitely not her friend, she didn't know where to start.

"Maybe I'll decide I don't want to drink, but like you said"—she glanced at Anna—"this is a safe place to try."

Rachel rubbed her hands together. "Let me get my iPad and I'll pull up a bartender site. Tonight the Moonshine girls are going for a taste drive."

It sounded great, and fun, and it wasn't until Rachel and Melody came back with a tray full of empty glasses and a bucket of ice that the words really registered.

Moonshine girls.

Rachel had included her as a part of that group, and something very much like butterfly wings set off in her stomach. She liked Trevor, a lot, but to be included as a part of his family was even bigger, and something she hadn't dreamed possible.

While the girls settled around the coffee table, all of them sliding onto cushions on the floor, Becky held tight to that flutter of happiness. In spite of the continuing worries for her sister, and the huge weight hanging over her head when it came to sex, she couldn't help but be delighted with the laughter and friendship surrounding her.

A glass appeared under her nose.

"We'll start you easy." Melody raised her glass in a toast. "To trying new things."

"Rum and Coke, in this case," Anna pointed out, raising her own glass in the air so she could clink it with the others.

There was only about an inch of liquid in the bottom of the glass, dark and sweet smelling. Definitely Coke, which she knew, with an aftertaste that made her shiver. "Should I keep track of these, or something? Because depending how many you give me, I'm not going to be able to remember what I've tried."

"Already on it."

Anna patted the table in front of her, and Rachel let out a hoot of laughter. "Seriously? You're taking notes?"

"Of course. How else is Becky going to learn? Especially after she's had a dozen shots."

This time it was Melody who snickered. "I'm so glad you're all about drinking responsibly."

Anna nudged her glass toward Melody. "Shut up, and pour me a regular-sized one. You can do the tutti-fruity drinks for you three. I'll stick to these."

Melody pushed the two-liter bottle of Coke and a full-sized bottle of Rum toward Anna. "She's all yours. I don't think from the face Becky made that one's on her keeper list."

Becky shook her head. "Coke makes my nose itch."

"Don't blame the Coke just yet," Rachel teased, taking back the glass and pouring two more things together, one from a small white bottle. "How's this one?"

Another cautious sniff made her curiosity rise. Coke again, but this time a scent like coconut. The first sip went down a lot smoother than the previous drink. "Oh, that was nice."

Melody nudged Anna. "Make a note. Our girl likes Malibu."

The drinks were so small it probably took eight different samples before she'd had a full glass, but by then Becky was already lightheaded.

"I need a break." She got to her feet, wavering for a moment before catching her balance.

"Bathroom is down the hall, first door on the right," Rachel offered, following after her to the kitchen. "Snack time. Anna, open up Netflix. We're gonna do a taste test on movies to see what Becky likes."

LAUGHTER ECHOED all the way to the road, the lights in the house dimmed to almost nothing as he and Lee headed up the walk.

"You're like a horse running to the barn at the end of the day," Lee teased.

"I'll take you back to Traders to beat you some more at darts," Trevor threatened. "Besides, Mitch will be here soon, so unless you want to hold up your own party until later, let me grab my girl and head home."

The sound of a motorbike moving closer echoed down the street. "That's Mitch now."

"And Steve is already here." Trevor pointed to their brother's truck. "It's a family reunion."

They stood at the sidewalk until Mitch arrived, smoothly manoeuvering his oversized bike onto the driveway.

Their brother-in-law pulled off his helmet and hung it from the handlebars, a cocky grin breaking free as he spotted them waiting. "Did the girls have a good time?" he asked as he uncurled himself from the bike and joined them.

"Don't know for sure, but from the sound of the shrieking going on, I'd guess yes." Trevor moved to one side, giving Mitch room to join them as they walked toward the house.

"Missed you at Traders," Lee offered.

"Missed being there, but I'm doing extra hours at the shop with my youngest brother still out of town. He should be back soon. We can go again then."

"Look forward to it."

Funny to think Trevor had once beat the crap out of the man now prowling beside him like a barely controlled tiger. Of course, Trevor had always wondered if he'd been *allowed* to beat the crap out of Mitch—luckily some things just weren't discussed, and now they got along gangbusters, and that's what mattered.

They marched inside only to jerk to a halt, Mitch and Lee bumping against his back as they discovered Steve standing silently in the shadows just inside the door.

The reason they were waiting was clear—three of the women were seated on the couch watching Rachel who was bathed in the blue light of the television. Music played in the background, but Rachel was the main attraction. Her hair fell in a riotous mess, the top buttons of her shirt undone, the tails hanging loose, and she was making the most *interesting* noises. Her eyes were closed, and one hand lay on her chest, the other curled over her abdomen as she undulated her torso.

Melody, Anna and Becky were laughing hysterically, gasping for breath as Rachel let out an exceptionally long moan, her head tilting back as if she were in ecstasy.

"Jesus, I wonder how much she's had to drink?" Lee muttered as he pushed past Trevor into the room. "Rach. What the hell—?"

Rachel snapped upright, her eyes popping open as the other women whirled on the spot, laughter turning to shouts. Anna howled as Rachel covered her face, and the whole room was filled with happy chaos.

Whatever they'd been up to, they hadn't expected company yet. "Do you want us to go away for a while longer? Or should we join the party?" Trevor teased as he marched to the couch.

Rachel straightened her clothes rapidly, her cheeks flushed red as Lee curled an arm around her waist and pulled her close. "All I know is whatever Rachel's having, I want part of it," he said, his voice full of innuendo.

She smacked a hand against his chest before tilting her head back to offer him a sultry glance. "Where do you think I got my inspiration from?"

Anna and Melody had finally caught their breath, rising to their feet and heading toward the kitchen as Trevor made a beeline for Becky.

"Ready to go home?" he asked as she stepped toward him, reaching out her hand. He ignored it, pushing past her fingers until their bodies came into full contact and he could give her a proper kiss hello.

Hell, yeah. She threw her arms around his neck and shimmied in close, warm curves nestled in tight as she opened her mouth and let him deepen the kiss.

"She can't answer with your tongue in her mouth," Rachel deadpanned.

"Maybe they've got that mental telepathy thing going on," Melody suggested.

"They got *something* going on."

Trevor pulled back reluctantly, keeping Becky at his side as he gave Lee a grin for his last comment. "Looks like everybody was having fun."

There was a shriek of laughter from the door followed by the screen door banging shut. They moved to the window to see Mitch strolling casually down the driveway with Anna tossed over his shoulder. She was laughing still, pushing up with her hands on his back so she could wave goodbye toward the window, seeming not at all displeased with being kidnapped.

"Our goodbyes were taking too long," Steve rumbled with amusement. He waggled his brows at Melody. "It sounds like a good idea to me."

Melody backed away as he reached toward her like he was about to pick her up. "Don't you dare," she warned, pausing to give Rachel and Becky hugs before heading out, her arm wrapped around Steve.

Trevor was eager to get home as well. Becky had slipped her hand into his, returning close by his side. "Ready to go?" he asked again.

She nodded, offering Rachel a brilliant smile. "I had such a good time. Thank you."

"You're welcome, sweetie. And you're not even drunk, so you can keep partying," Rachel offered with a wink, leaning back into Lee's chest. He curled his hands around her hips and rested his chin on her shoulder, looking very comfortable.

Looking very much like he had an agenda that would kick into gear the minute Trevor and Becky left, which was fine because Trevor had plans of his own.

Becky curled up against him inside the truck, legs on the seat, her hands wrapped around his biceps as he took them into the country. "That was so much fun."

"It sounded like it."

She giggled, hiccupping once before giggling again. "I'm not drunk," she informed him.

"So Rachel said." He still wasn't going to do anything unless she was completely sober, and from the way she was giggling, the *good time* had involved a fair amount of alcohol.

Only she hadn't gotten the memo about not doing

241

anything, because she shifted position until she could nuzzle her lips against his neck. "I did have some drinks, and I can report back on my favourites, but all I've been drinking for the past three hours is pop. And water. *Lots* of water, because Melody brought these things she said were made of buffalo, but they were so hot my tonsils were roasting."

"Buffalo wings," Trevor said, keeping his amusement out of his voice as best he could. "It means hot and spicy chicken wings. Did you like them?"

"Up until they attacked my taste buds, yes." She took a little nip at his ear lobe, and he gripped the steering wheel tighter to keep going in a straight line. "And then the girls showed me a bunch of their favourite movie clips. There was an awful lot of kissing in them."

And that explained Rachel's little role-playing at the end there. *When Harry Met Sally* was never going to get old. "Let me guess. There had to have been at least one scene from *Pride and Prejudice*. Mr. Darcy. Old-time clothing, and he dives into a lake."

Laughter escaped in the form of warm air rushing past his cheek. "Melody played that one, and the girls teased her for it. Then Rachel put on this clip that had someone doing weights and a whole bunch of bodies in a swimming pool. I wasn't quite sure what was going on most of the time, but it was hot."

Jeez. Trevor was laughing now as well, even as her tongue circling his ear was driving him crazy. "Rachel showed you porn?"

"No porn. That was a rule—it had to be a movie or TV show. I can't remember the title. Something about senses." Lips wrapped around his earlobe then she sucked, and he was perilously close to pulling over the truck to give her something else to put her mouth on.

"Want to go to your place or mine?" He had to grit the words out.

"I don't care." She undid the top buttons of his shirt, her hands slipping underneath to stroke his chest muscles. "I want to fool around."

God, she was on fire. "Those movies got your engine running."

"I guess. Mostly, though, *you* get my engine running. You're so sexy. I think about you, and it's like this match lights inside me, and I ache."

He passed her driveway, heading to his place, definitely going faster than the speed limit. "Hold that thought for three more minutes."

She dragged her fingernails over his chest. Talk about aching—his cock was sitting at an awkward angle for being at full mast, and there wasn't room to wiggle. He took the corner into his driveway on two wheels, roaring up to the front door and slamming into park.

The instant he turned off the ignition, his seatbelt clicked free, snapping away as Becky crawled into his arms. They tangled together as he shoved open the door and carried her with him, her mouth over his as she wrapped herself around him.

Trevor stepped forward blindly, drunk on the taste of her. He wasn't sure how he made it up the steps, or into his house, but moments later he had her pressed against the wall inside the door, desperate to satisfy his hunger as he licked into her mouth, teasing and making her gasp.

Even as he raced forward he checked for any complaints at his rough actions. Nothing, not words or physical retreat. In fact she jerked the front of his shirt hard enough a few buttons flew free, rattling on the floor as she desperately shoved the material from his shoulders.

"Take it off," she demanded when he let them up for air, her fists still tangled in the fabric as she tugged fruitlessly.

He didn't want to stop, not even to get naked. Her mouth drew him back like a bee to sweet nectar. But between kisses his clothes vanished. Shirt jerked forward over his head and tossed to the side. Her fingers on his belt, pulling it apart before she slipped from his arms and fell to her knees in front of him. She planted dirty kisses along his hipbones, her tongue tracing his skin and leaving behind wet streaks.

She tugged his jeans over his hips before reaching for his briefs and peeling them down his thighs. His cock sprang free and she hummed as if delighted. "My turn."

Trevor placed an elbow on the wall, leaning his body over her as she wrapped her fingers around his length, a delightful mix of inexperience and eager enthusiasm. "You've never done this before."

"I want to." She tilted her head back until her gaze met his, fire flashing in the brown depths. "I want to make you feel good, like you've done for me. And the idea excites me. Makes that ache inside turn brighter. Hotter."

He wasn't about to argue. "I get excited when I go down on you. Sex is fun, and it feels good to make someone else feel good."

She stroked him timidly, her hand gentle, her tongue slipping out to wet her lips. "Teach me?"

The sweet innocence of her request made him shiver with anticipation. "Use your tongue and lick all around the head."

He pressed his hand over hers to angle his cock downward slightly so it was easier for her to reach. She straightened her spine, and her mouth ended up in line with his cock as she leaned forward to obey his command. The first, tentative flicks with her tongue slowly grew more confident, until she covered him with her lips, licking up the spill of seed that had escaped.

She teased his slit for a moment and he moaned in approval. "Put your hand around me right at the base of my cock. That's it," he said, covering her fingers with his and showing her how hard to stroke. "Squeeze me, like that. Oh, hell *yeah*, that's right."

Becky stroked smoothly with a firm, strong grip. Pleasure rippled up his spine, especially when she put her mouth back on him, slowly moving her head over his length before pulling back. She did it again, a little deeper, repeating the motion until her lips finally met her fist.

"Fuck, Rodeo. That feels so damn good."

She didn't need lessons, or maybe he was so enthralled with her enthusiastic technique that he didn't give two hoots that she wasn't deep-throating him or something. The wet heat surrounding him made his cock hard and his balls draw up tight to his body.

His cock was completely wet, the moisture from her lips making it easier for her hand to slide. She pulled back to cover the head, teasing the sensitive spot right where he liked it best with the tip of her tongue until he was seeing stars.

She sped up her hand motion, twisting slightly at the end of each pulse. Trevor pulled his fingers through her hair, gathering it into a ponytail and looping the length around his fist so he could watch every second.

"So damn beautiful," he breathed, amazed that she would do this for him. Pushing away the urge to come because he wanted her to enjoy this as well. "Put your hand in your pants. Touch yourself while I fuck your mouth."

Her gaze flicked upward, a moment of confusion visible.

"Don't worry, I won't go too far." He pressed his other hand to her cheek and slowly rocked forward, holding her head in place and taking control.

He repeated it slowly, so slowly. The head of his cock barely resting on her lower lip before sliding forward just far enough she didn't pull away.

With her hands free, she undid her jeans and pushed under the pale white panties he could barely glimpse.

"That's it," he encouraged, waiting until she made contact with her clit, the tension in her body changing from anticipation to gathering pleasure. He tightened his grip on her hair, holding her motionless as he pressed forward again. Pleasure streaked up his spine, his gaze fixed on the way the material moved, pushed by her fingers as she increased the speed of her stroke.

Slow pulses now, barely more than the head of his cock in her mouth, but whenever she swallowed, whenever she closed around him, it sent an extra *zing* through his body.

She made a little noise, rocking gently, close to coming. When her lashes fluttered, Trevor lost it. Becky's hand jerked and a throaty cry echoed as she came.

He kept from driving forward, instead pulling from her mouth and grabbing his cock tight. Jerking frantically for one, two more times before losing control, his release spurting out with near violent pressure. He caught her on the face with the first shot before turning away and spilling on the floor, dark spots rising in front of his eyes at the sheer relief.

He rolled into the wall with a shoulder and slid to the floor beside her, cock still hanging out, tremours shaking him. Becky fell back on her heels in an untidy collapse of her own.

She pulled her hand from her pants, fingers glistening from the sweet moisture of her body. Trevor caught her hand and pulled it to him, licking her fingers clean as she stared wide-eyed.

They sat in silence, except for their heavy breathing, languid with pleasure. He was about to say something when she stole back her hand, wiping away the strand of moisture still clinging to her cheek.

She considered her fingers intently, then lifted them to her mouth, touching her tongue to his seed, all the while staring him in the eye.

"Sweet *Jesus*, Rodeo."

Her lips twisted into a filthy, satisfied smile. "Next time, I want you to come in my mouth."

He'd thought his head was done spinning, but he was wrong. "You're learning dirty tricks. I like that."

She batted her lashes, and they both burst out laughing, still breathless from what had gone before.

Trevor leaned in and kissed her before breathing an invitation against her lips. "Come on. It's time for bed."

Chapter Twenty-Two

IT DIDN'T make any sense to feel shy after what they'd done, but she did. Her cheeks heated as he helped her to her feet and they both straightened their clothes.

"Are you going to drive me home?"

Trevor linked his fingers through hers and pulled her down the hallway. "Stay with me," he said. "We don't have to fool around anymore, but I want to sleep with you."

Another first. Did she want this?

Her feet were answering before her mouth announced her decision, willingly following Trevor. "I don't have any pyjamas."

A low chuckle sounded as they entered his bedroom. "You really think that's going to be a problem, Rodeo?"

She was surprised when he threw her one of his oversized T-shirts, mischief on his face.

"You mean you don't expect me to sleep in the nude?"

He shrugged. "I'm not going to object if you do, but the shirt works. Go ahead and use the bathroom. There should be a new toothbrush in the drawer. I'll be back in a minute."

Becky waited until he'd left to slip into the bathroom, amazed yet glad to find herself comfortable at the thought of sleeping with him. She brushed her teeth quickly before returning to the bedroom to get undressed. She took off her jeans and folded them, leaving them on the chair beside the bed, then slipped his shirt over her head. Trevor's shirt hung to mid-thigh, the soft fabric caressing her skin as she eyed his bed.

It was big. Bigger than the beds she'd ever been in before. It was neatly made, enough that she couldn't tell just from looking what side Trevor usually slept on. She crawled under the covers and moved to the very middle, the sheets cool around her thighs as she waited, feeling very awkward and yet very mellow.

It'd been a *good* night. She'd enjoyed her time with the girls, and what had happened in the hall. And the idea of cuddling with Trevor all night seemed like the perfect end to the day. Only...

It really was a big bed.

"Such wide eyes," Trevor said softly as he walked in the door. "Are you okay with this?"

She nodded quickly. "I didn't know which side you want."

"Oh, right where you are."

Becky paused, not sure which way that meant she should move.

He laughed. "Don't worry, we're not going to take up that much room."

She wasn't quite sure what he was talking about until he stripped to his briefs and joined her, pulling her into his arms. He settled around her like a blanket, one arm over her stomach, his hand sliding up to cup her breast.

"*Oh.*"

249

Trevor made a soft noise, pressing his nose into the hair at the back of her neck. "Don't worry, I'm not gonna get you all riled up again. I've got early chores, and I'll probably be gone before you wake. I just like feeling you in my arms."

He fell silent, his chest rising and falling in an even rhythm, moving slowly against her back. The sheets had warmed up, and everywhere she was toasty warm.

She should've been exhausted, after a full day of work and partying with the girls, yet she was strangely alert, wonderfully satisfied at being limb to limb with him. The hair on his legs tickled slightly, and he might've said they weren't going to fool around, but his cock was *there*, pressed against her backside.

Not ten minutes later Trevor stroked her arm. "You're fidgeting. Are you uncomfortable?"

"Lying here with you? No, this is perfect. I'm not sleepy."

He kissed the side of her neck. "You had fun with the girls?"

"They're amazing. So easy to be with. I appreciate that a lot." She wasn't sure why she was surprised when good things kept happening. "I've been so lucky. Ever since I ran away, I've had nothing but good people come into my life."

"I'm glad."

Becky rolled under his arm until she faced him, pressing a quick kiss to his lips. "You're one of those good people."

"Well, I'm glad of that too. Nothing much I do that's special, though."

He had no idea. But his words made her think back. "That day I ran away, I wasn't sure what might happen. When Mark picked me up, there must have been guardian angels watching over me because I would've taken any truck that came along at that point."

Trevor stroked her hair gently. "Things could have ended badly."

She nodded. Maybe it was the combination of drinking and fooling around, but she was so relaxed she couldn't feel uncomfortable, not even bringing up her worst fears. "I was prepared for about anything, or at least I thought I was. I figured the worst that would happen was some driver would agree to give me a lift, but he'd want sex in exchange."

His grip tightened briefly before he went back to caressing her. "I'm damn glad that didn't happen."

"Me too, but in some ways, it wouldn't have been any worse than what had been happening back at the settlement. It would've been a step away from being trapped."

"I'm so sorry all that happened to you."

"I know." She considered. "Maybe Mark was my guardian angel. I mean, he could have left me at the next truck stop, and I would have been grateful, but he did so much more."

Trevor pressed his fingers under her chin and tilted her head back so he could kiss her. Once on the lips. Once on each eyelid. Once on the tip of her nose. "It's in your past. You've moved on."

"Paradise Settlement is still there, though," she pointed out, sadness making her ache inside. "That's still the world my sister faces every morning when she wakes up. Not the part about being shared—Abel never did that to her. But she's never going to get the chance to do so many of the things I've done over the past months. She's trapped, just like I was, and so are her kids, especially the girls."

Becky leaned her head against his chest and took a deep breath. Someday. Someday she'd be able to make a difference in her family's life.

The day caught up with her in a rush and she snuggled in tight.

"You getting sleepy?" he whispered.

"*Hmmm.* You should sing me a lullaby," she suggested in a whisper.

A soft noise snuck out from him. "You're an amazing woman, Becky Hall. Now go to sleep."

He did. Sing to her, that is. Not any child's song she recognized, but a soft collection of words that talked about oceans, and opening doors and dancing. But the loudest sound was his heart, beating solidly under her ear as it guided her into a deep, restful sleep.

THE ENTIRE day he'd done chores with his mind half on his task, and half on an idea that refused to go away.

Lee crawled back into the truck after closing a gate after them, bracing himself with a hand on the dashboard as Trevor drove slowly over the uneven ground toward the top of the ridge where the next cattle shelter stood. "I feel like something the cat dragged in, but you look as if you got less sleep than me. You going to last the rest of the day?"

"I slept fine," Trevor insisted. "We went to bed not that long after I picked Becky up."

That got him a low whistle in response. "So. I take it things are working out well. If you're spending the night together, and all."

"With me and Becky? Things are great." Other than that one unexpected issue, and he wasn't about to talk to his little brother about it. "I like spending time with her. She makes me feel good. And a bit guilty at how easy my life has been."

"I know what you mean," Lee offered, patting his shoulder briefly as they moved to dump bales from the back of the truck to the waiting cattle. "When Rachel was dealing with stuff with her ex, I felt useless. It was the most frustrating sensation ever—wanting to fix things and knowing there was nothing that I *could* fix."

Trevor flexed his biceps, lifting the bale by the binder twine and swinging it over the edge off the truck bed. The square bale landed with a gentle *thump* on the ground as the cattle moved forward eagerly. "Yeah. I pretty much know how to solve problems when it's things like fixing shit around the house, or if it involves a shovel or an axe. I don't know how to fix things that are hurting her on the inside. Or stuff like Dad being sick, and how frustrated he is with the whole situation."

"There's nothing we can do except be there for them," Lee said. "It takes time. If it's something bad, maybe suggest she talk with a counselor, but then everybody is different. You've got to let her decide when she's ready to do the next thing. "

Which is exactly what Trevor had been trying to do, so maybe he wasn't as stupid as he'd thought.

Only there was one thing not specifically related to Becky or his father, but connected to both that he *could* do. Of course, it involved one of his least favourite things ever, but screw it. He could handle a little mental torment.

He got home from chores and found a note on the table from Becky. A reminder she was working late, and that she'd see him the following day.

She'd signed it with a simple *B*, and a little smiley face, and the shorthand thrilled him more than anything—she was learning all the time. Finding her way in this big new world.

Trevor turned to a clean piece of paper and stared at it for a while before he decided what the hell. Maybe his words wouldn't be pretty, but no one would grade him on this.

It was something worthwhile doing, and in the end as he read his letter through before stuffing it in an envelope to be addressed and stamped, he figured it had turned out okay.

> *Uncle Mark*
> *It's strange to write to someone I don't know, yet I do.*
>
> *So much of my life has been spent with the Coleman clan that I can't imagine what it must've been like for you when you left. I'm not writing to find out what happened, or to see if there's any way I can convince you to come for a visit.*
>
> *I'm writing to say thank you.*
>
> *My father says I remind him a lot of you. I think that's a fine compliment when I consider what I know about you. What I've heard in the past few months. Whatever it was that made you leave Rocky, I think you're still the kind of man that my dad told me you were. Giving and kind.*
>
> *Maybe you're not a rancher anymore. I don't know—Becky told me you were driving a big rig when she met you, so maybe that's what you do for a living, but I think you're still damn good at making things grow.*
>
> *When you picked up that runaway at the side of*

the road in the middle of a snowstorm, you saved her life. When you took the time to help her find her feet and start again, you planted a seed.

Yeah, this is about Becky. We've become good friends, partly because of you. When you sent her north and set her up at your house, you gave her a chance to stand on her own two feet, and I thought you might like to know she's doing real good. She'd never write to you to say that, because she wouldn't want to interrupt, or make you feel obliged to do more on her behalf. And I'm not writing this so that you feel like you have to respond, but I wanted you to know thank you from one of your nephews.

I think if you'd been around while I was growing up, we would have gotten along just fine. I get that couldn't happen, but so you know, my door is always open.

Trevor (Moonshine) Coleman

Chapter Twenty-Three

JUST LIKE Trevor had promised at the start of the summer, a perfect August day had arrived. With nothing but sunshine and temperatures in the thirties, they'd made plans.

As they bounced down a back road in the truck, Becky held on tight, a wide grin making her cheeks ache.

"We all kind of start at the same time, but everybody floats at whatever speed they want." Trevor was explaining the logistics of the float trip. "Most of the time people chat for a while then float away, but I'll stay with you. The Colemans won't be the only family on the river today, not with these temperatures."

"And it's going to take three hours?"

"Maybe a little more. We're doing the main river, not the one through our land because it's late enough in the season the runoff is too slow." He offered a grin. "We've got food and drink, and the sun is going to make it stinking hot before we know it. The river is shallow for the most part, and I'll stay close when it's not. You'll have a blast."

"My dog paddle is better now that we've gone to the swimming pool a few times." He'd been so patient even as he worked to not laugh at her swimming attempts.

She was building memories full of joy.

There were over a dozen vehicles waiting by the bridge, a dozen inflatable boats in various stages of fullness. She recognized a lot of faces, including one that made her bounce on the spot with delight.

"Rachel's here."

Trevor pulled her out his side of the truck into his arms for a kiss. "Swear I should be jealous. You've got a serious girl crush on her."

She couldn't say much in self-defense. "I like her."

"She likes you too." He pushed a plastic bottle into her hands before reaching into the back of the truck. "Put on some sunscreen while I get our stuff together."

There was so much going on she wasn't sure where to look. Even as she rubbed lotion over her bare arms she eyed the coolers being lowered into small rubber dinghies. Kids were being rounded up and herded in the right direction. Not all of them were Colemans, although she thought she recognized a few from the Canada Day party.

But Rachel and Lee were there. They were enough for her to focus on.

Trevor was back, taking the sunscreen from her hands and pouring some into his palm before he motioned her to turn around. "Don't want you to burn."

He rubbed the cream over her back and shoulders, fingers lingering under the edges of the tank top she wore. "I still don't have a swimsuit," she explained in apology.

"You look great," he assured her, stroking his fingers along the edge of the shorts Rachel had helped her cut out of an old pair of jeans. "Daisy Dukes. *Hmm.*"

"I don't know what that means." She shivered at

257

his touch.

He stopped tormenting her, stripping off his shirt to apply sunscreen to his chest. "That means I'm going to enjoy the view the entire trip down the river."

Becky was enjoying the view now, his hands drifting over his chest and abdomen. "You missed a spot."

Trevor raised a brow then offered the sunscreen back.

She'd been teasing, but she wasn't about to give up the opportunity. She loaded her hands with sunscreen then moved around him slowly, pretending to touch up spots, even ones that were sufficiently covered that she wanted to touch.

She was mesmerized by one muscle in particular. The one that wrapped around his hip, a cut line by his hip disappearing under the edge of his shorts aimed toward—

"Oh, my."

Trevor caught her fingers before she could move any lower. "I think I have enough sunscreen."

His words came out a low growl, and she glanced up into his eyes, heart pulsing rapidly at the way he was looking at her. "I guess you do."

He leaned in, ignoring the people around them. "I'm glad that river is going to be cold, or else everyone would see exactly what you do to me."

She was glad the water was cold because it cooled off her flaming cheeks, although it was good to know she had that effect on him.

"Coleman party leaving ASAP. Everybody ready?" A shout from the riverside.

Trevor tilted his head toward the water. "That's Daniel. His boys are chomping at the bit. Let's put them out of their misery and get going."

It was a bit of a madhouse for a while as people settled into rafts and pushed away from the shoreline. Daniel Coleman had his three boys, early teens from the looks of it, another handsome young Coleman acting as a second wrangler.

Trevor held her raft as she cautiously settled into it, filling her in on the new face. "That's Jesse. Six Pack, Daniel's younger brother."

"Who's he here with?"

Trevor dropped himself into his raft, and a splash rushed over the side of hers, making her gasp as he propelled them into the faster-moving water. He held on tightly to the rope around her raft edge, the two inflatable boats spinning slowly as they caught the current.

Then he finally answered her question, rubbernecking to spot the rest of the group. "Doesn't look like anybody, for a change. I heard he promised his nephews he'd come along with them."

It looked that way to her. Jesse held a raft on either side of his, only it didn't seem to be to keep the boys close. It was so they could splash water all over him as he shouted and pretended to be attacked by pirates. "Three hours of that, and they're going to be exhausted."

"I think that's what Daniel's hoping for," Trevor joked.

"Wait for us," Rachel called from somewhere upstream.

Becky twisted, trying to see where they were, and the edge of her raft dipped rapidly. "Oops."

Trevor steadied her, kicking to turn them until they were facing the right direction. "You gotta move slowly," he warned, "or you'll go for a swim."

He rested his hand on the edge of her raft and she

linked their fingers together.

Rachel and Lee were in the same position, holding hands as they rested one in a raft, one in an inner tube. "Aren't you going to get cold?" Becky asked.

"After we've been floating for about half an hour, you'll be filling your boat up with water to stay cool," Rachel informed her.

Lee pulled on a rope attached to the side of his boat, reeling in the small raft floating along behind them. "Who wants what?"

It was like Trevor had described before. The cooler was full of snacks and drinks, including a cider Rachel passed over with a smile. "One of your top five."

"This is fun." Becky approved completely, paddling her feet slowly as their boats drifted, spinning in a gentle circle as the direction of the current changed. "Does the water get any rougher than this?"

Trevor wiggled a hand. "A bit, in a couple places, but we'll give you lots of warning before we hit those sections. They're still not much more than ripples on the water."

Floating and chatting became the order of the day. Like Rachel had warned, it soon got hot enough they took turns slipping into the crystal-clear water to cool off. Wiggling back into the unsteady plastic boats involved a lot of laughter and helping hands.

Shouts rang out in the distance, and they all turned to discover Daniel and his boys standing on the riverbank.

Trevor squeezed her fingers. "Rope swing. Anybody want to try?"

"I'm too lazy today," Rachel said. "But if you guys want to, I'll wait for you."

Becky glanced at Trevor. "Do you want to?"

He looked shocked. "Becky Hall. When was the last time you did a rope swing?"

It had to be a trick question. "Never?"

"Then it must be on your bucket list." He leaned forward and gave her an enormous grin. "I think Becky wants to try."

They kicked their way to shore, a bubble of excitement rising in her belly as she considered this new thing. "I really have never done this before," she warned Rachel as they pulled their boats onto the riverbank.

Her friend nodded. "I'll go first."

"I thought you felt too lazy?"

"Changed my mind." She pointed up the hill. "Watch how it's done."

The tree she pointed to was massive, one long limb reaching out over the river. A rope had been attached two thirds of the way to the end.

One of the teens wrapped his hands around the rope just above a thick knot. He jumped slightly, feet leaving the small extension of rock he'd been standing on.

The boy swung in an arc far out to the middle of the river before letting go, hitting the water with a shout that cut off as his head went under. Another of the teens caught the rope on its return journey, waiting near the riverbank to snag the long, wiggling rope before sending it up to where his brother stood waiting.

"This is a nice section of the river," Trevor said, pointing as he explained the rest of the routine. "It's not too deep, and there's not much current, so swim on an angle to get out right *there*. See that sandy section? Follow the trail back."

Becky nodded, leaning into Trevor's arm as she watched another couple people do the rope.

Trevor's cousin went, dragging a hand through his hair before grabbing the rope and offering her and Rachel a cocky grin. "If you want to know how it's *really* done..."

Jesse stepped back farther and took a run at it, throwing himself off the ledge and leaning backward to wrap his legs around the rope. Becky covered her mouth with her hands as he swung over the river, arms extended to the side as if he was about to dive in.

But he didn't let go.

"He's going to hit the bank." Becky clutched Trevor's arm tight.

"He's fine, damn showoff," Trevor muttered, waiting as Jesse swung toward land, still well above the ground. He swung back and this time, even though he wasn't as far over the river, he let go, vanishing beneath the surface with a gentle ripple.

"That looks like fun," Lee announced. "I think I'll try—"

"No way, José." Rachel caught him by the hand and jerked him to her side. "You're going to make my heart stop, you know that?"

Lee gave her a heated kiss before backing away, smirking. "Fine. I'll do it the old boring, *safe* way, just for you."

"I get to go first," Rachel shouted, racing past Lee to where Daniel waited, holding the rope.

"Bunch of kids," Trevor teased.

Rachel launched herself off with not quite as much enthusiasm as the teens had, but she still made it a fair distance over the water before letting go.

On the return swing the rope barely had time to reach the shore before Lee leapt for it, throwing himself off the rock and catching the rope in midair, arching over the water and landing beside Rachel before she'd floated more than a few feet.

She screamed louder than when she'd hit the cold water.

Trevor clicked his tongue. "He's going to get in shit for that," he offered with a chuckle.

"You shouldn't sound so happy your cousin is in trouble," Becky chastised as they made their way up the riverbank to where Jesse waited, holding the rope.

Jesse knocked Trevor in the shoulder. "You forgot to tell Becky part of the fun of getting in trouble is making up."

Trevor nodded. "That goes without saying."

He guided her into position, standing at her back as he checked her grip on the rope, his body right up against hers. "You saw how it's done. Just hang on tight, and once you're over the water, let go any time."

She hadn't realized how far above the water they would actually be standing. "Trevor..."

"You can do this," he said encouragingly. "It's not nearly as bad as crawling out on your roof."

"I guess."

Trevor pressed a kiss between her shoulder blades, his arm round her waist squeezing for a moment. "You don't have to do it. Totally up to you."

The rest of their group had made their way back up the path and were standing by their boats, and she didn't want to make them wait, but—

She turned on the spot and thrust the rope at him. "You go first. I need one more minute."

Trevor nodded then repeated his offer. "Or we can walk down and hop back in the boats. That works too."

She took a deep breath. Maybe she didn't have to do this, but part of her really wanted to. "Can you go first and catch me?" she asked.

He kissed her quickly then took the rope and got into position. "I'll see you in the water."

He glanced over his shoulder as he jumped off the ledge sending the rope twirling. He landed with a huge splash; legs and arms sprawled wide. His family on the shoreline cheered, flashing fingers for scores.

"What was that?" one of the teens shouted. "A triple salchow?"

His brother let out a hoot. "That's skating, not diving, you dumbass."

"Hey, no calling your brother a dumbass," Daniel reprimanded his son. "Or at least not where I can hear it."

Jesse ran up the hill with the rope in his hand and presented it to her with a smile, pointing to where Trevor was treading water to stay in one spot. "There's your target, mi' lady. Go get 'em."

She nodded, flexing her fingers over the rope, tiny frayed strands rough against her fingertips. "I can do this," she muttered.

There was no way she was jumping off the ledge, but stepping off had the same result. She swung in an arc, momentum carrying her over the water in mere seconds as gravity pulled her down and forward. It was exhilarating, it was scary...

...and it was over, and she was close to Trevor.

"Let go, I've got you." His voice so solid and reliable.

She wasn't sure how she got her fingers to obey, but the next second the thrilling ride was done, and icy-cold water engulfed her. She barely closed her mouth in time before going under.

Fortunately, one kick was enough to get her to the

surface, and then Trevor had her, one hand wrapped around her belly as he pulled her against his chest, rolling them to their backs to stare into the robin-egg-blue sky overhead.

"That was so much fun," she shouted, splashing her hands like a little kid.

Trevor guided them toward the shore where the rest of the family all shouted and offered loud applause. Becky stood on the riverbank feeling a little embarrassed, but far too excited to let this moment slip away. She bowed, getting another cheer from Rachel, before Trevor led her back to where their rafts waited.

The next part of the journey was sunshine and salty snacks. Sweet iced tea, and even sweeter kisses that Trevor stole as they floated along.

The trees along the riverbank stood like tall sentinels, watching over them as they drifted past. Trevor's strong arm rested across her body as he kept their rafts next to each other, and Becky leaned her head back on the soft plastic of the raft and sighed happily.

THEY PASSED under another bridge, the smooth slope and easy access to the water making it a great spot for floaters to get in and out of the river. Some people left at that point, new people joined in, including two familiar faces for their party.

By now the Colemans were spread out over the water. Daniel and the boys had raced ahead, barely visible before they'd vanish around another curve in the river. Others were farther behind, like Lee and Rachel who had gotten busy kissing, their rafts floating close enough to the shore to get stuck.

Trevor wondered with a laugh how long it would be before they noticed.

"Hey, Joel," Trevor called. "Thought you couldn't make it."

Joel kicked their larger raft over until it bumped into Becky's. "Vicki got back early from camp, so we decided half a river trip was better than none."

The petite brunette waved, her dark eyes taking in him and Becky with interest. "Nice to meet you," she said. They grabbed onto the ropes on the larger craft, staying close so they could talk. "I've been gone cooking at teen camp all summer," Vicki offered with a smile as she leaned against Joel. "Are you settling into Rocky nicely?"

Becky nodded, answering back softly. Her fingers were tangled with Trevor's, relaxed and at ease, so while the girls talked, he and Joel caught up with each other.

Joel played with a strand of Vicki's hair, seeming not aware he was doing it. "Where're my brothers and nephews?" he asked. "I thought they were supposed to be out here."

Trevor flicked his thumb over his shoulder, pointing downstream. "Daniel and Jesse have them running point to scare off the bears."

"*Bears?*" Vicki and Becky exclaimed at the same time, with the same tone of panic.

He and Joel snickered.

"No, I'm kidding," he reassured Becky.

Vicki gave them both the evil eye. "You guys are so bad."

Joel looked thoughtful. "If you girls want to talk, how about you share the big raft for a minute, and give me the single. We'll go burn off a bit of energy."

Trevor waited until Becky nodded her approval. "I'm good with that," she insisted. "Go play."

Joel leapt into the water, leaving room for her to crawl precariously into the raft beside Vicki.

They left the two girls happily chatting, their boat spinning slowly. He and Joel paddled hard in pursuit of their targets. Within minutes they had sight of the rambunctious group.

"They've been shouting and carrying on like that for over an hour and a half," Trevor said.

"You think we were any different at that age?" Joel teased.

Trevor shrugged. "I guess not, but damn, I wish I still had that kind of energy."

They were hidden from sight behind a bend, closing in on the kids who were using water guns on each other, their dad and uncle. Heck, anything they could soak down within shooting range seemed to be fair game.

Joel laughed softly, then lifted a finger to his lips. "Grab my raft," he ordered softly.

There was barely time to obey before he rolled backward, disappearing with a splash into the water. Trevor held the extra raft, drifting ever closer to the chaos, no sign of Joel anywhere.

Jesse spotted him and shouted a warning. "Avast, ye matey, here be pirates."

A thin ripple disturbed the water beside his raft, and Trevor chuckled. "I think you need to worry more about the sharks, cuz."

Confusion drifted over Jesse's expression. He leaned forward at the exact moment Joel appeared out of nowhere, flying out of the water and tipping his twin's raft.

The nephews shouted in surprise, and Daniel's

laugh boomed out as Joel and Jesse resurfaced, matching grins on their faces.

"Jerk," Jesse said, obviously pleased with being dunked.

"Ass," Joel replied with a smirk. He tilted his head toward the boys. "Shall we?"

Jesse's grin widened, and they turned to the nephews with evil laughs. Blood-curdling screams followed, accompanied by frantic splashing and much laughter as the uncles worked together to topple the teens into the water.

After all the boys were back in their floats, and settled down, Jesse and Joel returned to the rafts Trevor had held while watching with amusement.

"We noticed you didn't get wet," Jesse taunted, mischief lingering in his eyes.

"Someone had to be witness to your victory, or those hoodlums would claim they'd trounced you," Trevor pointed out.

"True." Joel gave his twin a brotherly sock in the biceps. "You're looking relaxed. Good to see."

Jesse shrugged, leaning back with his hands behind his head as he closed his eyes. "I'm always relaxed. Not a worry in the world for me," he gloated.

Joel rolled his eyes, but didn't taunt back. Trevor glanced upstream before he copied his cousin's position, letting the river take him. The girls were only a few minutes behind now, and he let the raft slowly spin as he waited for them to catch up.

The sun had made him drowsy by the time they approached, feminine laughter pulling him from his relaxed state. He opened his eyes to discover Jesse staring at Vicki, his expression unreadable.

Trevor wasn't surprised when his cousin silently

twirled his raft away into the stronger current, moving back toward Daniel and the nephews before he had to greet Vicki.

Joel sighed, but didn't say anything as he stared after his twin, his disappointment and sorrow clear as he switched places with Becky.

Trevor held a hand out to pull Becky to him, her shining eyes bringing him back to a happier place. "Having fun?"

She nodded, joy on her face.

In spite of the things that weren't right, this part was. He pulled her close and counted his blessings.

Chapter Twenty-Four

"WELL...*DAMN it.*"

Trevor shuffled up onto his elbows, amused and shocked all at the same time. "Holy shit, you swore."

Becky's eyes narrowed, frustration rolling off her and slamming into him like a fist. "I think it's allowed."

"It's *not* a big deal—"

"It is *so.*"

She'd jerked away from his cock in a panic, but still straddled his hips as he sprawled on the bed. Both of them were naked as jaybirds, and had been fooling around for a good solid hour before things had fallen apart.

Becky straightened up to glare at him, folding her arms across her body like a shield. The position framed her tits into erotic art, and his cock, which hadn't gone down since they'd started teasing each other during dinner, somehow got harder.

"You hear me complaining? I don't hear me complaining." Trevor skimmed his fingers over her nipples, squeezing her breasts and going out of his mind with lust. Debating if he should curl up the rest of the way so he could play with her a little longer. "So damn soft. You make my brain crazy."

"But I froze again," she said grumpily even as she caught his hands and held them to her, a flicker of desire sneaking through her annoyance. "It doesn't matter what position we try, I just can't do it."

"And I don't fucking care," Trevor insisted. "I mean, I *care*, but it's not the end of the world."

The debate was over. He was vertical now, lifting her by the hips so he could drag a nipple in his mouth. Nipping and sucking until she forgot to worry about the traitorous way her body kept reacting every time they tried to have sex.

He wasn't bullshitting her. As much as he'd always enjoyed full-out fucking, he was having a blast. Ever since the night she'd slept over, they'd been fooling around on a regular basis. At her insistence they'd made a half dozen attempts at going all the way. Each had ended with her turning into a statue, blood draining from her face and her breathing cutting off the instant his cock slipped into her pussy.

No, that wasn't right. They hadn't *ended* that way. They'd ended with him finding a different way to get them off, which he was about to happily do once again.

Becky undulated over him, barely brushing his cock, and suddenly as good as her tits were, he had something else in mind.

"Come here." He caught hold of her hips, pulling her forward until the heat of her sex rested firmly over his aching cock. A groan of rising urgency escaped. "Fuck me like this."

"This isn't...*fucking*," she muttered on a moan as he guided her through the motions until she took over. She paused, maddeningly, wiggling back. She stripped the condom from him and tossed it aside. "You may as well enjoy this as much as possible."

"I always do. God *damn...*"

She'd slid over him, her wet sex wrapping around his length. He angled his hips to slide through her labia, not giving two fucks that he wasn't inside her because he had a tunnel of heat over him, and it was so damn good. He swore again. And again, seconds away from coming.

Her palm landed over his mouth, and she leaned over, giving him a dirty look. "No more potty mouth."

Trevor snickered, then licked her palm.

Becky pulled back with a squeal. He caught her hips and ground against her clit until they both lost it, his belly coated with streaks of semen, his cock wet from her body, and every inch of him sated and satisfied.

Becky collapsed to the bed beside him, her breasts rocking with her heavy gasps. "That was..."

"Freaking *awesome.*"

Her next gasp was part laugh, part sigh. "Yeah, I guess it was." She rolled up to rest her hands in his chest, chin settling on top of that. "But I wish things were different. With sex."

"Even though we had fun."

She blew in his face and made him blink. "You know what I mean."

He blew back and she smiled.

This wasn't a solution, though. It mattered to her, so it mattered to him. "We can find someone for you to talk to. A counselor. Someone who's trained how to help. That's the best I can think of."

Becky made a face. "I don't want to talk to anyone other than you."

Damn.

They ended with a compromise. The stubborn woman refused to give in just yet, but she did say he could ask someone he trusted for ideas.

Which was why he found himself driving to the middle of nowhere to track down his cousin Travis. It was going to be the most awkward conversation ever, but the man was happily living with and fooling around with two other people.

He had to have some ideas that could help.

Trevor had found himself doing a lot of strange things lately—like this mission, and sending off a couple more letters to his Uncle Mark. He hadn't heard back yet, but he was hoping the borderline-newsie updates that had damn near killed him to write would make his uncle curious enough to write back. Maybe even consider a visit, down the road.

Maybe start to heal some hurts.

Finding his cousin was one thing, starting the crazy conversation was another. Trevor stopped his truck beside a horse shelter then waited until Travis pulled to a halt, swinging down from the tractor cab and removing his headphones.

He glanced around, concern on his face. "Something wrong?"

Trevor shook his head, then nodded slowly. If it weren't so damn important, he wouldn't be standing there feeling like a jackass. "No emergency, if that's what you mean. I've got a question for you."

One brow rose as Travis eyed him. "I bet it involves sex, because you're twitching like you just got caught trying to get into some girl's pants."

How the hell did he...? "What? I mean, yeah, it does, but...*fuck*."

Yup, awkward. Damn it.

A loud snort of amusement escaped his cousin. "Ha, I was kidding. Don't tell me you're actually going to

273

ask me for sex advice."

"Only if you're okay with it. I don't want to cross any boundaries here."

"There's something you want to talk about that you can't ask Steve or Lee?" Travis's eyes narrowed. "You're seeing Becky, aren't you?"

Trevor nodded.

"You sure as hell better not be asking me for any information about having threesomes, because there is no way on God's green earth that woman—"

Jeez. "Nobody's going to join us in bed, you're one hundred percent right on that." He swallowed hard. "The trouble is, we're not getting to the bed. Not really."

Travis stopped for a moment then sighed. "Pretty sure you don't mean you're having so much hot monkey sex you're doing it everywhere *except* in a bed."

"I don't want to share secrets," Trevor started in, hoping he could finish before he lost his nerve. "But Becky asked if I could find some ideas, and I'm at a total loss."

Travis folded his arms and leaned back against the tractor, all joking gone. *This* was the man Trevor had seen more of over the last year. A blunt-spoken but caring man he trusted would try to help *and* keep it quiet.

"This is going to be awkward as hell, so just spit it out," Travis suggested. "And seriously, the conversations me, Cassidy and Ashley have? There's *nothing* you could say that will shock me."

"She doesn't like sex."

Travis grunted in surprise. "Except that. Really? You mean you guys are doing absolutely nothing? No kissing, no touching, no going down each other, either way?"

"No, we're doing that stuff, and she likes it. So do I, but any time we try actual sex, she freezes and it's *hell, no.*" Trevor paced in front of his cousin. "She's got her reasons, and they make sense. Only she says she wants to keep trying, but every time it doesn't work, it frustrates her more, which isn't what I want."

"What *do* you want?"

"I want her to be happy with what we're doing," Trevor answered honestly. "I mean, yes. I like fucking, but she won't see a counselor right now, so I need ideas that might help get her past this trouble."

His cousin stared at him for a good long time. "Okay. Straight up, she likes everything except when you put your cock in her. That's what we're talking about here."

"Right."

"Hell. Thanks for asking me an easy one, cuz." Travis shook his head as he held up a finger. "For the record, you are having sex, asshole. Everything you've been doing is sex. Just because you're not sticking your cock in her doesn't mean you're not having sex. I've only got one dick, and I'm with two people. We can't all have *sex* at the same time if it's only about *insert tab a into slot b*, or I'd constantly have one person I'm not satisfying."

"It was easier to say *sex* than to say...cock in pussy, or something." Damn it, his cheeks were fucking hot like he was running a fever.

"You're such a dweeb," Travis muttered.

"Hey, you have two people you talk about sex with all the time, and one of them is Ashley who doesn't have a shy bone in her body. Give me a break."

"Dweeb," Travis repeated before growing serious again. "You say she's got good reasons for why this

275

happens. Don't tell me the details, but I can guess, and that fucking *sucks*. *Goddamn* screwed-up *assholes* in this world." He ground out the words, violence shaking his voice by the end.

"You can say that again." Trevor knew he couldn't change her past, but damn if he didn't wish he could, every single day.

Travis went on, calmer now, the anger that had burst out controlled, but not gone. "I'm not going to tell you she needs to get over it. I'm the last one to say somebody needs to drop what's important to them, or just forget about their issues. And *I'm* not an expert. I think you should get her to talk to someone who really knows how to help."

Trevor nodded slowly. "Yeah. I figured that was the best thing too, but she's not ready. I'm looking for ideas we can try in the meantime."

"I don't know. Visit a sex shop and buy some vibrators, see if they make a difference." His cousin stared off into the distance for a minute. "Don't tell me her issues, but if it's something like a lack of power, give power back to her. Get her a strap-on, and let her fuck you."

A shock wave struck, and Trevor swore. Loudly. "What the *hell?*"

An evil grin broke across Travis's face. "You asked for suggestions."

Trevor wasn't sure if he should kiss his cousin or punch him in the face. "Jesus, you're a damn menace."

"Go on—keep trying new things. And give it time," Travis encouraged. "Sex is fun, yeah, but it's also about connecting in here..." he banged a fist into his chest then tapped his forehead, "...and here. Until all three parts work together properly, something will always be missing. Not just dealing with Becky's problem, but big picture."

His brain was still reeling, but Trevor had at least one idea to try. "Thanks. For everything."

Travis turned back to the tractor with a chuckle. "Anytime."

SHE'D NEVER seen so many penises in her life. Or boobs, or...whatever that thing was that seemed to have more appendages than an octopus.

Everywhere she looked there was something else she wanted to examine in more detail mainly to figure out what on earth it was, but the idea of looking closer at the merchandise lining the walls made her heart pound faster, and another wave of embarrassment swept over her.

"Remind me I never want to meet your cousin and his partners," Becky whispered as Trevor tugged on their linked fingers and pulled her after him.

He chuckled. "Why? Just because he suggested we go shopping doesn't mean they own stock in the company, or that they use everything in here."

"I mean..."

Nope, she was speechless. He'd brought her in front of a selection of penises. The ones that were shaped like man parts, but florescent blue or green made her brain hurt. And the *sizes*—

"That's not possible." Becky pointed at one that was anatomically correct, but as thick and long as her forearm. "No. Way."

"People have different kinks, Rodeo. Each to his

own."

"There's no place on a human body that could fit in." Not without killing the person. Becky figured it might scare some of the mares as well, but she wasn't about to say *that* out loud. "That's just not right."

"Some parts of the body stretch more than others." His hand slipped from her waist to cup her butt cheek. "So, these on the left are called vibrators. They can go in you, or up against your clit. They can be fun."

She was still figuring out his last comment, turning to examine his face carefully. "Back up. People put these in their *butts?*"

"Some do. People who like it say it feels really good."

She shook her head. "That's an exit only."

He burst out laughing. "Hell, sweetie, let's not rush things, but remember you said you'd keep an open mind. We want new things to try, both of us."

"Not my butt," she muttered, grabbing down one of the packages from the wall and examining it intently before she realized what she was doing. "Good grief, it looks like a cactus with three arms." She read closer. "Pleasure pearls, tickling rabbit ears, vibrating anal experience..." She didn't know which part bothered her more—the anal comment or the rabbit bit. "I feel like I'm in a foreign country where I don't know the language."

But she was with Trevor, and that made things easier to handle. An hour later, after a lot of discussion and giggling on her part, they had picked out a bunch of stuff—including a rabbit, God help her—and were headed back to Rocky Mountain House.

"I'm glad we went shopping where I don't know anyone."

Trevor was unpacking their purchases onto the

278

dresser beside her bed. "People who work in shops like that try hard to make people feel comfortable.

It hadn't worked, but she saw his point. And now watching him lay the things they'd bought out in plain sight was doing something weird to her gut. "Are we going to fool around?"

He chuckled. "Not if you don't want to. We can go weed the garden or something, if you'd like that more."

She was scared that even with new things to try that they'd end up back where they always did, with her haunted by the past. She stepped forward to press her face to his chest. "I like everything I do with you, so why does this feel so strange?"

"Because you're thinking about it too much." Trevor kissed her. A sweet, lingering kiss that melted away a lot of her hesitation and got her on board with trying some of their new toys.

Especially when he shuffled her off to the shower, turned on the taps and stepped in with her. "There's not enough room for the two of us in here," she teased.

"Lots of room if we stay close," he murmured, slipping a hand around her waist and making contact between their wet bodies. His cock was already heavy with arousal, and even though he ignored it, she found it hard to.

He'd given her so much pleasure, it only made sense she should do the same for him.

Becky directed her hands over the solid muscle of his torso, shivering as he returned the favour, rubbing her until bubbles slicked her skin. The warm scent of raspberries rose around them, and she gasped in surprise when he leaned over to lick her nipple, soap bubbles and all.

"Edible oils," he murmured, lips against her skin.

279

"Although you taste delicious all the time without any help."

She breathed in deeply, letting the pleasure of what he was doing stroke her further and faster as he knelt before her in the tub, pressing kisses over her stomach. Her mound. His hands cupped her butt to hold her in place as he dragged his tongue through her curls, barely teasing her clit. Light, fluttering touches that sent individual streaks of lightning into her without setting off a storm.

When he slipped a finger into her sex, she'd been expecting it. Waiting for the sensation so she could try to analyze why *this* felt so good when other *things* didn't. He moved slowly, but insistently, stroking the front of her body, moving smoothly through the wetness he found. A second finger joined the first, sliding in deep as he increased the pressure of his tongue.

Trevor pulled out and skimmed his fingers at the entrance to her body, sensitive nerves making her moan with pleasure before a third finger stretched her, a split second of discomfort that skidded to pleasure so fast she didn't have time to complain.

He stabbed his tongue lower, into her body this time, then his fingers did the circle thing again, before drifting backward. He sucked hard on her clit right as he pressed a finger between her butt cheeks, and she shivered even as she uttered a warning. "*Trevor.*"

He chuckled against her body. "Just playing," he promised.

But he kept playing, teasing with the tip of his finger. She didn't tell him to stop because he also slipped his thumb into her sex, and combining that with what he was doing to her clit, she didn't have much to complain about. Stroking, sucking—it was triple overload, and an orgasm struck without any problem.

He had her wrapped in a towel and carried to the bed before she stopped shaking. "You didn't get to come," she complained.

"We're not done." Trevor pulled away the towel and sat back, delicious looking and oh so fine. A mouthwatering feast of masculine muscle wearing a cocky grin. "You have to promise to go careful with me."

He brought two of their purchases to the mattress, and Becky picked them up, turning them over in her hands. "I'm not feeling it," she warned. "They don't scream 'oh hey, you're going to love this' to me."

"Trust me, I'm as nervous as you." Trevor held up a small vibrator. "This one's for you. Not much different than what we did in the shower. This part is the same size as my thumb, and the rabbit sits against your clit." He pushed a button and the whole thing shook. "Vibrator."

She picked up the other thin shaft, not quite understanding. "If that one's for me, what are you going to do with this one?"

"I can't believe I'm saying this, but that's for you to use on me." Trevor let out a slow breath. "In the interest of trying new things, I'm willing to experiment. There's supposed to be this spot inside a guy that feels really good when it gets rubbed."

He took the purple thing from her and turned it on. The thicker head of the shaft shook against her palm as he pressed it to her hand.

Oh dear. "This goes inside *you?*"

He snickered. "Jeez, Rodeo, your eyes are like this big."

Trevor held up his hands to dinner-plate-sized circles, and she blinked, trying to hide her astonishment.

"But you like women, not men."

A louder laugh burst out of him. "This is nothing to do with that. This has to do with feeling good, so I shouldn't knock it till I try it."

Thankfully he stopped talking and started kissing her again, stretching out on the mattress and letting her take a breather. He caressed his fingers over her skin, using some of the massage oil they'd bought. She did the same, stroking her fingers across the top of his chest, slicking down the side of his ribs to that muscle she adored.

"I asked Rachel what to call this," she told him as she stroked along the length.

He eased his hips back to let her play, dragging his tongue along her collarbone as he moved toward her breasts again. "Of course you asked Rachel. And what she tell you?"

"*The muscle that makes you want to fuck their brains out.*"

His stomach muscles tightened under her fingers as he laughed. "She did not."

"She did, at first, but when she stopped laughing at the way I choked in surprise, she told me it's called the Adonis muscle, which pretty much means the same thing."

"You and Rachel are getting to be a lot of trouble."

She wrapped her fingers around his cock. "I'm trouble all on my own."

They spent another fifteen minutes touching each other, his fingers lingering longer and longer on the crease between her butt cheeks. "I'm going to put your vibrator in you now," he warned.

"Not in my butt," she insisted.

"No, in your pussy. I want to play with your butt."

He stroked the vibrator over her inner thigh, touching and retreating, again and again until she got used to the sensation. It felt good over her clit, and good at the entrance of her sex, and then warm as he slipped it in.

Becky waited for panic to arrive, but it never did. Instead, a tickling sensation tugged low in her belly, the same as when he put his mouth on her, only this was slower, less direct.

She sat on the mattress with the vibrator tucked inside her, pleasure on a slow drip. "Your turn," she whispered.

Becky pulled in her courage and touched him as well, copying his motions and using the oil as she rubbed his amazing butt. Fingers slipping over him carefully before retreating. Each time a little farther, a little more intimate.

He lay on his side facing her, and he seemed to be concentrating awfully hard. There was no sign he *didn't* like it as she kept touching him, so like he had in the shower, she pressed the very tip of her finger into him.

Trevor's eyes widened. "Umm, okay."

"Yeah?"

"Maybe."

She shimmied down the bed, keeping the vibrator between her legs, adjusting position until she could lick the head of his cock that stood hard and proud between them.

"Wait," Trevor ordered, tucking a pillow under her head before spinning himself around until they faced in opposite directions. He smiled at her. "Now we can both reach."

His cock was right there in front of her. "Convenient."

She caught hold at the base and angled him the right direction, licking the head happily before pulling him into her mouth. Trevor was busy as well, lifting her upper thigh and propping it over his body so he could take control of the vibrator.

He must've done something to it because suddenly the noise got louder, and the vibrations against her body increased.

Oh, *wow*. She hummed her approval around his cock.

"Damn, that feels good." Trevor angled his hips, pressing into her mouth. "Your mouth is fucking heaven."

His hands had returned, and between moving the vibrator and the finger that was back on her butt, Becky was close to overload.

But he'd said he wanted to try new things too. She rolled her finger over the oil on their skin, making sure it was slick. Then she sucked his cock into her mouth as far she could, and at the same time, reached over his hip and pressed her finger into him.

"*Jesus*, Rodeo. Go slow."

He didn't say stop, so she focused on what she was doing, ignoring the wildfire creeping into her veins. He stroked the vibrator in and out, his tongue replacing whatever had been touching her clit before.

She moved her finger in a matching tempo, and it was like they were fucking, only completely different, and yet completely right. She pulled back, lashing her tongue against the head of his cock as he groaned with pleasure.

"*Coming.*"

The word was barely recognizable. It was the tightness in his butt and the shaking of his hips that let her know what was about to happen.

Becky swallowed hard, dragging his release from him as he lost control. His cock jerked, filling her mouth with seed, his hips pulsing against her.

Everything he was doing stopped, the vibrator falling away to the mattress. She didn't care; it was so good to have him out of control and out of his mind. She'd done that to him—*her*—and it might not be where she wanted to end up, but it was a good beginning.

Trevor groaned, rolling to his back and panting like he'd just finished running a race. "Holy fucking *hell.*"

She curled up, grinning at him with satisfaction. "You liked?"

"I'll tell you when I get my brain to work again." He caught her gaze. "We're not done. Sorry I lost it before you came."

"Don't be." She leaned over and kissed him, settling in when he pulled her on top like a blanket. "We didn't use your toy, yet."

He narrowed his eyes. "I will not survive anymore today. And I don't know that I need anything but you." He caressed her back and offered a smile. "You're my favourite toy, all on your own."

It still wasn't *sex*, but it'd been incredible in all sorts of other ways. Becky laid her head on his strong chest, feeling very much at peace.

Chapter Twenty-Five

HOPE PRESSED her hands to her belly, gasping in pain.

Becky was around the cutting-board table immediately, catching Hope by the shoulders and guiding her to a chair. "You okay?"

She nodded, sitting gingerly. "That was one wicked kick. The kid got me in the bladder."

Becky pushed aside her worry best she could. "Don't *do* things like that to me," she complained. "It's too soon for you to go into labour."

Hope squeezed her fingers. "I have no intention of having this kid a moment earlier than his due date."

"Hopefully he got the message as well," Becky told her. "Are you sure you want me to leave? I can wait until Matt can come to get you."

Her boss waved a hand. "I'll be fine. I have paperwork to do."

Becky watched carefully for a moment, but Hope seemed to be telling the truth. She rubbed a hand over her belly, pulling forward notebooks and her laptop computer.

"If you need help, phone me."

"Go home, Becky. You'll be spending enough time

in the shop when I do have this kid."

Summertime warmth greeted her as she stepped outside, running shoes tightened for the long walk home. Every day as she paced along the road she thought back to the early days of making this trip, and how much her life had changed since then.

Becky was no longer an invisible person. She had ID. She had a phone, and her best friend, Rachel, had taught her the secrets of texting. She had a job with someone she enjoyed working with.

She had a boyfriend. A *lover* who cared about her—it never ceased to amaze her.

What she didn't have yet was a driver's license, but she'd work on that before the snow flew. It hadn't made sense to worry about it before she had the money to buy a car, but now enough funds were slowly collecting in her bank account to consider it.

Everything had gone so well over the past months, better than she had dreamed possible. But the one thing that was missing was the one thing driving her to do more as quickly as possible.

Paradise Settlement was still there. Sarah was still trapped, and Becky couldn't rest yet.

"Hey, Rodeo."

She shook her head, smiling because she should have expected it. She twisted toward the road to discover Trevor keeping pace with her, leaning out the driver's window of his truck.

"You're on the wrong side of the road," she teased.

He slowed to a stop, checking the highway before running across the road and scooping her up. He twirled her then gave her a mind-blowing kiss before setting her on her feet, dizzy for more than one reason.

"Let's go. It's your turn to drive."

She didn't refuse. The driving lessons were another step in reaching her ultimate goal. Besides, as he directed them along the back roads around the Coleman range, it was a nice change of pace. Something else they could do together, and she wondered again at how lucky she'd become. Glancing at him as he sat aside her, patiently answering her questions then leaning back as if completely confident in her skills.

He barely twitched when she hit a pothole instead of going around it.

Everything she had that was good shone with such brightness it threatened to steal her breath away.

They moved from driving lessons to gathering things from the garden, making a meal to share with Rachel and Lee who planned on coming over later that day.

This was what life was supposed to be like. Friendship and fun. A community that cared for each other. A place to call home where no one threatened that enjoying life would bring down fire and brimstone, or an eternity in hell.

Trevor paused in the middle of pulling carrots. "Where've you gone, sweetheart?"

Becky turned her face toward him. She'd gotten lost in thought, sitting on a stool near the edge of the garden, her hands steadily working to clean the beans she'd picked. She had to refocus to take in Trevor.

He was easy on the eyes when she did.

Tall and handsome. Rock solid as he leaned on a shovel and looked down with tenderness. Careful and caring, like always, and while the expression on his face sent heat through her, it also calmed her.

He turned her on, yes, but he also made her heart beat for other reasons. She trusted him.

That meant a lot. That meant *everything*.

Becky spoke quietly. "I've been thinking about this, and I know it might seem sudden, but I need your help."

He nodded. "What's up?"

"I want to go back to Paradise Settlement." It was the most important thing she could think of, and it had been too long in coming. "I want to go get my sister and her family."

Shock flashed in his eyes *"Jeez*, Rodeo. For a second there I thought you meant *you* wanted to go back, and I was going to tie you up and chain you to the porch railing until you came to your senses."

"I wouldn't go back at all, except she needs me." Becky took a deep breath. Just thinking about walking into the Settlement made her skin crawl. "I don't want to go, but I can't stand the thought that Sarah's still living there. That the *kids* are there. The only way for them to get out is to have somewhere to go." She waved a hand at the house and the garden. "I know it's not a lot, but it's a start. Sarah can find a job, even if it's something like watching kids or sewing. We can make it work, but I have to go back if she's going to have a chance."

"Have you written to her? What'd she think of the idea?"

Becky shook her head. "There's no use in writing. Abel would read the letter, and probably not even give it to her. We need to show up and get her, and then they'll be safe."

"Are you sure she'll come?" he asked softly, worry painting his voice.

She nodded immediately. "We talked about it. How it would be good to have a place of our own, and how there was more the world could offer the children if they weren't a few amongst the many."

"But she's the one who brought you to Paradise."

There seemed to be no way to explain how in spite of being mixed up, her sister was mixed up for the right reasons. "Because she loves me. Sarah didn't know what Abel was going to do, and Paradise Settlement *was* better than the military propaganda and fear in the community my parents belong to."

He stood like a statue, but she could tell he was thinking, hard. It was a huge thing she was asking, she understood that.

But it was the only thing she could do.

HER REQUEST was so not what he had expected.

He knew Becky had never stopped worrying about Sarah. He'd never found a way to stop the nagging doubts and anger from rising every time Becky brought her up. As much as she was also a victim, she'd had a hand in hurting his Becky...

Forgiving her for that wasn't easy.

He'd never quite figured out how he'd hoped the whole mixed-up, horrid situation would get resolved. It was an impossible situation with no clear solutions.

Trevor had enjoyed a few vivid daydreams about going into the cult with a convoy of RCMP so they could disband the entire commune while he personally laid into Abel and left him broken and hurting.

Going back to Paradise to convince Sarah to run away? He understood why Becky wanted it; he just didn't see how it would work.

He sure the hell didn't feel comfortable with her going anywhere near the cult without him. And no way was he letting her deal with the rest of it alone, either. So in spite of his fears, he did the only thing he could.

He reached down and lifted her to her feet. "If you're sure, and this is what you want, then I'll take you."

A sigh of relief escaped her. "Thank you."

His mind raced as he considered the logistics. He couldn't imagine the cult doing something stupid like attacking them, but they'd be safer with some backup, all the same. "Let me talk to my sister. Anna should come along—her and Mitch."

Becky wrinkled her nose. "I don't want to make trouble or have anyone arrested, Trevor. I want to go in as quietly as possible, and leave the same way."

"And I think having an RCMP officer along will help *keep* things quiet." Although he wished she would press charges, he wasn't going to make her go through what would be horribly traumatic all over again. "I need a few days to set things up."

"I need to talk to Hope, but the sooner, the better, since her baby is due in October." Her excitement was impossible to miss.

Ignoring how much this meant to her would be wrong, even as he worried how it was all going to turn out. "Then let's make it happen."

Becky curled her arms around his torso and hugged him tight, all warm and soft, and yet so strong. She felt perfect in his arms. Perfect in his life, in so many ways.

He couldn't say no to something she'd been working toward for months, only he would do everything he could to make sure she didn't get hurt more in the

291

process.

It took a week to coordinate things. Talking to Anna and Mitch, talking to his brothers and Hope.

The drive took six hours with Becky fidgeting for at least half the trip. She'd fallen asleep at one point, exhausted by the lack of sleep the previous two nights, too excited and worried to rest once she knew for sure they were leaving early Friday morning.

She'd finally laid her head in his lap and slept fitfully, trembling awake far more often than he hoped.

They made a pit stop at the closest RCMP station at Anna's insistence, not in any official capacity, but as a courtesy to say they'd be visiting the settlement.

The man behind the counter didn't seem to understand what they wanted. "Sorry, but I can't do anything. Not unless she's here to press charges."

Becky shook her head. "I just want my things."

They'd all agreed that keeping quiet about her plan to ask Sarah to leave was for the best.

Trevor wasn't sure what he'd expected, but the sight that greeted them as they entered Paradise Settlement wasn't what had popped to mind as he thought of religious cults. Part of him wished he could see blatant evil glaring back at him. Something that would make the anger in his belly more understandable.

Instead it looked like so many small, sleepy communities, he was shocked. Innocent and forgettable, the community probably didn't register on travelers driving by less than a mile away on the main highway.

Typical middle-class houses in a rural setting. Large yards, some of them with fences, some without. There were a lot of outbuildings and barns, but they made sense, backing onto fields that looked well maintained and nearly ready for harvest.

There were no kids around. He'd driven through Rocky at times and been totally confused at the lack of kids playing outside until someone had pointed out they were probably inside playing on their computers.

Here the kids wouldn't have that excuse, though.

They drove past another nondescript bi-level, and he squeezed Becky's fingers, checking in his rearview mirror again to make sure Mitch and Anna were still on his tail. "Where is everybody?"

"Not sure. Someone should be at home." Her voice was tight. "Take the next right. It's the yellow house, and you can park around the back. I'll see if Sarah's there, and if any of my things are still in my room."

They got out of the truck at the same time, Becky giving him a dirty look.

"Oh, hell no," Trevor admonished. "We talked about this. You're not going *anywhere* by yourself."

Becky sighed, then nodded, waiting for Mitch and Anna to join them as she walked to the back door and knocked.

There was no answer, not even when she tried a second time, so she opened the door and slipped in.

"I'll just be a minute." Her eyes were cast toward the floor, and all her fire and energy seemed to have vanished.

This wasn't his Becky. This was someone in hiding, downtrodden and abused. Muted fury rushed through him as he kept control for her sake. The sooner they left, the better.

He silently followed her up the narrow staircase to the bedroom at the end of the hall. Becky stood in the doorway, staring in without stepping any further. Her body trembled, and he moved in closer so he could hold her, trying to give her reassurance as she faced whatever demons possessed this place.

A simple wooden bedframe. A dresser. Thin curtains at the window. Nothing that looked like his Becky.

He stroked a hand along her neck. "What's the matter, Rodeo?"

She shook her head. "None of this is mine."

Dammit. "Nothing?"

"It's okay. I didn't have that much, anyway." She turned, forcing a smile to her lips that he knew she didn't feel. "Come on. I think I know where they might be."

It was like driving through some strange movie set. All of the buildings were there, but none of the actors had shown up. Becky leaned her head against his shoulder, taking deep breaths as he followed the loop to the largest building in the community.

Here finally were people—the full parking lot was the first sign, followed by the appearance of a few women with children in their arms standing outside the side door, obviously rocking noisy children during what must be a church service.

The faint sounds of organ music met them as they left the truck, Becky sliding her fingers into his. "In a way, this makes it easier. We can get Sarah and the kids, and it will all be done at one time."

Trevor had agreed to not take her supposed *husband* apart, but it wasn't enough. "Nobody touches you," he warned. "I won't go in and pick a fight, but if anyone tries to hurt you, I'm not standing there and letting them."

She stopped, worry on her face. "Trevor, you promised."

"He promised not to start a fight," Mitch grumbled softly. "Neither of us promised not to finish one."

Damn right. "Anna, I like your choice of husbands."

His sister straightened her jacket, putting on her cop face. "He's a keeper." She gave Becky a direct look. "Remember, all you can do is ask. It's up to Sarah, because no matter what the guys just implied, there will be no fighting today."

In some other place, at some other time, Trevor would've called his sister a spoilsport, but this moment was far too serious for joking.

Becky tightened her grip on his fingers and led them up the stairs.

The soft, churchy music had stopped, and someone was talking over a loud speaker. Nothing earth-shattering or demonic. Something about harvests and a fall gathering. Only, as Becky walked them past the back row of dozens of pews, the man standing behind the pulpit faltered, his voice trailing off into nothing.

People turned to see what he was staring at, the wooden pews creaking like a chorus of ghosts, shock on faces the clearest thing Trevor could see.

And then the whispering began.

Becky's fingers were ice cold in his, but she kept walking, chin jutted out, bravery in every step. The same kind of bravery that had taken her through a world of change over the past months.

He'd never been prouder.

Trevor had also never been more afraid in his life—not for himself, but for her. Having to face the people who had held her trapped for so long? He just wanted to get the hell out of there and take her with him.

"Rebekah?" A slim woman stood in the front pew, eyes wide in her white face. The family resemblance was there in the lines of her cheekbones and chin, although her dress was from a former generation, her hair braided back plain and proper.

Becky slipped her fingers from his and stepped forward, rushing to wrap her arms around her sister. "Sarah. I've missed you so much."

For one moment Trevor thought in spite of his misgivings it was going to be a grand reunion like he'd seen on TV shows, or heard about on the news. Long-lost family reunited, and there'd be tears of joy in celebration, then they'd move on to the next thing—

But while Becky was hugging her sister, Sarah hadn't moved. She stood stiffly, arms hanging at her sides. The sound in the room was no longer made of muted whispers, but anger and confusion.

He stepped forward, certain things had just gone to hell.

Chapter Twenty-Six

BLOOD POUNDED in Becky's ears, making it hard to focus on what was being said around them, but it was easy to tell *something* was wrong.

Sarah stood like a statue, icy cold and rigid in her arms. No welcoming hug, no joyful exclamation, or questions about where she'd been.

Becky released her, looking into her sister's face and trying to read what she saw there. Nothing. No warmth, but no dismissal either. Just a completely blank slate, as if Sarah wasn't really there.

Confusion made her hesitate, and then Trevor was at her side, the familiar feel of his hand taking hers centering her. Giving her an anchor to hold on to as she took the next step.

"I've come to get my things." Becky glanced around at the familiar faces of the family. People she'd spent years with. Children she'd helped raise, women she'd worked alongside in the kitchen.

Men who'd—

She glanced at Trevor in sudden concern. Maybe she should have made sure he waited for her outside.

He was also examining the congregation. There was fire flashing in his eyes, and tension along his jaw,

297

but he wasn't staring at anyone in *particular* offering death threats, which was about the best she figured he could do at that particular moment.

"There's nothing here of yours."

They turned toward the front of the church. Nausea turned her stomach as Abel stepped forward from where he'd sat to one side of the podium, probably waiting for his turn to stand and preach whatever message he wanted to control his flock with this week.

Tall and confident, his dark hair shot with silver all in perfect place. His blue gaze examined her closely, but there was more kindness and relief on his face than malice or anger.

Her first impression was the same as always. She'd always thought he was a good stand-in for the devil. Satan wasn't red with a pitchfork and a tail. He was handsome—charismatic even. There was no way someone ugly or straight-up *obviously* evil could convince good, decent human beings to do terrible things. That took a man who was impressive, if only on the outside.

Trevor took a partial step forward before she jerked on their hands, bringing him back to her side.

Abel looked Trevor over before his gaze traveled toward Anna and Mitch who had waited at the back of the church. His brows went up as he examined the tattoos plainly visible on Mitch's bare arms, but he focused on Anna as he spoke. "This is a private gathering. Unless you have official business here, Constable, I'll have to ask you to leave."

"As soon as my friend collects the possessions she left behind." Anna's voice rang out strong and confident, but polite.

"Then she can leave. Sadly, when we heard nothing from her for the longest time, we concluded the worst. All your things were given to charity." Abel turned with open palms toward her and spoke kindly, like a benevolent benefactor offering a wonderful alternative. A gift he couldn't imagine anyone turning down. "But you could stay. Return, Rebekah. Return to the family where you belong. You only need to ask for forgiveness, and you can come home."

Trevor muttered softly, his grip on her fingers tightening to the point of pain. "No fuc—"

"No," Becky interrupted before Trevor lost control. She shook her head. "I have *nothing* to ask forgiveness for, and I'm not returning. I came back for my things," she repeated. "That's all."

"There's nothing here for you." It was Sarah who spoke, her tone making Becky snap to attention. The blank wall of emotionlessness was gone and in its place was barely controlled fury. "We do not suffer evil to live amongst us. Liars and thieves are cast out of paradise to where there is no joy, no happiness. Only eternal suffering, with weeping and gnashing of teeth."

"*Sarah?*" Her sister reciting scripture wasn't out of character, but what she was reciting was—*hell and brimstone?*

Sarah took in Trevor, staring at their joined hands with disgust. "*Adulterer.* I didn't believe it when they told me you were so willing to sin, but I see that it's true."

Oh my *God*, what kind of lies had Abel told?

"I came for you, Sarah. You and the children." Becky spoke in a rush, trying to get out as much as possible in the hopes that *something* would register. That somehow she could turn around this terrible, out-of-control situation. "You're my sister, and I love you. I have a place for all of us now. I have a job. I have enough money that we can—"

"I have no sister. My sister is dead," Sarah whispered.

Sheer determination was the only thing that kept Becky's legs from buckling. "You don't mean that."

For one brief instant she imagined she saw a crack in the wall. A fleeting moment of emotion in Sarah's eyes that looked like hunger and sadness, then it was gone, replaced once again by indignant righteousness.

"This is a private gathering," Sarah repeated Abel's words from moments earlier, cold and formal. "Leave us in peace."

Breathing was impossible. Her throat and lungs were cased in ice. Pain stabbed into Becky's heart as she saw little Mary's eyes peeking from behind Sarah's skirts, and she realized she'd lost them. Not just now, but maybe forever.

She hadn't been able to save them.

"Constable, I suggest you escort your friends out now, or I'll be forced to call our local detachment and have you all charged with trespassing." Abel. Reasonable, calm.

The devil incarnate flinging her out of paradise.

Trevor slipped an arm around her, carefully turning them and guiding her out of the building.

She let him lead her blindly; staring over her shoulder for one more desperate glimpse at the only part of her sister she could still see. A tiny slice of her profile as Sarah kept her gaze firmly on Abel at the front of the room.

Becky's heart shattered into a million pieces.

SHE'D CRAWLED into his truck without a word, staring straight ahead as he, Anna and Mitch stood helplessly in the parking lot.

"That's it?" Trevor demanded. "We pack up and go home without *anything*?"

"We can't make Sarah change her mind," Anna said softly, resting a hand on his arm as Mitch stood in silent support behind her. "We knew it was a long shot in the first place. It's not an easy thing to leave behind everything you've ever known, even when someone you trust is waiting for you on the other side."

Frustration and anger strengthened the urge to go back in and wipe the smirk off the bastard's face, but his family knew him too well.

Mitch stepped between him and the church doors. "I know that look. No, Trevor, we can't go beat the crap out of them."

"Fucking *watch* me."

His brother-in-law shook his head. "As much as I'd love to join you and give out a few righteous beatings, there's not a lot you can do to help Becky from inside a jail cell, which is where we'd both end up. Pull it together and think of her."

Becky. Trevor turned and hurried to his truck as his sister called after him, "Stop at the café in Maple Creek. We'll meet you there."

Then he was inside the truck, pulling Becky into his arms and squeezing her tight. "I'm so sorry, sweetheart. I'm so fucking sorry."

She nodded, but still didn't speak. Not even when he cupped her chin and looked into her eyes. As if she were frozen with worry and disappointment, and he didn't blame her one bit. The last thing she needed right

301

now was for him to push her any further.

"You okay if we head home?"

Another nod, then she pulled away from him, moving into the passenger seat before buckling up her seatbelt. She leaned against the window, staring straight ahead and ignoring everything as he drove slowly out of Paradise.

They stopped at the café briefly before Mitch suggested they grab food from the truck-stop gas station instead of sitting in a booth like they'd come from a funeral. "We may as well put a few more miles between us and that fucking place."

Trevor agreed with the sentiment, although Becky refused to eat anything he offered her. Refused to talk too—just stared out the window without making a sound.

Six hours of near silence was enough to make Trevor want to turn around the instant he dropped Becky off, return to Paradise, and burn the place to the ground. If he'd hated them before for what they'd allowed to happen to Becky, he was now ready to go to war.

Instead, he brought her all the way into the kitchen of her house, pulling her back into his arms and holding her because he wasn't sure what else to do.

"Tell me," he begged. "Tell me what you need."

She lifted her eyes to his, the deep brown depths filled with hopelessness like he'd never seen before. Never, not once since the day he'd barged in on her, crawling onto the roof. He'd seen her scared; he'd seen her determined. Mostly, though, he'd seen her laughing. Full of life and hope even as she found her way in a world where she hadn't known any of the rules.

"You're so strong," he whispered. "I know this isn't what you wanted, and I can't imagine how you feel right now, but I'm here for you."

"I know." Her voice was brittle, as if she hadn't spoken for days. "Thank you for trying. I need a little time."

He pressed her head against his chest then stroked his fingers through her hair. "Take all the time you need."

Silence again, but this time not as painful. More like the soundless motion of raindrops trickling their way down a pane of glass. Slow, silent. Unstoppable as gravity deliberately dragged them downward.

Becky took a deep breath. "I'm tired. And you must be exhausted from all the driving."

Adrenaline and anger had fueled him with energy, along with far too many cups of coffee. But he had to agree. "It's been a long day."

She stood, awkwardly moving away from him. "I'm going to take a shower then go to sleep early. I'll talk to you tomorrow."

Which was a deliberate brush-off if he'd ever seen one. Still, he had to try. "Did you want me to stay? I want to stay," he admitted, not caring two shits what that made him sound like.

"I need time to think," she confessed, turning back to him and pressing her lips to his cheek. "I'll call you tomorrow," she promised.

He wanted to argue. He wanted to crawl into bed with her and hold her all night long, but ignoring her request was exactly what he'd sworn he would *never* do—override her decisions. Go around her.

So as much as he hated it, he nodded. "Tomorrow."

She walked away toward the front of the house. The stairs creaked under her slow footsteps. He waited until he heard the water come on in the shower.

Trevor locked the door behind himself, heading back to his truck and getting behind the wheel before staring ahead blindly, uncertain where the hell he wanted to go.

What he *wanted* was to be inside that damn house with her. Beyond that, his mind was a blank.

Frustration slammed into him again, and he threw the truck into reverse, spinning out his anger in the gravel under his tires. Shoving the beast back into gear and roaring down the secondary highway, headed for nowhere.

Trevor would never understand people, or how they could be so fucking cruel. Hell, he got the pleasure in a good practical joke, although sometimes even a joke could go wrong and feelings got ruffled. But causing long-term hurt or hanging on to bitterness made no fucking sense.

He passed his parents' house. His father stood on the porch, and Randy waved before turning slowly and hobbling toward the chairs that faced the sunset.

Another frustration—Trevor knew his dad's illness wasn't his fault, except not being able to do more than offer platitudes and hopeful comments seemed a shitty way to help.

He couldn't turn in and stop and visit. Couldn't add another disappointment to the day, so he kept going straight on past like he hadn't seen.

He stopped at the mailbox and pulled out his mail. A mindless activity, done mostly by rote.

One envelope in the pile was so out of place from the flyers and bills it caught his eye, and he ripped the slim paper open, curiosity edging through his gloomy mood.

Trevor—
Got your letters. Glad to know Becky is doing okay. It's not much, what I did. Anyone would have. I'm glad she's fitting into Rocky, and making friends. Seems the type to land on her feet.
  As for the rest—this might sound cruel, but Rocky isn't home for me anymore. It's not been for a long time. I guess I'm saying, while I'm glad for the update on Becky, I don't need you to write to me anymore.
  Sometimes it's better to let old hurts alone.
Mark

Fuck.
Fuck it all.
Trevor tossed the papers onto the passenger seat and took off, driving in circles to escape the sheer hopelessness washing over him. His inability to change things in people's lives made him all the more miserable.
What the hell good was he anyway?
All the fury and frustration drained out of him as hours later he stood in the middle of his yard. The sun had long ago vanished behind the mountains, dusk following. The temperature dipped and left him standing in the dark, chilled to the bone and utterly spent.
Reality sucked, and then reality slapped him upside the head. He was *no* fucking good, but that wasn't the answer his family needed, and it wasn't the answer Becky needed.
So in spite of the truth, tomorrow he'd get up and do the shitty best he could all over again. He'd keep trying.
But it was a bitter pill to swallow, to think that his best wasn't good enough to help the people he loved.

Chapter Twenty-Seven

BECKY HAD forgotten to close her curtains before she'd stumbled into bed, head aching, heart aching. Now sunshine streaked across her face, the gold and yellow bands painting the room with far too much cheerful light for the pit of sadness in her stomach.

And yet—the sun shone.

Her sister's seeming betrayal and lack of trust *hurt*. Becky wasn't going to deny how much it had hurt, and she was nowhere near over being sad at how things had turned out.

She wasn't willing to give up completely yet either.

There had been that moment when she'd thought Sarah would say yes before she'd changed her mind. Maybe there was a reason for staying in the settlement. Maybe there was something Becky didn't know about...

Yeah, she was probably just dreaming, but it was a dream worth having.

In the meantime, she would start writing letters. If even one got through, it might plant the seed for the future. It was a fool's hope, but she refused to give up. Sarah was family—she deserved more than a second chance.

She deserved all the chances she needed.

Another flash of light struck Becky in the eyes, bouncing off the picture frame beside her bed. She grabbed it up, staring at the snapshot taken of her and Trevor one day when they'd gone riding with Melody and Steve. She looked *happy*, and Trevor looked crazy about her and...

It was a reminder of everything she'd gained, which was more than what she'd lost. As disappointed and hurt as she was, she wasn't going to wait and pout and let life pass her by while she hoped for another miracle. She'd already had one dream come true—*she* was free, and she wasn't going to take any of that for granted. Not any of what freedom entailed.

Especially not Trevor.

Becky put the frame back in its place and got to her feet, moving to the window to stare into the sunshine. Warmth surrounded her like a blanket.

She'd needed last night by herself, though, to get her head back on straight and let go of her regret without crying all over Trevor, although she'd been tempted.

Today she would totally let him pet her and make her feel better, and she'd do the same for him. It couldn't have been easy for him to take her all that way only to face disappointment.

Only he didn't answer her call, the line saying something about *out of service,* which was another word for some technology she hadn't yet figured out.

So she pulled on jeans and one of her rodeo shirts, kind of like a peace offering, because she knew they made him smile, then made her way over to his place.

His truck was parked in the yard, but no one was home. It wasn't until she peeked in the shed that she noticed the larger tractor was missing. He must've driven it somewhere on the ranch to work.

Maybe it was stupid. He was working, and this wasn't *that* urgent, but something made her bold.

Besides, the keys were in the ignition.

She drove Trevor's truck over to the Moonshine ranch house to track him down.

Kate opened the door, took one look and swept her into an ironclad embrace. "I heard. I'm so sorry."

Okay. Becky had done all right up till this moment, but the sound of tender concern in Kate's voice pushed her over the edge. Between one breath and the next, she lost it. Tears burst free and she buried herself in Kate's bosom, weeping quietly and feeling slightly guilty for enjoying being babied.

Strong arms held her while Kate made soothing noises, patting Becky's back gently.

"That was not what I came over here to do," Becky complained after she'd pulled herself together, wiping her eyes before joining Kate at the kitchen table. She accepted the cup of tea the other woman pushed toward her.

"I'm glad you came. I know you've got Trevor and your friends to talk to." Kate eyed her carefully, hesitant, but like she had something on her mind. "But...well, straight up, if you're mad at God, and want to discuss that..."

Oh boy. Becky took a deep breath and told the truth. "I don't blame God for man's behavior. I never have."

Kate breathed out slowly. "Some people aren't very good at understanding basic truths. Makes them act in ways that are about as far from righteous as can be." She caught Becky's fingers and gave them a squeeze. "Some of us are still trying, though. To live life in a way that makes a difference."

"I know—and some people do it without knowing that they're making a difference." It wasn't faith that had ever hurt her. She offered Kate a smile. "If I ever need to talk, I'll call."

"You do that."

Becky was itching to get moving, though. "What I came to ask is if you know where Trevor is today. I couldn't get a hold of him on my phone."

Kate gestured to the north. "He's in the dead zone. The one spot on the Coleman land where no one's cell phone works. He'll be gone all day."

She could wait until tonight to let him know she was okay, or...

"Can you tell me how to get out there?"

The other woman's lips twitched. "You sure you want to do that? He's spreading manure."

She didn't care. "I'm sure."

Kate grabbed a piece of paper, sketching a few lines on it. "Tell him to stop by the house later. His dad got good news yesterday. That last set of tests that Trevor bullied him into taking found out the trouble. Randy's gone to town this morning for the first set of treatments."

The sheer relief in Kate's face made it easy to be happy for them. "It's something simple they can give him medicine for?"

She nodded. "I have warned those boys for years not to go drinking out of the mountain creeks, and sure enough, turns out Randy has a severe case of giardia. It can hide in your system for years, only flaring up every now and then before hiding again, which was making him sick *and* making it impossible for the doctors to diagnose. And the longer you have it, the more side

309

effects hit your system. That aching in his bones might never go away, but at least it shouldn't get any worse."

"Trevor is going to be excited," Becky said. "He's been so worried."

"All of us have been. And if it hadn't been for Trevor, we still wouldn't know." Kate stood and passed the piece of paper over. "Close the gates behind you—" She held up a hand when Becky would have assured her she knew enough to keep the animals safe. "I know you will, but I'm the mom. I get to tell that to all my kids before they head out. It's tradition."

Becky swallowed hard, the acceptance and kindness in the other woman's eyes almost more than she could bear. She stole another hug before heading to the truck with her directions.

It took a while to get where she was going. First she stopped at the house to grab something she thought she might need. Then she had a challenge following the directions, opening the gates, getting the truck through, *and* keeping the cattle out of the field when they would've followed her.

It seemed Trevor's truck was the Pied Piper of the Coleman range, calling all the cattle to follow it.

She was smiling over the fact she knew that story as she topped the ridge to where Kate had put the big X on the map as the best spot for her to track down Trevor.

Becky stomped on the park brake hard before crawling into the back of the truck. She stood as tall as possible, checking over the hillside. The land seemed endless, but it was clear she was in the right place by the pungent smell carrying on the breeze.

Sweet smell of the country. The words hit her in Rachel's teasing lilt and made her smile harder.

Something lit up inside as a tractor came into

sight, and maybe it was silly, but what she did next felt right. She picked up the hand bell Trevor'd left for her on the porch so long ago, lifted it overhead and *shook* it.

The sound seemed to echo back from the mountains in the distance—it was impossible, but she could have sworn it did. Each shake was like a peal of laughter, spreading across the land and coming back to wrap itself around her.

The tractor paused then broke pattern, turning toward her at a ninety-degree angle, leaving a new trail over the previous dark rows as Trevor closed in on her.

Becky didn't stop ringing the bell until he turned off the tractor and opened the door. Then she was over the side of the truck box and racing toward him, her feet sinking into the freshly turned soil, an aromatic scent all around her.

But up ahead of her was Trevor. She kept her eyes on the target and didn't stop until she could throw herself into his arms.

HE THOUGHT his heart was going to stop. It wasn't so much his truck showing up unannounced—that part was fine. It was the clanging bell that followed, its tone cutting through sounds of the tractor engine and making him wonder if he was hearing things.

Spotting Becky on the ridge sent his heart pounding, fear driving him to push the tractor to top speed in his rush to reach her.

And now she was in his arms, and he was trying to loosen her off so he could make sure she was all right. "Becky. Stop. Tell me what's wrong."

She clung even harder. "Nothing's wrong, but I needed to see you. I needed to tell you *thank you.*"

Once his heart had kicked into gear again, he took a deep breath and fought for balance, both his feet and his head. He held on to her, face toward the sun as he soaked in its heat and the sensation of how right it was to have her in his arms. "You scared the shit out of me," he whispered. "I'm glad you're okay."

"I'm sorry." She wiggled slightly until he reluctantly let her down, keeping her hands stretched around his neck so their bodies were close together. "I couldn't wait. I was terrible to you last night, pushing you out of the house like that, but I'm—"

Trevor shook his head. "Don't you dare apologize. You didn't do a thing you need to be sorry for."

She tilted her head to the side. "Well, I'm still sorry, but I wanted you to know things are okay. I'm sad, and disappointed, and I might start crying again in a minute if I'm not careful, but I really am okay."

"It was a pretty big disappointment," he said. "I wish things were different."

Becky nodded, smiling at him with that sassy attitude that he'd always gotten such a kick out of. "Trevor?"

"Yeah?"

Her nose wrinkled. "It really stinks out here."

He nodded. "Go wait for me at the truck. Or really, you can go home. I'll come see you after I've had a shower."

She lifted her chin. "You trying to get rid of me?"

Jeez. "Of course not. Only you might be better off waiting for me somewhere else."

"I was just pointing out the smell. I wasn't done telling you something."

He waited patiently.

A smile broke out, dazzling bright. "I stopped by your mom and dad's place, and they want you to drop in later. Your dad got back his test results, and everything's going to be okay. He's getting treated, and it's not perfect, but Kate was really excited—"

"Wait. *What?*" He dragged a hand through his hair before replacing his hat. His brain spun with shock. "They found out what was wrong all this time?"

She nodded, damn near dancing in the soil underfoot. "I'll let them explain the rest because some of it slipped over my head, but that's good news, right?"

It was great news, but he couldn't quite believe it, nor could he wrap his head around how bubbly Becky seemed to be.

Had he dreamed the whole disastrous clusterfuck they'd experienced yesterday? Last night he'd thought they'd hit a rock-bottom point that would take a hell of a long time to crawl out of, and yet here she was, holding on to him and looking as if there was nowhere she'd rather be than standing with him in the middle of a stinking mess.

He looked her over again more carefully. "Have you been drinking?"

"Of course not." A furrow appeared between her eyes. "What's wrong, Trevor? Where's my Tigger? Where's the man I know who bounces through life?"

"He's standing in front of you, confused as hell, and his bounce is broken."

Becky stroked a hand down his chest. "I'm sorry. You're probably exhausted from all the driving you did yesterday, you went straight back to work today, and now I'm interrupting you. I wanted you to know I couldn't have done any of this without you."

A snort of disbelief escaped. "I haven't done anything but screw up."

Her fingers curled around a fistful of his shirt, tightening as if she could hold him in place. "You keep saying things I don't understand."

Trevor took her in, her shining eyes, all of her so strong and resilient, and this crazy sensation rippled through him. The realization that if she wasn't in his life it would be like giving up oxygen.

"I feel like I've let you down," he admitted, ready and willing to do anything necessary to make sure he stopped being such a fool. "I'm sorry, and I'm gonna do everything I can to make it up to you."

"There you go again, making no sense." Becky cupped his face in her hands. "You've never let me down. You're the most incredible man I know."

He shook his head, or he tried to, but found himself trapped by a set of steel vises that refused to budge. She was glaring at him now, a spitfire mix of anger and delicious attitude as she held him firmly and refused to let go.

"I never do anything important," Trevor insisted. "I'm just me."

"Trevor Coleman, you listen to me, and you listen to me good. I don't know what it is you thought you needed to do to be *important*, because for the last four months you have been *exactly* the kind of man I needed in my life. And if you think what you were doing wasn't good enough, we're going to stand right here in the middle of this stinking field until you get your head out of your ass and admit that you're perfect for me."

"Oops, Rodeo, you swore." The quip escaped before he realized it, and her lips twitched into a smile. "Stop that," he ordered.

314

"I can't, because that was *my* Trevor, teasing me and making me smile even as he's so careful to make sure I'm happy and not afraid." Becky slipped her arms around his waist, leaning their torsos together as she tilted her head back to stare into his eyes. "You can't fix everything for me. You can't fix everything for everyone else all the time, either, but you do an awful lot of good just being yourself. Making people smile, whether it's because you're poking them or offering them your truck."

"Offering them my truck *is* poking someone," he admitted. She waited as he tried to think of the simplest way to explain it. "When you get car insurance, they look at a chart to see how risky it is to own a vehicle in the area. I told them they were crazy to have Rocky in the same category as Calgary or Edmonton. I bet them I could leave the keys in the truck, even offer for strangers to drive her, and I'd still have no accidents for a year."

"You made a bet?"

He nodded. "They changed the zoning for the entire area in June because of it."

Becky's lips curled upward. "You're perfect," she repeated. "For me, and for the rest of your crazy family."

There had to be something he could blame for what happened next. Like maybe a short circuit between his brain and mouth, because suddenly the words escaping were exactly what he'd been thinking, but they were popping out at what had to be the shittiest moment ever.

"Marry me."

This time it was Becky's eyes that widened. "Wha... *what?*"

Jeez. He'd only missed a half-dozen steps.

"I'm such a damn fool." He kept her close, standing there in the dirt as he tried to straighten this

315

out. "Let me try that again. Becky, I *love* you. Will you marry me?"

Her mouth still hung open in surprise. "Trevor?"

The stupid part was he hadn't said it before now. "Is that so impossible to believe? This is me, being a perfect Trevor, and I'm announcing that in spite of feeling like I have nothing to offer you, I still want this more than anything. I want to be with you. Because I love you."

"Am I imagining this?" She blinked hard, seeming dazed.

"I didn't expect to fall in love," he admitted, "but hell, Rodeo, you snuck right in and lassoed my heart."

Talk about impossible things. Waiting for Becky to respond seemed to take hours even though seconds after he'd spoken, she slipped her hands up his arms until she was once again hugging his neck. "I love you too."

Exchanging *I love you*s while standing ankle-deep in well-manured soil. Damn if he wasn't the most romantic man on the face of the earth.

He picked her up, holding her tight as he kissed her. Her fingers around his neck, squeezing him close as a sweet breeze blew through the garden, sending his hat flying and ruffling Becky's hair around them both.

Becky smoothed her fingers through his hair as he settled her back on her feet. "Listen to everything I say before you get mad. Yes, I love you, and yes, I want to be with you, but no, I won't marry you."

Trevor waited for a punch line, but none came. "You better explain a little more."

She shook her head. "I wouldn't make a very good wife."

"You said that about not making a good girlfriend,

and look how well that turned out." Trevor wasn't sure where he'd gotten the set of horseshoes he possessed at the moment, but while he had the advantage, he was going to push aside all of his doubts and get *everything* he wanted. "I don't want to just be with you, I want it to be official. On paper *and* with the government."

What he *wasn't* saying must have rung through loud and clear because she swallowed hard. "Will you stop being so damn perfect?"

He raised a brow at her swear.

Becky ignored him, building up a head of steam so she could roll him over with her protests. "It's not fair for you to marry me. I still don't like sex, even though that might get better down the road. And if we don't have sex, I can't have children, and I don't know if I can have them anyway, because if I didn't get pregnant in five years, chances are I can't."

Trevor listened to her breathless complaint carefully. "Do *you* want kids?"

"Not right away. I want to do so much first. There are so many things that I haven't learned yet."

He nodded. "I've always joked about not liking kids, but I'm kind of on the fence now. I still don't really like other people's, but I think if you and I had some, that would be fine. And if we didn't, that would be just fine as well."

There should be smiles or laughter happening, but Becky was still not cooperating.

"So you want to be together, but not be married...?"

"I want..." She frowned. "I don't know what I want, but I don't like sex."

Trevor snickered. Okay, now she was complaining about something he did know how to answer. "You think waiting is a problem for me? Good grief, Rodeo, I'm a rancher. Waiting was programmed into me before birth, or at the latest, by the time I cut my eyeteeth."

"But—"

He twisted her in his arms so she could look over the land. Where they stood, the rise of the land let them see nearly all the way from Six Pack land over the Moonshine spread to the rental—to *Uncle Mark's.*

"We broke this land about five years ago. Harvested all the trees, hauled out the roots. We had burn piles the size of the houses scattered all across the field, then we had to wait until the middle of winter until the snow was deep enough it was safe to light them. It took three more years of harrows and hoes, planting a cover crop, turning it under—all before we even tried to grow anything."

The patience of a rancher. She had no idea who she was arguing with. Trevor's confidence was back, rising by the second.

He turned her to face him. "And then when we do decide it's time, it's not like your garden where a couple of nights of hard labour get the weeds out and the seeds in the soil. We drive those damn tractors in circles, row after row, and field after field. Turning and seeding and cutting and raking. By the time we've got the first bales dropped, we've probably been over every part of the land a hundred times or more."

"And that teaches a man to be stubborn?"

"Stubborn? We call it patience. And some years you seed and it doesn't rain, or you cut and it pours, and in either case your dreams and cash lie barren in the ground."

Becky stared with big eyes at him. "I don't want you to ever feel like you lost out by choosing me."

318

Trevor curled his hand under her chin and tilted her head back so he could kiss her. Soft and tender. "We do it all over again the next year, don't we? Because we're stubborn fools who just won't quit."

"Not fools." Becky stroked his cheek, amazement in her eyes. "Stubborn, I'll give you, but a fool? Never."

He kissed her again because he had to. And then once more because she hadn't given him the answer he wanted. "Say yes, Rodeo," he murmured against her lips.

"I'm stubborn too," she warned. "Yes, but not until I'm ready."

Trevor could live with that. "Just don't make it too long, okay?"

"I thought you had all sorts of patience," she teased.

"I do, but I want to beat my kid brother to the altar. Lee and Rachel have been engaged to be engaged for months, so we can't wait forever."

She laughed against his chest. "It's not a contest."

"Hell, yeah, it is." He picked her up and carried her back to the truck, setting her down on the tailgate. Trevor stepped between her legs and pulled her to him. "Now, about the rent I charge for using Esmeralda…"

Becky's face wrinkled in confusion. "*Esmeralda?*"

He patted the tailgate. "My pride and joy. You didn't think I'd let you use her for free, did you?"

She laughed, pulling him to her and planting a big, steamy kiss on him, distracting him all over from what he was supposed to be doing.

Which was exactly where he wanted her—in his arms, and in his life.

Epilogue

December, Rocky Mountain House

"WHY THE hell didn't you boys tell me you were bringing them in?"

Trevor and Lee glanced at each other then pointed at Steve. "His fault," they said in unison.

Randy stomped to a halt outside the stables, pushing back his hat to glare at his oldest son who was patting the nose of his horse and looking far too satisfied. "You were supposed to let me know when you were heading out to get the mares," Randy complained.

"Didn't need four people to do it," Steve said calmly.

"Then you should have—"

"*Shhhh,*" Steve warned. "Don't upset her. She's sensitive right now."

That was all it took to make their dad clam up, his body relaxing as he leaned his elbows on the railing and stared in at the pregnant mare.

He lowered his voice and spoke to her, ignoring the rest of them. "Pretty girl. Yeah, you're a good girl. I'm not upset with *you*, just with this trio of jackasses who keep treating me with kid gloves."

The mare turned toward him, nostrils flaring briefly as Randy soothed a hand over her nose.

Steve patted her withers before slipping from the pen. "For the record, the *trio of jackasses* are totally not treating you with kid gloves. We're letting you pick and choose your work list, except when it means going out in freezing weather to do a job that doesn't require extra hands."

"Besides, these are Lee's favourite weather conditions," Trevor said. "We need to get him snowed in again this year, for old time's sake."

They all moved toward the door. Randy kept stride with them easily as he checked about work plans for the rest of the day. Trevor slowed so he could watch, but other than a faint hint of a limp at times when he overdid it, his father was back to his old self.

It had seemed like a fast cure after a long time coming, and every time Trevor noticed, the changes made him happy all over again.

"You coming into the house?" his dad asked, hand on the door as he waited.

Trevor shook his head. "I'm done for the day. Started at five—and Becky is home early today as well."

"You're bringing her by for lunch on Sunday, right?"

"We'll be there." So would the entire lot of the Moonshine clan, and Trevor couldn't wait.

The past months had been filled with settling in and setting new paths. He'd joined Becky in the rental, which gave him an excuse to write to Uncle Mark on a regular basis without *really* ignoring the request not to. He was careful not to push an agenda, but keep the door open, even if just a crack.

Becky had begun to write to Sarah. Trevor still tasted rage when he thought of how much pain her sister had caused that day, but Becky—his sweet, forgiving, *giving* Becky had convinced him there were layers of reasons for the betrayal they might not be aware of.

He was still working on forgiving Sarah, but for the kids' sake, he could hope for a different future.

So once every couple of weeks they both sat down and found something to share. Maybe, some day, what they were doing might make a difference. Might make it possible to have family join them.

He slipped behind the wheel and cranked on the heat for the short trip home. December had teeth, sharp and bitterly cold, but he spent most of his days in a happy haze, Becky's warmth enough to carry him through the coldest tasks.

He was one cheesy, lovesick fool, and he didn't mind one bit.

The sun vanished far too soon these days. Even done as early as he was, by the time he pulled into the driveway and parked next to her secondhand Ford, the sky behind the house had already faded to dim twilight.

But from the windows, a warm, flickering glow welcomed him home. Trevor left the keys in his truck with a laugh, more than ready to get to spend another evening with the woman he loved.

He paused. Lights flickered by the front door, so instead of going to the back like usual, he took the front stairs two at a time, pausing to admire the mess of tea lights on the chair placed outside on the porch.

Becky was up to something.

Inside the house candles were everywhere. Wineglasses and snack plates sat on the stairs and seats of chairs, small honey-scented candles flickering as the air currents caught them and turned the entire house into an invasion of fireflies.

"Hey, Rodeo."

He listened for a moment, the low sound of bluesy music drifting to him from the living room.

Trevor moved slowly, taking in what had to be over a hundred flickering lights. They'd been lit long enough ago to melt, the small tin containers holding the liquid wax safely.

It was pretty, but more, his curiosity had shot to maximum. "Sweetheart? Where're you hiding?"

He didn't have to go far to find an answer. The lights led him in the right direction. The living room was awash with candles, the obvious source of their firefly invasion.

Trevor stepped through the doorway and his throat tightened.

Becky lay propped against a pile of pillows in front of the fireplace. She wore white lingerie—a barely there bra and a pair of panties that must've been in heaven, snugged up against her perfect body.

"There's an angel in my living room," he said. She blew his mind every single day.

She lifted her chin and curled herself up, a seductress set on teasing him, the weight of her breasts dipping forward as she moved. "I've been waiting for you."

He lowered himself onto the coffee table as she sat back on her heels, a tempting vision. "Looks as if you got something on your mind."

She nodded. "I have something to tell you, but first, go grab a shower."

Fuck. "Wait right here."

"Hurry." She teased her fingers up her rib cage, skimming them over her breasts, and then Trevor couldn't see what she was tormenting him with because he was out of the room, up the stairs and into the shower for the fastest scrub-down ever.

There was barely time for steam to build before he was done. She'd snuck in while he was under the taps and left him clean clothes on the counter. Black jeans and her favourite shirt of his.

He didn't know what he was getting dressed for when she was in nothing but her underwear, but like he was going to argue.

Walking out of the bathroom, he discovered all the candles had been extinguished except for a single trail leading down the hall to their master bedroom.

This was getting more and more interesting.

She waited for him by the window, her seductive outfit covered by a dress of palest pink.

"It's hard to complain when you look so pretty, but I hope I get to unwrap you. Soon."

Becky held out her hands, and he took them, waiting for her to make the next move. She took a deep breath. "I love you, Trevor Coleman."

He was never going to get tired of hearing that. "I love you too, Rodeo."

Her lips twitched into a smile. "It's time. I'm ready to get married."

Jesus. Trevor opened his mouth but no words came out. He wasn't sure his brain was still functioning.

"I know you want to do it up all formal, and I'm willing." Her words were soft but deliberate. Her eyes mesmerizing. "It won't change what we've already committed to, like being there for each other. Like you've been there for me the past months."

Happiness and concern warred together as his protective instincts shoved into overdrive. He didn't want her to push herself too far, and as pleased as he was that she'd agreed to get hitched, he was worried that's where this was heading.

Trevor cupped her face carefully, putting every bit of love he could into words. "I'm glad. And we'll get started on planning right away, but...what's up with tonight? Why the pretty dress and sweet candles?"

Becky hesitated. She caught his wrists, tugging one hand downward so she could place it on her chest. "Feel that? That beats for you. My body *sings* when you touch me. There's nothing I want more than to be with you every way possible."

Under his hand her heart fluttered like the wings of a bird, and his soul ached. "Sweetheart..."

She touched her fingers to his lips, smiling softly. "Don't panic, Tigger. Talking with the counselor has helped, but I've still got a long way to go. I know I'm not ready, not for some things, but you keep telling me that it doesn't matter. You've said it, and you've shown it. In words and in everything you do. So I'm finally finished with feeling I'm not enough, or that I'm holding you back. Because you've spent every day showing me how much you love me."

Sheer relief flooded him. "I'm not disappointed in anything about us being together," he said again.

Becky nodded. "I know. And someday, well, maybe I'll be ready for more."

She trusted him. She loved him. Trevor took a step of faith and pushed aside his fears. "What do you say to a test run tonight? Sort of to make sure we've got some practice?"

Her eyes lit up. "That's what I was thinking..."

"Because you're brilliant as well as beautiful." He turned her into the light, watching candlelight flicker over her face, lighting up her eyes with love. "Becky Hall, will you do me the honour of becoming my wife?"

A shaky breath escaped her, as if she'd been prepared to fight for a lot longer. "Oh, Trevor, *yes*. I love you so much."

He had to have been to a dozen weddings over his lifetime, but damn if he could remember what the official words were supposed to be. So he took both her hands again, turning her until the candlelight lit her face. Then he said what he needed to say.

"I remember that first time I saw you, standing on the ridge of this house. My heart nearly stopped, because I wanted to make sure you were safe and at the same time, I wanted to shake you. You know what? Every second of every day since then has been filled with those same emotions."

A laugh snuck out from her perfect lips. "You caught me."

"Just as much as you caught me." He lifted their hands so he could kiss her fingers. "You make me feel protective; you make me laugh. You make my heart beat so damn fast my head starts to spin, and then you bring me right back down to earth and give me roots when you look at me with those big eyes all full of trust."

Like she was looking at him now, staring into his heart.

"I will always be there for you," he promised. "No matter what the future brings."

Shining eyes, shaking fingers. Becky stroked a hand over his cheek, his unshaved stubble rough against her soft skin.

She didn't seem to mind.

"I will always be there for you," she repeated. "No matter what the future brings."

Best damned vows he'd ever heard.

They stood staring at each other before Becky wiggled on the spot. "I think this is where someone would say *you may kiss your bride*," she whispered.

Hell, yeah.

Trevor dipped his head toward her and kissed her softly. The way he would down the road when they did this at the front of a church, with all of his family watching.

And in spite of this being a practice run, he knew damn well the rest of the family was going to want to know the play-by-play of everything that had brought them to this moment.

The rest of the evening, though? Was for them alone.

Starting now.

He deepened the kiss, pulling her against him. He pressed his hand more firmly to her lower back, keeping her so close their bodies barely took up any room.

She trembled under his touch, but when he pulled back he saw nothing but desire flashing in her eyes. Like always—

"Think it's time I got to unwrap my bride," he whispered.

Becky stepped back, hands demurely by her sides. "Yes, please."

HE'D SAID he was going to unwrap her, and that was the closest thing she could compare it to.

Trevor paced around her slowly, kissing her neck, drawing his fingers down the long row of buttons at her back. "How the heck did you get into this thing by yourself?"

"It's a secret," she teased. She wasn't going to tell him there was a hidden zipper along the side. The buttons were there on purpose, to drive him wild.

"It's going to take me forever to get you undone," he complained.

She laughed, twisting in his arms to plant a kiss on his pouty lips. "Then I guess you'd better get started."

He turned her again, smacking her butt lightly. "Maybe what I need is every time I undo a button, I get a kiss."

"We *will* be here all night."

A rumble of amusement escaped him, his fingers brushing the hair at the back of her neck. "I'll keep count. One. Two..."

His lips settled at the base of her neck, a soft kiss followed by a tiny nip that made her squeal. "No teeth," she gasped.

"You didn't include that in the rules. Three..."

This time she felt his tongue, moisture landing along her spine as he undid buttons as rapidly as possible. Gentle as he pushed the dress from her shoulders, setting her skin quivering from his very touch.

"That's a very pretty dress," he whispered from his position behind her, tugging the fabric away as she stepped out of it. His lips caressing the slope of her back.

"It's my wedding dress. I wanted it to be pretty, but something I could wear any time we have a special occasion."

He hummed in approval, but she wasn't sure if it was about the dress or about the fact he'd stood, now close behind her, hands placed on either side of her hips. He tucked his chin over her shoulder, the scruff on his face scratching the soft skin of her neck and sending shivers racing.

"You wear this pretty underwear any time you want. I promise I'll always make it a special occasion when I take it off you."

Those shivers he'd started continued as he trailed his fingers up her ribs and below her breasts, cupping her carefully as he bit down on her shoulder. Massaging the weight of her, his thumbs and forefingers catching her nipples, making them tighten with need.

Becky let her head fall back on his shoulder as he played. One moment her bra was there, the next it was gone as his hands returned this time to bare skin.

Making love like this was right. It might not be typical, but it was right for them.

His erection pressed her hip, thick and heavy, and she rubbed back, teasing him, knowing what they'd have in the end would leave them both satisfied and connected.

Perfect for them, just like his vows of love, and all the signs of caring he'd shown her over the past months.

"Something about you, Rodeo, fits me. The way you smell. The way you taste." He skimmed his hand down her hip, catching hold of her panties dragging them away. "The way you feel. I love everything about you."

He turned her, staying on his knees.

"That's a good look," she teased.

"The way you taste, the way you smell," he repeated back, cupping his hands around her butt and pulling her to his mouth.

Oh, she had no objections at all to the way the evening was progressing. This was the way making love was supposed to be. Unique and special, everything she wanted it to be.

It *was* their first time. In a way.

She drew her fingers through his hair, luxuriating in his attention as he played with her clit, teasing it lightly with his tongue until her legs grew so shaky she could barely stand. "Trevor, I'm going to fall over," she warned.

He scooped her up and laid her on the bed, returning between her legs as if he were starving. He didn't stop until she was quivering, the orgasm ripping through her taking out all control.

Becky sucked for air. "That...was amazing."

"Just wait, I'm not done."

She didn't want to wait. When he would have teased her more, Becky rolled over him, taking control. She pressed her hands to his chest and pinned him in place, sliding her sex over his cock. She was wet enough the motion was smooth, rubbing them together like sexual kindling.

Teasing him made her body light on fire as well. Trevor's eyes nearly rolled out of his head. "*Fuck.*"

"We're going to," she promised. She tilted her head and gave him the most provocative smolder she could. "At least the way *we* fuck. I promise to be gentle with you."

His laughter rang out, perfect and strong, so much a part of them as it poured over the bed. He gripped her arms carefully and rolled again, his body over hers a soothing weight of firm muscle and passion.

"Forever," he promised.

Their lips met as the tiny candles all over the room sent flickers of starlight dancing on the walls. This was where she belonged, with this man and in this place.

A paradise not formed by human rules or twisted ambition.

A paradise made by love.

Trevor slipped his cock between her closed thighs, angling to rub her clit on each motion. Experimenting had given them a multitude of positions they enjoyed, each offering pleasure in its own way. Right now he was wrapped around her like a cocoon, a strong barrier that nothing but love could get through.

There was no place in this bed for nightmares or the past.

He stared into her eyes, love and laughter shining in the depths. "Welcome to married life, Ms. Hall."

"Coleman. I'm taking your name," she told him, shuddering as they lined up just right. "Oh my *goodness*, that feels perfect."

Trevor pulled his hips back slightly, rocking forward so slowly she felt every single inch. Pleasure cascaded, and she moaned, flexing her hips to get more of the sensation. Every bit of pleasure he'd given her up until this moment amped up ten times over.

"Shit." He stilled, hips tight to her hers. "Give me a second."

The words came out tortured, and she looked up anxiously to find his face screwed up tight as if he was in pain. "Trevor?"

"Oh, *fuck*." He offered a wry smile. "How the hell do you do this to me? I barely touch you, and I'm ready to burst. We might have to fool around a few times because I'm going to be a little fast on the trigger this first go-round."

Becky laughed, the sound filling the room, turning into a sigh of pleasure as he thrust against her, not holding back.

She had no complaints about how fast they were going, because no way could she last, either. His hands skimmed the sensitive tips of her nipples, drifting over her stomach as he kissed her. Seducing her senses with his lips and teeth and tongue. And touch—his cock connected with her clit over and over, and it was no longer pleasure stroking her, it was wild fire, burning away all her inhibitions and dragging her willingly to the precipice with him.

Anywhere *he* took her, she'd go.

They were rocking the bed, his thrusts powerful and yet loving as he looked into her eyes and made love to her. Every bit of him focused on her, on them together.

Before Trevor she'd never understood what it meant to be one body. It had nothing to do with a physical act—had everything to do with what was in their hearts and souls.

They came at the same time...or maybe not. Maybe she fell first, and then him, or the other way around—Becky wasn't sure because she was overwhelmed with pleasure. Sexual satisfaction burned through her, deep emotional connection tangling them into no longer Trevor and Becky, but one person.

"*Trevor.*"

His name came out the closest thing to a prayer that she'd uttered since the night she'd run away.

He pressed his forehead to hers, and it was so familiar and right as their eyes met. "Rodeo."

She squeezed his shoulders and curled into him, delight playing in her heart echoing the warm light from the flickering candles. A dance of joy offered by a million fireflies.

They lay there for a long time, stroking each other's arms and gazing into each other's eyes before

332

Trevor traced his finger over her lips. Swallowing hard before he spoke.

"I know you're the one who fell off the roof, but I'm the one who fell even harder. You've changed my life. Forever."

It was the perfect benediction for what had turned out to be the perfect night.

"Forever," she whispered.

New York Times Bestselling Author
Vivian Arend

invites you to meet the Colemans. These
contemporary cowboys ranch the foothills of
the Alberta Rockies. Enjoy the ride as they
each find their happily-ever-afters.

———————————⟡———————————

Six Pack Ranch
Rocky Mountain Heat
Rocky Mountain Haven
Rocky Mountain Desire
Rocky Mountain Angel
Rocky Mountain Rebel
Rocky Mountain Freedom
Rocky Mountain Romance
Rocky Retreat
Rocky Mountain Shelter
Rocky Mountain Devil
Rocky Mountain Home

VIVIAN AREND has been around North America, through parts of Europe, and into Central and South America, often with no running water. When challenged to write a book, she gave it a shot, and discovered creating worlds to play in was nearly as addictive as traveling the real one.

Now a *New York Times* and *USA Today* bestselling author of both contemporary and paranormal stories, Vivian continues to explore, write and otherwise keep herself well entertained.

CPSIA information can be obtained
at www.ICGtesting.com
Printed in the USA
LVOW04s1756200116
471541LV00023B/1648/P